THE TREASURE OF THE GRAN VENTURA

by Robert Rahula

ALSO BY ROBERT RAHULA

NOVELS:
Messieurs
Panamaniac
Island of Misfits
Day Another Paradise In
One Last Fling
Bathhouse Stories
Conversation in a Belgian Bar
All the Yage in Reno
Exigent Circumstances
Uninvited Guest
A Modest Summation of Things
To Die in Toledo

SHORT STORIES:
Horror Stories for Children
Behind the Pearly Gates

POETRY:
Trigger Points
Dentro Del Corazón Bloqueada
Camino
Migration
I Sing the Body Politic
Wonderland
From Whose Bourn
Poemas Españoles
Expat Poems
Old Dogs New Poems

ANTHOLOGIES:
Half Life
The Essential Dan Landes
50 Years Down the Drain

Alma-gator Press
Barcelona • Madrid • La Chorrera

"There is no torrent like greed."

-Buddha

PROLOGUE

It was not until after the whole mess was over that Dan Landes was able to figure out what had triggered the series of murders that came to be known as the San Servando Massacre. Like all catastrophes in life, it began with something innocuous, something simple and innocent. That's what always makes it so difficult to avoid the huge tragedies of life: you can't foresee them because they always begin innocently. By the time you grasp that your life is about to be a train wreck, the train is already upon you, and you are tied to the very tracks that you built.

It was about a year before the troubles began that Dan's old friend Ricardo Mendes had decided to sell three old Spanish coins on eBay. He had bought them about fifty-five years earlier from a street vendor in Toledo, Spain. He believed that they were silver maravedis, a type of coin that preceded the Spanish reales of the mid-fourteenth century. Ricardo was fond of old Spanish coins because he associated them with a happy time in his life—when he was a young American bumming around Spain. But these days, well, he was getting old, and didn't need them anymore. He had been living in Panama for more than fifteen years, and the Spain of his youth was long gone. There comes a point in life when people start divesting themselves of their possessions, and Ricardo was way past that point. He was not sure what the coins were worth, so he took them to Matzel Davis, a local historian in Villa Rosario who was reputed to know about coins. Matzel took a quick look at the first two coins and told Ricardo he should list them for two hundred dollars each but be willing to take less. But he studied the third coin for a while, turning it over and over in his hand, and finally examining it under a microscope. When he came back to the counter with the coin, his hands were shaking. He told Ricardo that the coin was very rare, so rare that it would not sell for much on the open market, because nobody would recognize how unusual it was. He told Ricardo that if he listed it on eBay, he would not get more than a few hundred dollars for it, because, he said, "people are stupid." Then Matzel said that he did not want Ricardo to be cheated out of the coin's full value, and so he would offer Ricardo five thousand dollars for the coin on the spot. Ricardo was stunned, but also suspicious. He told Matzel that he wanted to know more, more about the history of the coin, more about why Matzel thought it was so valuable. He promised Matzel that he would sell him the coin if Matzel could prove that five thousand dollars was a fair price. And so, Ricardo began meeting with Matzel each week, to listen to Matzel's story about this particular coin. Over time, they became friends.

Of course, Dan Landes knew nothing about all this when Ricardo phoned him in the early morning hours, one year later.

CHAPTER ONE

Dan was fast asleep when his cell phone rang. It was so rare for his phone to ever ring, that at first, he couldn't figure out what obscene sound was cutting through the silence of the night. For a nanosecond he thought he was back in the States, maybe in some hotel room, and the fire alarm must be going off. He flailed against the tangled sheets, trying to get them off so he could get up and escape. By the third ring, he realized he was home in Panama in his small apartment in the town of Villa Rosario. There was no fire. It was just his phone.

"Jesus fucking Christ," he said out loud. He sat up, switched the bedside light on, and looked around the room to locate his phone. It was there, over on the table. He pulled himself out of the bed and walked naked over to the table to grab it.

"What?" he barked.

"Sorry Dan," came a voice he recognized.

"Ricardo?"

"Yeah, listen Dan, I need help. Can I come over?"

"Right now?!"

"Yeah, sorry. This is important. I need help."

Dan peeked through the blinds of his bedroom window. It was way past midnight. Villa Rosario had no streetlights, so the only illumination was the ghostly light from the half-full moon which lent an eerie glow to the mango trees that lined the dirt road in front of his apartment building.

"Yeah... sure, of course, Ricardo."

"Thanks, I'll be there in five minutes."

Dan clicked his phone off and put it back on the table. His t-shirt, underwear, and shorts were still on the chair by the table where he had left them hours earlier. He put them on and then went to the bathroom to splash water on his face.

A few minutes later there was a soft knock on his door. Dan opened it, and Ricardo slipped quickly into Dan's apartment. He was dressed in long pants, a long-sleeved shirt, and was wearing a small backpack. Even in the cool nights of Villa Rosario, no one wore long-sleeved shirts. These were traveling clothes.

Dan's hand was still on the doorknob, but Ricardo eased the door shut.

"Going somewhere?" Dan asked.

"Yeah," Ricardo muttered. He slipped the backpack off and let it slide to the floor. Then he sat down in the chair by Dan's table and pointed to the nearby recliner, indicating that Dan should sit down. Dan looked at Ricardo's face. This was not the relaxed easy-going countenance he was familiar with. Ricardo looked worried, almost panicked. Dan sat down on the edge of the recliner and started to speak, but Ricardo interrupted him.

"Look Dan, I know this looks crazy, but I don't have time to explain the whole deal. I've got a taxi waiting downstairs, so just listen. I'm going to disappear for a while. I need you to do me a favor. Don't tell anyone you saw me tonight. Just wait about a week and then call Silas Edwards. Do you remember him?"

Dan nodded yes.

Ricardo reached over to Dan's desk and grabbed a pen and a blank 3x5 card from a stack of cards that Dan kept there. He scribbled a phone number on the card.

"Okay, good. Here's his number back in the States. Call him and tell him you haven't seen me for long while, at least two or three weeks, and that you're worried. Then do whatever he tells you to do. Whatever you do, don't say you saw me tonight. Just tell him you're concerned. Okay? Can you do that for me?"

Dan pursed his lips but nodded slowly. He had known Ricardo for more than fifteen years. He trusted Ricardo. Besides, this was Panama, and Dan knew better than anyone that strange things happen in Panama.

"You gonna be alright?" he asked.

Ricardo just shrugged. "Hope so."

"Where are you going?"

Ricardo's eyes darted to the left and then down to the floor.

"I don't know." He paused, then said, "But I need to go. Remember, you didn't see me tonight. Wait a week, then call Silas, and just say you were wondering if he's heard from me because you haven't seen me in at least two weeks—no, make it three weeks—and that you are very concerned. Then do whatever he says."

"Got it," Dan said.

Ricardo stood up, grabbed his backpack, and turned towards the door. "Thanks Dan," he said over his shoulder. He paused at the door for a second, as if he was going to say something else, but evidently decided not to, and then he simply went out the door without looking back.

Dan just sat on the edge of the recliner, shaking his head. He heard a car door shut, and then heard a motor start and the sound of a car driving away.

He sat and thought about what had happened. He felt fully awake now. A small part of his brain wondered if he had been dreaming. He tried to remember how much he had had to drink earlier. He looked at the whisky bottle that was still sitting on his desk. No... no, he hadn't drunk that much. He got up and peered through the window blinds again. He wasn't sure why he did this—the street was as deserted as he expected it to be. He looked back at his desk. There was the 3x5 card with Ricardo's handwriting lying there. No, this had actually happened. It had not been a dream.

"Well, fuck me," Dan said out loud. "That was weird."

CHAPTER TWO

Dan did just as Ricardo had asked him. He went about his normal life in Villa Rosario for the next week and didn't say a word to anyone. Dan was good at keeping secrets and acting normal. He was retired now, and so his normal life was easy to keep. He would sleep until mid-morning, make a lazy breakfast, do some grocery shopping in the local mercado before the sun got too hot, siesta in the afternoon, make dinner, and then head down to El Balcón to drink when the evening turned cool. Still, some occupational habits die hard. So, he did take a walk by Ricardo's apartment and tried the door. It was locked. He knocked, but as he expected, there was no answer. The blinds on his front window were closed. He didn't notice anything out of the ordinary about the front of Ricardo's apartment or his balcony. And he did very discretely inquire among Ricardo's friends about the last time they had seen Ricardo, how he appeared to them, and whether he had said anything unusual. None of them reported anything out of the ordinary.

The following Wednesday, Dan took the 3x5 card out of his wallet and dialed Silas's phone number.

He had never spoken to Silas before, but he knew who he was. Silas Edwards was Ricardo's literary agent in New York City. Ricardo always claimed that Silas was a good agent, and that he had worked hard over the years to get Ricardo's books published and marketed. According to Ricardo, Silas was one of the founding partners in an agency called Herrell, Facela, and Edwards.

At first, the receptionist didn't want to put Dan through to Silas.

"What publishing house are you with?" she asked.

"I'm not with any publisher. I'm calling on behalf of Ricardo Mendes."

"Are you a client of Mr. Edwards?" Her tone was starting to get condescending.

"I am not. I'm a friend of Ricardo Mendes, who *is* a client of Mr. Edwards."

"Well, Mr. Edwards is very busy. Why don't I give you our corporate email, and you can just send him a text."

"Uh, no," Dan said slowly. "Why don't I wait on the line, and you get him for me."

"I'm sorry, *sir*, but Mr. Edwards is not available right now, but I'd be glad to take your number and give it to him."

Dan slowed his voice down even more, putting a menacing pause between each word. "Miss - just - tell - Mr. - Edwards - that - I - am - calling - on - behalf - of - Ricardo - Mendes. - If - *he* - tells - you - that - *he* - wants - you - to - take - a -message - *then* - I'll - leave - a - message."

There was a pause on the line, then, "Just a minute please."

A few minutes later, a male voice came on the line. "This is Silas Edwards," the voice said. It was an aristocratic voice, Dan thought, very precise, with just a slight British accent... precise but guarded.

"Mr. Edwards, my name is Dan Landes. I'm a friend, a long-time friend, of Ricardo Mendes down here in Panama."

There was a long pause on the other end. Then Silas said, "Ah yes... Mr. Landes, of course... Ricardo has spoken of you." The voice was smoother now, trying to sound friendlier, but still guarded.

"I'm sorry to bother you, Mr. Edwards, but the reason I am calling is that some of us are concerned about Ricardo. We haven't seen him in about three weeks, and it's unlike him to simply disappear. And we were wondering if you had heard from him. Yours was the only number that we had of any friend of his back in the States..."

"Ah, yes, Mr. Landes... well, I am glad you called. Yes, I'm very glad you called... because I didn't have your number, and I had no way to get in touch with you. Yes, Ricardo is fine... I... I spoke with him recently. He's back here in the US.

He's decided to stay here for a while... to do some writing... a new project... I'm not at liberty to discuss the project, but Ricardo's very excited about it... and he asked me to ask you if you could send him some of his things... from his apartment, where he was staying... He needs his computer, all of his computers if he had more than one, and he wants all of his manuscripts, documents, and any notes that he left behind... And so, I was wondering if I could impose on you to go to his apartment and collect any of his manuscripts, notes, whatever papers he's left there, and any computers, hard drives, thumb drives, whatever he's been working on. Then you can give me a call and we'll figure out the best way to ship all of that up here to us... so we can get them to Ricardo..."

Dan was listening carefully. He had no doubt that Silas was lying, improvising, making the story up as he went along. There were just too many "tells", too many pauses, with too much speeding up and slowing down of phrases. Besides, the whole story was absurd. If Ricardo wanted Dan to send him something, he would have just called Dan himself. Dan did not believe for a moment that Ricardo was in the States working on a writing project. But he remembered Ricardo's instructions to do whatever Silas wanted.

"I'd be glad to help, Mr. Edwards. Any friend of Ricardo's is a friend of mine. I'll go over to his apartment and sort through his papers. I'll have to get permission from his landlord, so it might take a few days, but I'm sure I can get it done."

"I would be most grateful, Mr. Landes, and I'm sure Ricardo will be too."

"No problem. I'll give you a call when I've collected everything."

After some more thank-you's, Silas Edwards hung up. Dan put his cell phone down on the table and went outside onto his balcony to think. Despite the decades that had passed since he had worked in Special Investigations back in LA, Dan still knew how to think like a detective. He automatically laid out all the possibilities like imaginary cards in rows on a table in his mind: Ricardo had always said that Silas had been a good literary agent and had always treated him right; Ricardo had told Dan to do whatever Silas instructed him to do, which would imply that Ricardo trusted Silas completely; Ricardo had left town suddenly, taking only a small backpack; Silas had said that Ricardo was back in the States, which on its face could be plausible; Silas had said that Ricardo needed his computer and notes which, given how Ricardo had left Villa Rosario, could also be logical; Silas had also said that he had spoken to Ricardo recently, which also might be plausible. Except... except that Dan *knew* that Silas was lying, and if he was lying about that, then he was lying about everything else. Dan's experience over countless police investigations was that no matter how the facts appeared, his intuition about people was always more accurate. Silas had clearly lied to Dan about having spoken to Ricardo, which meant that Ricardo was not, in fact, back in the States, and that he had not asked Silas to ask Dan to ship his computer and papers to New York. But what conclusions could he draw from this?

Dan watched two vultures soaring in the sky high above. They seemed to be floating on the wind. Assuming that it was a fact that Silas had lied—and Dan did take that as a fact—then that fact contradicted one of his earlier facts, which was that Ricardo trusted Silas. Maybe, Dan thought, Ricardo's trust was misplaced. Ricardo might have felt that Silas was trustworthy when in fact Silas wasn't. Or, maybe Silas was trustworthy, but lying to Dan for some unknown reason that would make the lie necessary and understandable. Or, it might be that Ricardo *didn't* trust Silas. Dan meditated on this a bit... that would make some sense out of Ricardo's request that Dan lie to Silas—his asking Dan to tell Silas that he hadn't seen Ricardo for a couple of weeks—and it would make some sense out of Ricardo's instructions to do whatever Silas said. *Maybe* Ricardo was trying to test Silas. But why? If he didn't like his literary agent, he could just fire him and hire another agent. No, there was more to this, Dan thought. But he needed more information. He would follow Ricardo's instructions, but he would be vigilant about observing what transpired.

He watched the two vultures make two wide circles in the sky and fly away.

His first problem would be how to get into Ricardo's apartment. Dan knew the man who Ricardo rented from. He was very security-minded and would not let Dan just traipse into one of his tenant's apartments and start removing things. Dan decided to call Ted. Ted was not only a friend of his and Ricardo's, but he was a longtime respected landlord in Villa Rosario. He had rented to both Dan and Ricardo in the past. Ted knew Ricardo's landlord and had influence over him. Ted could talk him into letting Dan into Ricardo's apartment. Dan would have to continue Silas's ruse and explain to Ted that Ricardo needed his things shipped to New York.

CHAPTER THREE

Nothing happens fast in Villa Rosario, and it wasn't until the next evening that Dan and Ted were able to get inside Ricardo's apartment. They started going through all the drawers and closets, but there were no notes or manuscripts anywhere. The only electronic device they found was Ricardo's laptopp computer which was sitting on his desk.

"Yeah," Ted was saying, "I remember Ricardo talking about that Silas guy. When Ricardo first rented from me, he put Silas's name and number under the emergency contact part of the application. He said he didn't have any next of kin and that Silas was his only contact person."

"Was that when Ricardo told you he was a writer?" Dan asked.

"Yeah," Ted said. "But he didn't elaborate. He just said that he was a writer, and that this Silas guy was his agent. That was the only number Ricardo ever gave me. Even when he traveled to Europe and I would ask how to get in touch with him, he would always just give me that same number. I never did talk to the guy."

Dan was going through some boxes in the back of Ricardo's closet, but they only contained old clothes.

"Did he say he wanted *all* of Ricardo's notes? *Everything*?" Ted asked.

"Yeah. He told me he would pay to ship everything that Ricardo had written or was working on."

"Why everything?"

"I'm not sure. Probably he's just being thorough. Maybe he wants to make sure Ricardo gets the manuscripts he needs... and maybe Silas wants to keep the rest, you know, in case they might be valuable someday," Dan said.

"No disrespect to Ricardo, Dan, but I didn't think he's that famous of a writer."

Dan had nodded his head and said, "I don't think he's that famous either, Ted, but he's written a lot of books and he's made a living at it, so he must have some kind of following. Maybe he'll be like Van Gogh, you know, only really famous fifty years after his death."

"So, what exactly are we looking for?" Ted asked.

"I'm not quite clear. Silas just asked me to save anything that looked like manuscripts, notes, journals, handwritten notes, drafts of books... anything like that, and then to call him."

But as Dan and Ted went through the closets and drawers, they only found clothes, boxes of books, knick-knacks, and miscellaneous personal items.

"I guess I'll just ship Ricardo's laptop to him," Dan said. "That makes it easy."

"Yeah," Ted said, "maybe he keeps all his notes on his computer anyway."

Dan looked around. "Did we check everywhere?" He opened the closets one last time, and then walked back into the laundry room.

From the laundry room he heard Ted say, "Oh wait, here's something." When Dan stepped back into the bedroom of Ricardo's apartment, he saw Ted down on his hands and knees, pulling a large suitcase out from under the bed. It was one of those cheap soft-sided black cloth suitcases with rolling wheels and a telescoping handle, indistinguishable from thousands of similar suitcases that tumble down baggage carousels in hundreds of airports every day.

"It's heavy," Ted said as he hoisted the suitcase off the floor and placed it on the bed. Dust flew into the air as Ted undid the zipper and flipped open the top.

"Wow," said Dan. "This is what Silas must have meant."

Inside the suitcase were stacks of spiral notebooks, all different sizes and colors. They almost filled the entire suitcase. Dan picked one up and thumbed through it.

"These must be his journals," he said. He picked up a second and then a third one. Each was full of handwritten notes, paragraphs, and individual lines, some in careful neat handwriting, some in barely legible scribbles.

Ted picked up one of the notebooks, opened it, read a few lines, then closed it and put it back in the suitcase. "It's kind of creepy, Dan, to look at someone's diary," he said.

"Yeah," Dan responded, but continued to flip through the pages. "Although these are more like just random notes—you know, ideas and thoughts—here's a page marked 'ideas for new book' with a few different lines... and here's a page with a poem... interesting... Well, I could just ship this whole suitcase to Silas. Hmmm, no, maybe not... this suitcase is pretty old and flimsy. I'll just take it home and call him and see if he wants me to box these notebooks up in some kind of shipping crate. At least I can wheel it home in the suitcase."

Dan closed the notebook in his hand and placed it back on the pile.

"There's just enough room for the computer," he said, and grabbed the laptop from the desk and placed that on top of the journals and then zipped the cover shut.

"Did you ever read any of his books?" Ted asked.

"Yeah, a few," Dan replied. "He wrote a lot of short stories. I liked those the best."

"He gave me one of his books once," Ted said, "after he had lived in the apartment building a while. I told him I would read it, but I never did. I didn't want to tell him that I wasn't into gay literature."

"Hmmm, I don't think of his books as gay," Dan said. "Which book did he give you?"

"I think it was called *Another Country*," Ted said.

"Oh yeah, I've read that one," Dan said. "It's not bad. You might like it. It's not gay. Besides, Ted, I'm not sure Ricardo was totally gay. I remember when I lived at your building, he had that girl from the States who came down to stay with him. Remember her?"

"Yeah, she was stunning," Ted admitted, "but he also used to have that waiter from that restaurant he liked in La Chorrera come over too—what's the name of that place?"

"Los Cuñados?"

"Yeah, that place," Ted said. "There was that waiter who worked there—this was years ago, of course—but he was hung up on that guy, and he would come over and stay the night pretty often."

"Uh huh," Dan said, "but he's also been a regular customer at Jenny's for years, you know that."

"True, but also at that bathhouse in La Chorrera," Ted retorted.

Dan laughed. "Yeah, well, let's just agree he's active."

"Yeah," Ted said, "we can agree on that."

"You know, I asked him about it one time," Dan said. "I asked him how he defined his orientation, and he said he preferred the term 'eclectic' rather than gay or bisexual. He told me that if he thought someone was beautiful, it just didn't matter to him what their gender was... But anyway, that book he gave you is worth reading."

"Yeah, well it's been a number of years. I'd have to dig it out from wherever I put it."

"Here, I'll save you the trouble of looking," Dan said and walked over to a bookcase that held dozens of books stacked two-and-three deep. He reached down to the bottom shelf and pulled out a copy of *Another Country*. "He's got plenty of copies here. I don't think he'd mind if I gave one to you," he said and handed the book to Ted.

CHAPTER FOUR

Dan wheeled the old suitcase back to his apartment. The wheels weren't much use on the broken sidewalks of Villa Rosario, but the suitcase was too heavy to carry, so Dan walked slowly, steering the suitcase along, navigating the gaping holes in the uneven concrete. His route took him by the Parque Central and the old Catholic Church. Funny, he thought: there had only been one time that he and Ricardo and Ted had been inside that Church together, and that was about five years ago, when the three of them had been pallbearers together and had to carry the body of that poor girl Magali from the church up to the cemetery for burial.

"This is probably where I'll end up," Dan had thought to himself that day at the cemetery. "All my travels and I'll probably end up here in this tiny cemetery with Magali and the rest, here in Villa Rosario, four thousand miles from what used to be my home in California." He supposed it could be worse. Villa Rosario felt like the closest thing to a home that he had even known. Despite the drawbacks of being an expat, he liked it here.

He wheeled the suitcase through the gated entrance of his apartment building and up to the stairwell that led to his second-floor apartment. He tested the weight of the suitcase again. It felt even heavier than it had at Ricardo's apartment, plus Dan noticed that he was out of breath. It was going to be too difficult to carry it up the one flight of stairs. He would have to wheel it up, step by step.

And so, he did. Finally, he reached the second-floor landing and rolled the suitcase down the tiled balcony to his little apartment. He undid both locks on the door, stepped inside, turned on the lights, pulled the suitcase inside, and stood it up over in the corner.

"I'll deal with it tomorrow," he thought, and went into the kitchen to pour himself a whisky.

He took his drink and sat down in his large recliner and looked at the suitcase. Dan thought of the decades of recorded memories contained in those journals. The suitcase reminded him somehow of a suit of armor: a knight standing mute in the corner, a dusty old vestige of a bygone era, like the journals it contained. There was a time when people recorded their thoughts—when people still had thoughts. He took a sip of whisky and let his mind wander.

Dan had moved to Panama about two years before Ricardo showed up in Villa Rosario. They had met at Ted's apartment building where Dan had also been renting an apartment. Was that really fifteen years ago? Or longer? Dan tried to do the math in his head, but the whisky was already starting to work its numbing magic, and he couldn't remember the exact year he had met Ricardo. It was back when Dan still had his motorcycle—that wonderful vintage Yamaha Virago that he had shipped down to Panama. In fact, Dan recalled that it was because of that bike that he had met Ricardo. He had been in the courtyard cleaning the bike when Ricardo walked up to admire it and introduced himself. God, that was such a long time ago. He wouldn't risk getting on a motorcycle now. His reflexes were not what they used to be.

Eventually, both he and Ricardo had moved out from Ted's building, but the three of them had remained friends. Ricardo had moved to the edge of town and rented an apartment—that very same little apartment that Dan and Ted had scoured this evening—and had never moved from it. By then, Ricardo had met Magali, that poor sweet prostitute who worked in Jenny's brothel. Magali had moved in with Ricardo, but that relationship didn't last. About a year after that, Magali and Dan started seeing each other. But that didn't last, either.

Dan took another sip of whisky. The memories of fifteen years floated through his head. After his affair with

Magali, Dan had gone back to the States for a while, but eventually he returned to Villa Rosario. That was a fucked-up time for Dan. He was drinking heavily and indulging in certain psychedelics that were indigenous to the area. But after Magali had died, he straightened out... more or less. Now he limited his intoxicants to a moderate intake of whisky. Maybe that was a function of age. Those wild years were mostly a haze to him now. But he did remember that during that same time Ricardo used to travel frequently back and forth to Europe. Age had eventually slowed Ricardo down, too. Over the past few years, Ricardo had reduced the number of his trips abroad. Time moves on, Dan thought sadly. Time moves on and does what time always does—plucks the people from our lives, one by one. Magali had died too young... way too young. Father Lopez—the old Catholic priest who represented the Villa Rosario of yesteryear—had also died. Dan's best friend José Fernando—who had been the police chief of Villa Rosario forever—had recently announced that he was going to retire in six months. His health was not so good now, and he had already reduced his hours to part time. The police chief of the nearby city of La Chorrera, Jorge Manuel (who also happened to be José Fernando's nephew) was helping to cover the other half of José Fernando's hours while the city council searched for a permanent successor.

It made Dan feel old to consider all these things. He got up and refilled his glass. Whisky had been a steadfast companion throughout all of life's whips and scorns. He thought of Magali again. Somehow, he and Ricardo had remained friends despite the fact that both of them had loved her. He thought again of when he and Ricardo and Ted had carried Magali's casket from the church up the hill to the cemetery. That seemed like light years ago now. Where did it all go?

He looked over at Ricardo's suitcase again. Tomorrow, he would go through all those spiral notebooks and see if there were any clues to why Ricardo had left town so suddenly. And he would look through all of them *before* he called Silas.

CHAPTER FIVE

The next morning after breakfast, Dan poured himself a second cup of coffee and sat down to go through the suitcase and categorize the contents. He placed the suitcase on a low bench and started leafing through each notebook. After perusing each one, he placed it on one of several piles. Those notebooks that seemed to contain entries about dreams or dream-like paragraphs, he put into one pile. Those that contained poem fragments or rhymes, he put into another pile. Those that contained single phrases or questions or undecipherable notes, he put into a third pile. A fourth pile contained ideas for books or short stories. There was a fifth pile of notebooks that were completely empty. About halfway through his sorting, he found two notebooks that seemed to be unique. One was a complete manuscript, handwritten, that was entitled *A Modest Summation of Things*. Dan read through several chapters. It appeared to be a series of essays on the meaning of life, or at least the meaning of Ricardo's life. The number of crossed-out lines and editing notes indicated to Dan that Ricardo had intended this to be a book. He placed that notebook on his desk. The other notebook contained a series of hand-drawn maps. Each map was of the same scene, but each was drawn with more detail than the previous one, with the final map being quite dense with names and notations. But none of the references were familiar to Dan. He was sure they were not maps of any place in Panama. Dan wondered if they were ideas for a new book Ricardo might be working on. There was a squiggly line that suggested a river that appeared on all the maps. It was marked "Tagus". There was a hill marked "Azor" and sketches of many buildings with arrows marking distance. One building was drawn to resemble a castle turret with the abbreviation "San Serv" written beside it. It had many arrows coming out of it with notations of distance to other buildings. All in all, there were eighteen maps followed by a half page of notations, indicating direction and distances. The notations were all cryptic, such as "four meters due west of NW corner of San MigAlto." At the very end of the page of notations was the name "Matzel Davis" followed by "3 pm coins". This name Dan recognized. Matzel Davis was an old German expat who ran a small bookstore in Villa Rosario. Dan assumed Ricardo must have had an appointment to talk with Matzel at three in the afternoon, but that appointment could have been for any day in the past fifteen years. Dan placed the notebook on his desk with the other notebook of essays.

By one p.m., Dan had gone through all the notebooks. There were five stacks on the floor and two notebooks on his desk. Not counting the stack of empty notebooks, there were fifty-four notebooks with entries. Some were completely full; some half-full; and some only had a few paragraphs or lines. Only the manuscript of essays seemed like a complete book. Dan didn't know what to make of the notebook of maps. The rest of the notebooks were simply random thoughts, dream fragments, ideas for books that Ricardo never wrote; starts of paragraphs, etc. They were no different than anyone's private thoughts, meaning that they were mundane. And they offered no clues as to why Ricardo had left. He wondered if Silas would want them.

*   *   *

After a late lunch, Dan called Silas's number in New York. Again, it took forever for the receptionist to patch him through to Silas.

When Silas finally got to the phone, he apologized for the delay.

"I'm so sorry to keep you waiting, Mr. Landes. I was on a different floor. What news do you have?" Silas said.

Dan smiled slightly to himself. He was always bemused by the North American businessman's custom of getting straight to business. That would never happen in Panama. In Panama, there would be at least ten minutes of inquiry into one's health, the health of one's family, the general state of business, maybe even some gossip, before two men would get down to business. Dan accepted that it was different in the States, but somehow, he expected more from Silas, maybe because of that slight British accent. Dan assumed that the British tended more towards conversational chit-chat than North Americans. He made a mental note to ask Silas—if he ever got the chance—about his background. He really knew nothing about him other than that he was Ricardo's agent.

"Well, I was calling about Ricardo Mendes, of course," Dan replied. "We went through his apartment last night, and discovered a whole suitcase of journals, notebooks, and what looks to be a manuscript of sorts..."

"Really?" Silas interrupted, "A large suitcase?"

"Pretty big. I did an inventory this morning. There are fifty-four notebooks in total... well, there's a couple more that are blank, but there's fifty-four notebooks with writing in them, but almost all of the notebooks are just random notes, thoughts, questions, nothing sequential, a few words, maybe a line of poetry... but to be honest, I didn't find anything particularly memorable in those fifty-four notebooks except for one—and that notebook looks like a complete manuscript for a book. It has a title page called *A Modest Summation of Things* and it's divided into chapters, all of which appear to be essays—essays that flow sequentially. It looks pretty good. You might be interested in that. And of course, there's Ricardo's laptop computer."

"You're very thorough, Mr. Landes."

"Well, I just wanted you to know what you would be getting before you shell out a lot of money in shipping fees. Anyway, I thought you might be interested in this manuscript of essays. I could mail that to you."

"Well… actually… I probably would want to see *all* the, um, items… and the computer of course. When you say notebooks, what exactly do you mean?"

"Like the kind students use in school. Some have spiral wire on the spine that holds them together; others are just regular notebooks without the spiral wire—just normal notebooks."

"I see… and you read through all of them?"

"Oh no, no," Dan lied. "I just glanced at the pages to get an idea of what each notebook was, you know, so I could organize them into piles. Like I said, all of them were just short notes, paragraphs, nothing much really, except for that manuscript of essays, oh, and a notebook with some maps, but the essays seem worthwhile and I thought…"

"Did you say *maps*?" Silas interrupted again.

Dan did not like being interrupted. He bristled.

"Yes," he answered curtly.

"What kind of maps?" Silas asked.

"Hand-drawn sketches. One notebook had almost twenty maps, diagrams really, but I couldn't figure out what area they were, or if they were a real area at all."

There was a pause on the line. Then Silas asked, "Were there any words on these maps?"

"Yeah, lots of them. Hang on." Dan reached over and grabbed the notebook with the maps from his desk and flipped it open. "They're Spanish terms, but I don't recognize them as anything around here in Panama. Here we go: Acantara, Juanelo, Tagus, Plaza San Justo… names like that… There's a drawing that looks like a castle tower labeled *San Serv* and a lot of arrows with numbers. I really shouldn't call them maps. They're more like doodling, crude sketches."

There was another pause on the phone. "I see… interesting… very interesting. Well Mr. Landes, I greatly appreciate you securing these notebooks. I would like to see them all. Could I ask a huge favor? Could I ask you to ship all of them to me? Is there a Federal Express down there? We'll pay the freight of course."

"There's a DHL office in Panama City. I've used them before."

"Yes, of course. I tell you what—give me your number and I'll call you back in five minutes. I need to get our DHL account number so that you can write that on the bill of lading."

Dan gave Silas his phone number and hung up. Then he began to think about the call.

He had noticed that Silas's was much more interested in the maps than the manuscript for Ricardo's book—more interested than he wanted Dan to know. Silas's speech pattern had sped up when Dan had mentioned the maps... and then Silas had stretched out the word "interesting" twice to slow down and give himself time to think. But maybe there was an explanation... maybe the maps fit into some other manuscript of Ricardo's that Silas was getting ready to publish. Still, it was odd that Silas—Ricardo's literary agent—didn't seem interested in the completed manuscript of essays.

Dan refilled his coffee cup and sat back down at his desk. He opened the notebook of maps and idly flipped through the pages. He let his eyes scan through the words on the maps as he sipped his coffee. Again, none of them rang a bell. On a whim, he opened his computer and pulled up Google Maps and typed in the phrase "Tagus River," and a map of Spain came up. There was a Tagus River that flowed through the middle of Spain. He looked it up on Wikipedia and learned that the Tagus River is the longest river in Spain. Well, that made sense, Dan thought. Whenever Ricardo went to Europe, he always spent most of his time in Spain. He typed in some of the other words and abbreviations on the map into Google maps, but nothing else seemed to generate a more specific result than just Spain. Okay, Dan thought, so this is a map of some town in Spain. Big Deal. Ricardo did like to vacation there.

The phone rang. It was Silas calling him back with his agency's DHL account number. Dan had shipped DHL before so he knew he could simply put that number on the bill of lading and Herrell, Facela, and Edwards would pay the shipping charges. Dan wrote down the account number and the address of Silas's agency.

"I'll get these shipped to you as soon as possible," Dan said. "I'll have to box them up first."

"Yes, of course," Silas said. "We want to protect them. Ricardo Mendes was not our biggest selling author, but he had a very loyal readership. They might be interested in seeing excerpts from his journals."

"Well, I'll leave that up to you," Dan replied. "As I said, there's not much content to these notebook entries, except for the notebook full of essays. That looked like a full book. I'm not sure I would even call the other notebooks *journals*."

"I'll have the editors pour over them," Silas responded, "and see what they think. Do you think you can ship them overnight express today?"

"Hmmm, no," Dan said, looking at his watch. "Today is Friday, and I wouldn't be able to box these up and get to Panama City by the time they close. And they won't be open this weekend. I can ship them out Monday."

"Why aren't they open tomorrow?" Silas asked.

"Because this is Panama," Dan said curtly. He was beginning to get irritated at Silas.

There was a pause on the line.

"I see," said Silas. "I see... Well, we're anxious to see them, but I guess we'll just have to wait... Do they have overnight express down there?"

"Oh, I doubt it, Silas. I think they have what they call expedited shipping. But I'll find out what they have and use the fastest."

"And the most secure," Silas added.

There was another pause on the line.

"Panama City..." Silas said. "How far is that from Villa Rosario?"

"It's about an hour away."

"Yes, I see... Ricardo always said that your little town didn't have much in the way of modern services," Silas said. "One of my colleagues was asking me about the state of technology down there, whether you had scanners for sending documents and the like?"

Now Dan *was* irritated. He had already spent most of the day reviewing and categorizing all these notebooks. He wasn't about to spend any more time scanning them to Silas just because Silas was a big-shot New York agent.

"No," Dan lied. "Things are pretty primitive in this little town. No scanners, no copiers."

"I see..."

Dan decided to change the subject. "Oh, by the way," he said, "when Ricardo's landlord was letting us into Ricardo's apartment, I was explaining to him that Ricardo was back in the States, and his landlord of course was concerned about how long he was going to be away, or to put it more precisely—his landlord asked how Ricardo was going to pay his rent from the States."

"Ah, well... I'm not sure how long Ricardo will be here... This project that he's working on is pretty big... Hmm, why don't I do this? I'll have Ricardo's lawyer call you and make arrangements to pay the rent."

"Okay," Dan said slowly. "Who's his lawyer?"

"David Ortega. Nice fellow. I'll give David your number and have him call you. You can assure Ricardo's landlord that he'll get his rent money. No problem."

"Excellent," Dan said. "And I'll get these notebooks boxed up and sent out to you."

After he and Silas had hung up, Dan sat and thought some more. The quickness by which Silas assured him that the rent would be paid was another sign that he was lying about Ricardo being back in the States. People are never eager to pay the debts of another. If Ricardo was in the States, Silas would have said something like "I'll pass that on to Ricardo." And the fact that he promised to pay the rent without even knowing the amount indicated that he had a financial interest in keeping things calm, keeping things status quo. But why?

Dan picked up the notebook with the maps and started typing the words into Google Maps again. This time he tried pairing up some of the words. After a few combinations, he typed "Tagus River" with "Plaza San Justo," and a map of the town of Toledo, Spain, came up. There was a park named Plaza San Justo near the Tagus River in Toledo. He started zooming in on different streets in Toledo, looking at the names. After a minute, he found the Iglesia San Miguel, the Church of Saint Michael. Well, he thought, there was that abbreviation "San MigAlto" on one of the maps. Then he found a castle marked San Servando. Maybe that was that castle turret drawing on the maps marked "San Serv." Maybe these maps were of Toledo, Spain. He looked at the shape of the Tagus River on hand-drawn maps. It was like a sideways S, and that matched the shape of the Tagus as it flowed through a part of Toledo, around the jutting-out piece of land where the Plaza San Justo was located. Maybe these were all different drawings of a section of Toledo, Spain. Of course, he could be wrong. Every river in the world probably has a section where it curves like a sideways S. He sat and thought some more. He didn't like being lied to. It pissed him off. It made him want to start digging for the truth. It hooked his old investigative "cop brain."

Then something occurred to him. He wondered if that was why Ricardo had chosen him to confide his disappearance plan to. Ricardo could have picked any one of his friends, but he had picked Dan. Did Ricardo know that Silas was going to lie to Dan? Did Ricardo know that Silas would piss Dan off and make him dig for the truth? It seemed like a weird thought, but it made some intuitive sense to Dan. He wondered if Ricardo had anticipated Silas's lie and then asked himself, "What would Dan do?" Maybe he wanted Dan to act like a detective, to investigate something, although Dan had no clue what he was investigating.

Dan sat and thought about this for a while. Then he decided to go see Matzel Davis.

CHAPTER SIX

Dan assumed that Matzel Davis, like most of the shopkeepers in Villa Rosario, kept irregular hours at his bookstore. For that reason, he would have preferred to call Matzel first, before walking across town, to see if he was open. But phone books and 411 services do not exist in Villa Rosario. So, Dan started walking the twenty-minute route to Matzel's bookstore on the other side of town. Dan was used to walking everywhere. Since he didn't have a car, it was how he normally got around town. But it was mid-afternoon, and the sun was fierce. He took the streets that kept him in the shade of the tall whitewashed concrete walls that surrounded most of the houses. The streets of Villa Rosario were narrow and curved, built that way to offer pedestrians the most shade possible. As he walked, Dan thought more about Ricardo. He visualized his mental table again, with "facts" written on 3x5 cards arranged in rows. Ricardo was not in the States—Dan believed that was a fact. But where was he, then? He had told Dan last week that there was a taxi waiting for him downstairs. Taking a taxi meant he was going somewhere he couldn't get to by walking or by bus. Plus, it was logical he would use taxi because he had come over past midnight, so no buses would be running. But then Dan realized there probably wouldn't have been any regular taxis operating at that time of night, either. The taxi business in Villa Rosario was mostly a daytime operation. Ricardo would have had to call a pirate taxi—one of the many unlicensed taxi drivers who were on call 24/7 for their group of regulars. Ah, yes, Dan realized: Ricardo would have called Minor. If Ricardo had to take a pirate taxi, he always hired Minor, because he felt sorry for Minor's family.

They were poor, and Minor worked very hard as a pirate driver to support them. Yes, Dan thought again: Ricardo would have called Minor. He needed to hunt Minor down and ask him where he had taken Ricardo that night after Ricardo had visited him... assuming Minor would divulge that information. Pirate taxi drivers were very loyal to their regular customers and did not gossip. Many locals depended on the pirates to transport them discretely to the brothels in nearby La Chorrera without their wives or neighbors being the wiser.

As he was thinking this, Dan realized he was only a block from the Parque Central. Maybe Minor would be there. Most of the pirate taxi drivers hung out on the south side of the park when they were in between fares. Dan decided to take a short detour. He turned left and headed down a side street.

The Parque Central, situated across from the large Catholic church, was the centerpiece of the town. It was a green park that took up the whole block, lined with mango trees and concrete benches. The open-air vegetable markets were held there each morning. All the locals walked through the park at least once a day, usually taking a *paseo* in the early morning or in the cool of evening, to meet and chat with neighbors. The lottery ticket sellers stood on the corners of the park calling out the daily prize amounts, trying to entice the public to buy a lottery ticket. There was usually someone with a cart selling snow cones or cold drinks during the heat of the day. And in the late evening, a few hookers would make the rounds. It was a splendid place, to be sure.

But as Dan got to the shaded corner of the park where the pirate taxi drivers all gathered, he could see that Minor was not there. He was probably out on a fare, or maybe he went home to take a siesta. So, Dan turned east again to head to Matzel's store. But halfway up the street, Dan saw a display that he had never seen before at the park. It was a display of eight electric bicycles, all lined up in a row, under the shade of a tall palm tree, with a big sign beside them indicating that they could be rented by the hour. Two young men in company shirts stood by them.

Dan walked up and examined the bicycles. These were the pedal-assist type of electric bicycles. He had read about these, how they had the motors in the rear-wheel hub, and a battery in the frame. Dan wondered if he might find such a bicycle useful for getting around town.

One of the young men approached Dan and introduced himself. His name was Mark, and he had the rapid-fire speech of a self-assured young salesman. Dan asked him how the rental system worked, and whether he had to leave a deposit. Mark said no, and explained that the whole process was handled online. He handed Dan a brochure that outlined the process. The company was called Todo. In order to rent a bike, Dan would have to first set up an account with Todo and link that account to his credit card. Dan could then simply walk up to any of the bikes and focus his cellphone's camera on the QR code, located on the handlebars. His cellphone would tell him how much battery power was left in that particular bike, what the estimated range would be with that much battery power, and it would ask him if he wanted to rent it. If he clicked yes, his meter—so to speak—would be running. When he finished riding, he could leave the bike wherever he was, and his credit card would be charged for the time he used the bike. He just had to focus his cellphone's camera on the QR code again to terminate the ride. Each bike had a GPS device built inside them. No matter where in town he left the bike, the company would drive around each evening and pick up all the bikes, charge the batteries up overnight, and place them back in the park the next morning.

Dan nodded his head as Mark explained the process. He thought to himself: Finally, technology was coming to Villa Rosario. He wondered how many of the locals would use such a modern system. He wondered how many locals even had cellphones.

"What's the hourly rate?" Dan asked.

"One balboa," Mark replied.

A dollar an hour? Dan thought to himself. That can't be right. He asked the young man again. Yes, it was only a dollar an hour. But if he used less than the full hour, he would still be charged the whole dollar.

"That's an amazing price," Dan said to Mark. "I don't see how you can do it. What's the catch?"

"There's no catch," Mark said. "It's a special promotion, but it gets better. If you apply for one of our Todo debit cards, we will give you five hours of ride time for free."

Mark held up a black Visa debit card embossed with the Todo logo.

"The card is offered through our Todo Bank, so it's totally safe. You can open an account instantly online by transferring money from your credit card, and then we can either mail you a Todo debit card or you can use your phone as the debit card. This card will replace all your other credit cards. You can transfer money internationally with no international exchange fees. And every time you use our card, you generate Todo Points which you can redeem for cash. And the best part is that you can use your account to buy and sell cryptocurrency. We even have our own crypto coin, the TodoCoin, which is one hundred percent backed by our Todo Bank."

"Do I have to apply for your card to rent the bike?"

"No, of course not. You can just use your own credit card. Our goal is to make it easy for you."

Mark had a smooth salesman's touch, Dan thought. He checked his watch. It was time to go.

"I've got to meet someone now, but I'll look into this tonight," Dan said. "Are you here in the park every day?"

"Yes, seven days a week from eight in the morning until eight at night."

Dan thanked Mark, stuck the brochure in his back pocket, and headed off again to Matzel's bookstore. He wondered again what the catch was, how the company could make a profit in a small town like Villa Rosario renting out electric bicycles at a dollar an hour. He made a mental note to look them up later tonight. But then he turned his attention to the more pressing issue at hand.

He thought again about his interaction with Silas. He again visualized his imaginary card table with a stack of cards, each one containing a fact. He turned each card over, placed it on the imaginary table, and looked at it. Ricardo always talked positively of Silas, not so much as a friend, but as an agent... an agent... one who acts on behalf of another... one who acts with the other person's interests in mind... but clearly that had changed. If Silas was on Ricardo's side—looking after Ricardo's best interests—Ricardo would have clued Silas in to what was going on. Silas would have said, "Yes, Ricardo told me he had talked to you and that you would call." Or, Ricardo would have told Dan to call Silas and tell him the truth—that he had come to Dan's apartment in the middle of the night and had to get out of town. But Ricardo didn't do that. He told Dan to lie to Silas. So Dan added another card to the table: Silas was not operating in Ricardo's best interests. Then another card: Ricardo didn't know what Silas would tell Dan to do. That's why Ricardo told Dan to do whatever Silas told him to... because Ricardo didn't know what Silas would say.

Dan then thought about Matzel Davis. He didn't really know much about Matzel except that he was old and had lived in Villa Rosario for about ten years. Dan had never spoken to Matzel, but had overheard him once in the open-air market. There was a slight German accent to his Spanish. Plus, he looked German. Even in the tropical heat, his white shirt was starched and pressed. And his shirt had that small collar one sees men wear in Germany. He had a short square body, not fat but thick, solid. And his neatly combed white hair and small gold-rimmed wire spectacles added to the Germanic impression. But it was just an impression. A lot of Europeans had settled in Panama over the centuries: Germans, Jews, Austrians, Swiss, Poles... Matzel could be from any of those countries... or none of them. All Dan knew was that he owned a small bookstore—a bookstore that also sold a bit of jewelry and some antique coins.

As Dan approached the street where Matzel's store was, he could see that the store appeared to be open. There was a medium-large picture window with shelves that displayed older used hardcover books at the back and new paperbacks in the front. Most of the books were, of course, in Spanish, but Dan noticed a few titles in English, and even one in Portuguese. The lights appeared to be on inside. Dan went up the three steps to the front door and opened it. A tiny bell over the door chimed as he stepped inside.

The shop obviously had been an old house that had been converted to a bookstore. The large front room must have once been a living room. Shelves had been added to all the walls, from floor to ceiling, to hold as many books as possible. A small counter had been built in the center of the room. There was an old-time cash register on the counter along with a modern credit card reader. Dan wondered how much use either of them got. Small hallways led to other rooms in the back. There was a staircase that led to a loft upstairs, whose walls were also lined with shelves full of books. And there was the characteristic smell of old bookstores: a certain odor that millions of paper pages slowly give off as the years pass, as all the bleaches, formaldehydes, chlorines, and starch binders in the pages gradually decompose, molecule by molecule, drifting into the still air that hangs in old bookstores.

Dan walked up to the counter and waited for someone to appear. He looked down through the glass top of the counter and saw various old coins laid out on glass shelves, each in a cardboard and plastic coin holder. The prices were written in pencil on the cardboard part of the coin holder. Dan looked closer. Some of the coins were priced at five or six hundred dollars. How odd, he thought, to put such valuable objects in a glass case so close to the front door in a shop that had no security guard. In fact, there didn't seem to be any employees about. Dan looked around the store. He was simply standing there alone. Maybe Matzel was back in the bathroom, he thought. He looked back down at the coins. How easy would it be, he wondered, for some robber to step inside, smash the glass, grab the coins, and run out? He tapped on the glass. His tapping made a dull thick sound. He looked closer. Then he recognized the glass type. It was thick bulletproof glass. Even though the counter appeared to be an old antique store counter, the underside of each piece of wood was reinforced with a metal framework. And there were very thin electrical wires running the length of the glass. He then spied two tiny cameras at either end of the top shelf, aimed up through the top glass counter, aimed to record any customer who would be standing there. Interesting, he thought: the appearance of a nineteenth-century commercial wood and glass countertop, yet with bulletproof glass, an alarm system, and cameras. He glanced around the ceiling of the room. Tiny cameras were mounted very discretely in the dark shadows of each wooden beam. He looked closer. There had to be at least ten different cameras. It reminded him of all the cameras in the ceilings of the casinos back in Nevada.

He wondered how long he would have to wait, but after another minute, he heard a door open and the shuffling of feet. Matzel Davis was slowly walking up a hallway to the counter where Dan was standing.

Before Dan could speak, Matzel said, smiling, "I was watching you. You spotted my security system. Very observant."

Dan wasn't sure how to respond, so he just launched into an introduction.

"Mr. Davis, my name is Dan Landes. I'm a friend of Ricardo Mendes..."

"Yes, I know who you are. Ricardo pointed you out to me one time. What can I do for you?"

"Well, sir, this is about Ricardo. He's—well, he's kind of disappeared. None of us has seen him for a while, and we were worried, and wondered if you had any idea where he was."

"And why would you think *I* would have any idea where he's gone?" Matzel asked.

"Because his landlord let us into his apartment, and we found some notes that indicated he had an appointment with you at three o'clock." Dan looked down at the coins in

Matzel's display case. "An appointment to talk about some coins."

"Ha... an *appointment*, that's funny," Matzel said. "Ricardo used to come over here often to visit, probably two or three times a week. He didn't need an appointment. He would drop by in the afternoons, and we would talk. And yes, we would occasionally talk about coins. After all, they are a... hobby of mine."

"When was the last time you saw him?" Dan asked.

Matzel thought for a moment. "It was two weeks ago. Yes, he came by on a Friday right before we closed. Exactly two weeks ago."

"And what did you two talk about?" Dan asked.

Matzel smiled. "Things... just things... the kind of things old men talk about."

Dan couldn't help but smile himself. "Sorry," he said, "I didn't mean to pry. It's just that I can't shake this feeling that Ricardo's in some kind of trouble."

"Oh, I doubt that," Matzel said. "Ricardo's pretty good at taking care of himself."

"True. But still, I'm worried. Do you have *any* idea where he is?"

"No, no I don't. I didn't know he had gone anywhere. But, if I had to hazard a guess, I would guess he's gone to Spain."

The mental image of Dan's card table of facts flashed briefly in his mind. On an impulse he asked, "To Toledo?"

Matzel's eyes widened just a bit, and then he smiled. "And why would you think he went to Toledo?"

"Because I saw some maps he drew," Dan said.

"Ah... you *are* the detective that Ricardo said you were. And how did you come to see Ricardo's maps?"

"Well, like I said, his landlord let us into his apartment. We were worried. We thought maybe he was sick. But then he wasn't there, so we were looking for clues as to where he might be. I just happened to see some maps he drew..."

"*Just happened,*" Matzel said in a mocking tone. "Do you know much about Toledo, Mr. Landes?"

"Not a thing."

"Well, Ricardo is very familiar with it. Toledo is just about an hour's drive southwest of Madrid. Ricardo lived in Madrid back in the sixties, did you know that?"

Dan nodded. "Yes, he told me about that."

"Well, when Ricardo was living in Madrid, he spent a lot of time in Toledo. Interesting city, Toledo. You know how you can read the history of an entire forest—an entire area—from the rings of one tree? That's Toledo. The history of all of Spain is contained in the story of that one city. Controlled by the Romans almost two centuries before the birth of Christ. They thought it was a delightful little town. But then, of course, the Visigoths conquered Rome. The Visigoths liked Toledo, too. They made it their capital for almost two centuries, until the Moors came up from Africa and conquered Spain. The Moors also liked Toledo; made it their cultural center; built great mosques and palaces there; turned it into a magnificent city. But then came the Reconquista, and the Christians took Toledo back. Yes, Toledo was very popular for conquering armies. After the Reconquista, Toledo became an economic powerhouse and was basically the capital of Spain until about 1561, when the king of Spain... let's see, that would have been Philip II... when he decided to move the capital to Madrid."

"I was never much of a history buff," Dan said. "And I didn't think Ricardo was, either."

Matzel shrugged. "History is fascinating, Mr. Landes. You can learn so much from it. Although, to be fair, understanding history is like trying to understand a dream. All you have are fragments and they fade very quickly. But history has always interested me. However, I agree with you; I don't think Ricardo was much interested in history until recently. I think when he was young, he was just fond of Toledo. It's a very beautiful city, high up on a hill. I think Ricardo loved the city for its spectacular views. He only became interested in its history about a year ago. That's why he would stop by, so we could talk history. I've got an odd memory for facts and dates, and he used to quiz me. I think he liked trying to stump me. He would do a bit of research and then come and question me about what he had read."

Dan thought about this. Ricardo had never mentioned Toledo to him, nor had he ever talked about history.

"So... you think he's gone to Toledo?" Dan asked.

"Oh, I have no idea where he's gone. As I said, I didn't know he was out of town. I only said that if I had to *guess*, I would guess he went to Spain. You were the one who said Toledo."

Dan looked at Matzel. Here was someone who liked to play cat and mouse, he thought. Dan decided to be direct.

"Look, I'll be honest, Mr. Davis. I didn't go rummaging around his apartment just because I'm nosy. Ricardo is my friend, and I have good reason to believe he's in some kind of trouble. The last time I saw him he was spooked about something. I know he's smart and capable of fending for himself. But this is different. This is serious. He's disappeared, and no one knows where he is."

Matzel frowned. He seemed to be thinking. Then he said, "Well, if I were you, I would put those maps in a safe place."

"Why?"

Matzel just shrugged.

"I think you know more than you're telling me," Dan said.

"Of course. I'm a historian. Historians always know more than anyone. But why don't you read up on Toledo? Then come back and talk with me." Matzel took a watch out of his pocket and looked at it. "I have to close now, but I open tomorrow at noon. Saturdays are always slow. Why don't you come by, say at a quarter after twelve? We can chat some more then."

With that, Matzel turned and shuffled back down the hallway he had come from, leaving Dan standing alone at the counter.

CHAPTER SEVEN

That was frustrating, Dan thought to himself as he walked home. Not horrible, but frustrating. Matzel clearly knew more than he was letting on. But at least he hadn't lied, as Silas had done. Maybe Matzel was just being careful, discreet. Why did he want Dan to read up on Toledo? What was Ricardo researching that he would question Matzel about? And most importantly, why did Matzel tell him to guard the maps?

"Put the maps in a safe place" was what Matzel had said. That obviously was contradictory advice since Ricardo had told him to do whatever Silas said, and Silas had told him to ship the notebooks to him. But now there were two people signaling that the maps were somehow valuable. Dan didn't understand how they could be valuable—they were just crudely drawn maps—but Silas was clearly more interested in them than in Ricardo's completed manuscript of essays. And Matzel had just warned him to keep them safe. The smart thing to do, Dan thought, would be to make a copy of them, just in case.

Despite what Dan had told Silas, Villa Rosario did have scanners and copiers... at least one... and that was in the local police station. It was not available to the public, but Dan was good friends with don Fernando, the outgoing police chief, and thus Dan had free access to the copier and the scanner. Even if don Fernando was not at work today, all the officers at the police station knew they were friends, and wouldn't stop him from using the equipment.

So, Dan walked home, retrieved Ricardo's notebook with the maps from his desk and headed down to the police station. The sun was bending towards the horizon now, and the long yellow shafts of light that poured through the streets didn't hold the heat of just thirty minutes earlier. Dan's route took him back by the Parque Central and the huge Catholic Church that sat on one end of the park. He looked again for Minor, but again, Minor was not there. Dan thought about the hundreds of times he had walked this route before, down to the police station, to visit his friend don Fernando.

José Fernando—or don Fernando, as everyone called him—had been the police chief of Villa Rosario for more than forty years. He got the job in his early twenties because the locals all believed he had killed a brujo who was terrorizing the town. Dan had never asked him whether there was any truth to that story, but Dan never disbelieved it. Villa Rosario still was known as the "town of witches" to the locals, and Dan had personal knowledge of at least one brujo whose death don Fernando had arranged. But Dan no longer believed there were any brujos left around Villa Rosario. They had all left, or died, or had been killed, or, like everyone else he knew, simply aged out of the system and disappeared. No, Villa Rosario had been free of brujos for many years now. It was no longer the town of witches.

The desk sergeant looked up from his paperwork when Dan walked into the police station. He just nodded at Dan, gestured with his thumb down the hallway to indicate that don Fernando was in his office and went back to his paperwork.

Dan walked down the hallway and stuck his head into the open doorway of don Fernando's office.

"Hola, mi amigo, can I use your copier for a minute?"

Don Fernando was sitting at his desk, his dark eyebrows in a perpetual frown, staring at some reports. He looked up and nodded at Dan.

"Of course, Dani."

Dan continued down the hall to the copy room. The copier/scanner/printer that was there was a beast—a huge machine that would have been an antique in any North American office, but was state of the art here. Dan took Ricardo's notebook, folded it open flat, and made a copy of each page, folded the copies, placed them in his pocket, and headed back to don Fernando's office.

Don Fernando was still sitting at his desk with the same scowl when Dan walked in and took a seat facing him.

Dan ventured a guess. "Crime up?" he quipped.

"Crime is always up, Dani. It rises with the population, and my little town is growing. Did you know that the provincial government wants to rename us Ciudad Rosario? They claim we are too large to be called a villa any longer, so they want to call us a city. The town council is in favor of the change because they think it will bring more development, more condos, and more tax revenue."

"Ah yes, the almighty dollar," Dan said.

Don Fernando picked up the report in front of him, waved it at Dan, and let it fall back to the desk.

"But it's not the amount of crime that bothers me. It's the type of crime we're getting now. It's not the simple home burglaries or petty thefts that we've always had. More and more it's computer fraud, credit card fraud, more sophisticated crimes. Did you know that we caught some kids trying to put a skimmer on the ATM at the Banco Nacional downtown last week? A skimmer!"

"No. I didn't see that in the paper."

"It wasn't in the paper. The bank kept it out. They didn't want people to lose confidence in their ATM."

"Yeah," Dan said, "I get that. You say you caught the criminals?"

"Well, they were just kids. One was only sixteen. Dumb local kids. They didn't know what they were doing. They took so long trying to install it that a night guard inside the bank saw them. But the skimmer they were trying to install, well that's another story. It was a very sophisticated piece of machinery—much too complicated for these kids to have built."

"Really?" Dan started to get interested. "And where did they get it?"

"Ah, we don't know. They wouldn't tell us. There was a day, Dani, when I could have squeezed that information out of those two punk kids, a day when I could have beaten it out of them, but I can't do that anymore. The parents think they have *rights* now. And the newspapers all have online editions. If I rough them up, I would be in trouble. I don't know how they expect me to control crime anymore."

"So, what happened to the kids?"

"We had to release them to their parents."

Don Fernando opened his desk drawer and took out a police evidence envelope and removed a small green plastic object and held it out to Dan.

"But look at this skimmer, Dani. It's so thin, so compact. If they had gotten it on the ATM machine successfully, no one would have noticed it. They could have stolen the credit and debit card numbers of every single person who used that ATM. We only have four ATMs in town! And the one at Banco Nacional is the most popular because of its location."

Dan stood up and stepped over to don Fernando's desk and took the skimmer from don Fernando's hand and examined it. It was designed to fit right over the ATM card input slot of the ATM machine. Dan peered into the slot. There was a tiny magnetic reader inside that would read and store the information from the magnetic strip on any ATM card that an unsuspecting customer inserted into the ATM machine.

"I remember seeing these years ago when I worked in L.A., don Fernando, but they were so much bigger than this one," Dan said.

"I have never seen one so tiny, so well built," don Fernando replied. "I even sent pictures of it to the FBI lab in Virginia."

Dan looked at don Fernando in surprise. "In Quantico? Since when did you start asking the FBI for help?"

"Ah, Dani, times have changed. Villa Rosario is no longer protected from criminals because of our remoteness. As criminals become more sophisticated, law enforcement has to adapt." Don Fernando furrowed his brow. "Actually, it's not that criminals are any brighter now, but they are more international. And new faces from other lands bring new ways of doing bad things. Did you read about those two *usureros* that were murdered last month in La Chorrera?"

"Yeah, I read about that. They were loan sharks, right? Something about loaning money to taxi drivers at high interest rates and then beating them up when they didn't pay on time?"

"Yes, but these loan sharks were not Panameños, not even Latinos! One was from Italy and the other was from the Czech Republic. And that hit was professionally done, which means that some gangs—foreign gangs—are fighting over the money lending business here in Panama. In the little town of La Chorrera! We never had that in my father's day. And we still don't know who did it... No, things are changing alright. We're always one step behind the criminals; we cannot afford to fall back further. And so yes, I talk with the FBI often these days. I want to create relationships now while I can, so that Jorge Manuel will have some resources when he takes over my job."

"I thought the city council was going to be considering applications over the next few months," Dan said.

Don Fernando laughed. "Ha, yes, but luckily some things don't change. They'll take applications alright, but my nephew will get the job."

Dan knew don Fernando's young nephew Jorge Manuel. He was the police chief of La Chorrera, a job that don Fernando had secured for him several years ago. Jorge Manuel might have gotten his job through nepotism, but he was smart and dedicated. Dan had grown to respect him over the years.

Dan turned the skimmer over in his hands. He noticed how there were two tiny spring-loaded clips on each side designed to hold the skimmer securely to the ATM's credit card slot.

"Interesting," he said out loud. "You'd need some special tool to affix or remove this."

Don Fernando reached into an evidence envelope and held up a small L-shaped prong. "Those kids had this on them. That's why they got caught. They couldn't figure out how to use it."

Dan took the L-shaped prong and saw how it could be used to reach into the slot of the skimmer to open or shut the clip. "It's a nice design, don Fernando. The old skimmers just used double-stick tape. This is craftsmanship."

"Yes, that's what worries me, Dani. We don't have that level of sophistication here in Panama. This came from outside the country."

Dan nodded his head and handed the skimmer and the prong back to don Fernando.

"And the other thing that was strange Dani, is that whoever was behind this didn't go after the customer's passcodes. The FBI explained to me that usually with ATM skimmers the criminals either install a tiny camera or a fake keypad to read the customers' passcodes. But we searched those kids and scoured every square inch of the ATM machine and the walls around it. No cameras and no fake keypads."

"Maybe they were planning to come back later and install those," Dan suggested, but then paused. "Or if it was a group outside of Panama behind this, maybe they just wanted the credit card information. There's a huge dark web market in Russia that buys and sells credit card numbers…"

"Exactly," said don Fernando. "Either way, bad juju."

Dan smiled. "Juju? You been vacationing in the Caribbean recently? Picking up some slang?"

Don Fernando shrugged. "Koke explained the phrase to me," he said, referring to Jorge Manuel by his family nickname. "Anyway, Dani, was the copy machine working today?"

"Yeah, thanks. In fact, I want to talk to you about this. Have you got a minute?"

"For you, Dani, of course. What's up?"

"Well," Dan began, "you remember my friend Ricardo?"

"Oh course, Dani. I have not seen around recently."

"He's left town for a while, and that's the problem. I don't know why he's left. He showed up at my door a little over a week ago, in the middle of the night, all packed to go somewhere, but he told me he wasn't even sure where he was going. It looked like he felt he had to get out of town quickly."

"Ah, yes. Gringos…" don Fernando said. "Is he in trouble?"

"I don't know. He told me to wait a week and then call his agent in New York—the guy who sells his books for him—but he told me to tell the agent that I had not seen him in *three* weeks, not one but three. And he told me not to tell anyone else about his visit..." Dan smiled and said, "Oh course, that does not include you, amigo."

Don Fernando nodded his head in appreciation. Dan continued, "But this is where it gets weird. I called the agent and the agent lied to me and said that Ricardo was back in the States working on a project, and that Ricardo had asked him to ask me to send him all of Ricardo's manuscripts and papers. I know that's not true. This guy was lying, but Ricardo had explicitly told me to do whatever this guy said, so I'm going to ship him Ricardo's papers on Monday."

"Yes... gringos," don Fernando repeated. "Gringos always have problems... except you, of course, Dani. You are the only gringo I know who doesn't have—how do you say it?—*first world problems*. With all other gringos, it's always the complicated problems..."

Dan smiled. "So anyway, I got Ricardo's papers, and I noticed there were some maps he had drawn, and I happened to mention that to the agent, and he got all excited. And I could tell he didn't want me to know he was excited, but he was *very interested* in these maps, which makes no sense because they are just crudely drawn maps, like something a child would do..."

"Maps of what?"

"I think they are of a town in Spain called Toledo. Turns out that Ricardo has been spending time talking to Matzel Davis about this town. You know this Matzel guy?"

"Sí, Dani. El loco moro."

"Moor? I thought he was German. Is he Muslim?"

"Everyone thinks he is German because of his accent, but he is from North Africa, Dani."

Dan thought about this for a moment. Don Fernando had been the police chief in Villa Rosario forever. He knew everybody. If don Fernando said that Matzel was from Africa, then Dan could take it as a fact.

"Is he Muslim?" Dan repeated.

"I do not know his religion," don Fernando said. "I only know he is a Moor and a bit crazy. But I think crazy like a wolf. He keeps to himself. Has never caused me any problems. He does a lot of business with German tourists. The bookstore is just a hobby. I don't know if he even sells any books. He makes his living dealing in old coins... and in gold. The locals know they can pawn wedding rings to him for a fair price. He used to buy a fair amount of gold from the Colombian *oreros* who would slip across the border."

Dan knew that the slang term oreros meant illegal gold miners, mostly poor people desperate to feed their families, who panned the rivers in Colombia or worked in shallow mines, and who usually died from mercury poisoning from breathing mercury fumes from their homemade gold smelters.

"Really? Is there a lot of illegal gold trafficking here in Villa Rosario?"

"No, not anymore. There used to be, years ago, but now the oreros don't come here. They all go to Panama City now and sell directly to the Colombian cartels."

"Wait. The Colombian oreros come here to Panama to sell gold to the Colombian cartels?" Dan asked.

"Absolutely, Dani. Because the cartels have US dollars and, thanks to your government, the US dollar is legitimate money here. You can't spend dollars in Colombia—they're not accepted. But here in Panama, the cartels can pay for gold with dollars, and no one questions the oreros when they go to the currency exchanges to convert their new dollars to Colombian pesos to take back home. That's why there is so much money laundering in Panama—because it's so easy. The cartels ship drugs to the US to sell, then smuggle the dollars down to Panama City and exchange them for gold the same day. Then they can easily fly or sail the gold straight north to the offshore banks in the Cayman Islands or the British Virgin Islands, the Bahamas, or even Bermuda."

"Do the banks launder the gold for them?"

"No, no Dani," don Fernando laughed. "The banks just *store* the gold for them. The cartels have regular accounts there. It's really the perfect system: The cartels convert all the dollars that are smuggled out of the United States by buying gold, then they store the gold in offshore banks, and then set up shell companies that use the gold as collateral to get loans from those same banks to buy property all over the world. These offshore banks have more gold than your Fort Knox, but they don't have to reveal anything to the US authorities. It's a very good business model for the banks because they hold the collateral for the money they loan, so they have no risk. And it's a good business model for the cartel bosses, because they can legitimately say they borrowed the money that they are using to invest in property, and even write off the interest charges. It's a win-win situation."

"Interesting," Dan said, "interesting and depressing... but Matzel Davis is not involved in that, is he?"

"No. In terms of gold, he is just a small-time pawnshop... The cartels deal in thousands of kilograms of gold. He is of no use to them."

"What else do you know about him?" Dan asked.

"That's about all, Dani. As I said, he keeps to himself and has never caused me any problems. But he is a bit loco, so be careful... so what were you saying about maps?"

"Well, Matzel seemed to know about these maps. It seems that Ricardo used to go and talk with him about this Toledo town in Spain. And Matzel kind of warned me I should guard these maps."

"And?"

"Well, that's it, really. Ricardo disappears but tells me to call his agent. His agent lies to me. Ricardo left behind some hand-drawn maps that I think are of Toledo. His agent seems inordinately interested in them. Matzel seems to know about Ricardo's interest in this Spanish town. He also knows about the maps and warned me to keep them in a safe place... that's about it."

"I see," said don Fernando. "Is that what you were copying—the maps?"

"Yeah."

"Are those them?" don Fernando asked, pointing to the notebook in Dan's hand.

"Yes," Dan said, and handed don Fernando the notebook. Don Fernando leafed through the pages.

"You see, there's not much there," Dan said.

"I don't know, Dani." don Fernando said and smiled. "It could be a treasure map."

"I don't think so, amigo. It's more like just random notes and sketches. I think he was just working on ideas for a new book."

Don Ferando handed the notebook back to Dan. "Well, as I say, Dani, gringo problems. You gringos are like onions—many layers, no center. But what you are telling me is that Ricardo has left town, and he has a loco friend in Matzel and a lying agent in the States. Seems like a typical gringo scenario to me. But let me know what happens."

"I will."

Dan racked his brain to see if there was anything else he could ask his old friend about Matzel, but there wasn't, so he stood up to leave.

"Okay amigo," he said, "I'm off. Don't work too hard."

Don Fernando just grunted and picked up his reports and began to study them again.

Dan walked out of don Fernando's office, down the hallway, and out of the police station.

The sun was setting, and the streets were getting dark. Usually, from don Fernando's office, Dan would cut through the Parque Central to get to his apartment. But tonight, he took the route around the circumference of the park, to walk by the corner where the pirate taxis park. He was still looking for Minor. But Minor was still not there. "Probably gone home for the night," Dan thought. He made a mental note to look him up tomorrow, and see if he could get him to confirm that he had brought Ricardo to his apartment, and more importantly, where he had taken him from there. If he had taken Ricardo to the airport, Dan hoped he could deduce which planes might have been flying at that time and maybe get an idea of where Ricardo went. He wasn't sure what use this information would be, but he had learned long ago as a detective that the more information you gather the better. It all becomes useful eventually.

As he made his way uphill from the Parque Central to his apartment, he thought about his day tomorrow. He could not ship the notebooks to Silas in that flimsy suitcase. He would have to buy some type of shipping crate. There was a general all-purpose hardware store on the other side of town. He could go there tomorrow and see what type of crate or box they might have, assuming they were open. Or he could simply take the suitcase to the DHL office in Panama City on Monday, and he knew from experience that they would box it up for him—for a hefty price. But that was probably the easiest course, because they would put the charges for the boxing-up on the bill of lading so that Herrell, Facela, and Edwards would pay. Yes, Dan thought, that was the way to go. Besides, that would free up his day tomorrow to research Toledo and go back and see Matzel, plus track down Minor.

He thought about his liquor supply at home. He knew he had sufficient whisky for tonight, but he decided to stop at the liquor store anyway. After all, it was on the way. Besides, he had to open his liquor cabinet anyway. In the back of his liquor cabinet was a secret compartment where he kept important documents like his passport and extra cash. He was going to put the copies of the maps in that secret compartment. And since he had to be in the cabinet anyway, he might as well add another bottle to his collection. No sense in risking running out.

CHAPTER EIGHT

The next morning, after several cups of coffee, Dan started scouring the internet for information on Toledo. Matzel had implied that he would be more forthcoming if Dan knew something about Toledo. The problem was that Dan had no idea what type of information he was looking for. But Matzel had said more than once that he was a historian. So, Dan started with the history of Toledo. And he was surprised by what a dense and tangled history it has.

He read how the Iberian Peninsula—now called Spain and Portugal—had been home to successive invasions and cultural migrations over the past 2,500 years. This included the Romans, the Visigoths, the Jews, the Moors, and the Christians. Located on a hill overlooking the Tagus River, Toledo was the perfect spot to build temples, mosques, synagogues, churches, castles and fortresses in order to control transportation up and down the river. The Romans took control of it in 192 BC. But Rome fell to the Visigoths in 476 AD. The Visigoths then advanced west into the Iberian Peninsula and made Toledo their capital in 570 AD. But then the Moors from North Africa invaded Spain in 711 and conquered Toledo. The term "Moor" did not define one people; rather, it was used to describe Arabs, North African Berbers, or any group of Muslims. There were many different groups of "Moors" who fought for control over the Iberian territory. But different Christian groups also wanted the land. In 1085, King Alfonso VI of Castile, with the help of the Knights of Templar, wrested Toledo away from the Moors and made it a Christian city. In 1469, Queen Isabella I of Castile married Ferdinand II or Aragon, combined their armies, and united their two great kingdoms to form the country now known as Spain. By this time, the Catholic Church had gained immense power. The Spanish Inquisition began in 1478. And in 1492, Isabella and Ferdinand drove the Moors out of the last Moorish city of Granada, and issued the Alhambra Decree, expelling all practicing Jews from Spain. In 1502, any remaining practicing Moors were likewise expelled from the country.

Dan wrote all those dates down on a legal pad and stared at them. *So what?* he thought. *How does this help me?* Maybe there was some other angle. Don Fernando said that Matzel made his money from coins and gold. So, Dan started reading about the Moors' use of Syrian gold dinars, and how they brought those coins to Spain. The Moors started striking their own gold dinars in Spain sometime after 912 AD. When the Christian "reconquistadores" began re-acquiring territory in Spain, the continued the practice of minting gold coins modeled after the dinar, but called them maravedis after the name of the Muslim Almoravid empire they were fighting. Evidently, it didn't matter what the coin looked like, nor what it was called. So long as it was gold, it was good. But as the reconquistadores began winning battles against the Moors and forcing them further outside of Spain, the maravedis began to get smaller, with less gold. In the late 1200s, the maravedis were made with silver. Around 1350, King Pedro I of Castille introduced the more valuable reales, silver coins which eventually replaced the maravedis. Later came the gold escudo coins, called doubloons.

But the more Dan read, the more his eyes glazed over. All these nomenclatures just were names to him, nothing more. By eleven o'clock, he had taken in enough information. He made himself a quick lunch and decided to go see Matzel despite the fact that he did not know much more about Toledo except that it had a complicated history with lots of different cultures and rulers.

Dan gave himself enough time to go by the Parque Central and see if Minor was there today. The sun was bright, but the day was cooler than yesterday. Dan even enjoyed walking on the side of the street where the sun hit. He made his way from his apartment down the hill to the park, then turned left and headed to the side where the pirate taxi drivers hung out. He noticed that the display of electric bicycles was not there today, nor were the two young men in company shirts anywhere to be seen. Odd, he thought, because they had told him they were there seven days a week. But maybe all the bikes were rented out. He remembered that he had meant to look up the Todo company last night and see about opening an account with them so he could try out the bikes. But he had stopped at the liquor store last night, and that had erased all his good intentions.

Down the street, he could see Minor sitting on a concrete bench, smoking a cigarette and talking to the other drivers. Dan waved at Minor, and Minor instinctively got up and went to his old car and climbed into the driver's seat.

Okay, Dan thought, *"I guess I'll take a little taxi ride.* He walked up to Minor's car and got into the front seat passenger side.

"Where to, señor Landes?" Minor asked in Spanish.

"Just drive around, Minor, I want to talk."

"Sí, señor."

Dan thought for a moment about how to launch into this topic. He decided to be direct.

"Look Minor, I need your help. My friend Ricardo is in some kind of trouble, and I need to find him. I know that you dropped him off at my apartment last week." Minor gave Dan a nervous look but said nothing.

"I know you waited for him while he talked with me, because he told me you were downstairs waiting for him. And he told me he was going to leave Villa Rosario for a while. And I know you took him somewhere after he left my apartment. But something has gone wrong with his plan, and I think he's in trouble. I want you to tell me where you took him."

Minor looked very nervous now.

"Señor," he said, "I never get involved with my client's personal lives."

"Well, you *are* involved, Minor. Because if you don't tell me, and something bad happens to Ricardo, it will be your fault."

Dan paused for a moment to let that sink in before continuing. "You know me, Minor. And you know I'm Ricardo's friend. I won't tell him or anyone else what you tell me. But I need to help him. I think he's in danger and I need your help to find him."

Minor pursed his lips, but nodded, and then said, "Sí, señor. I know you are his friend... It was a very strange evening. I could tell that señor Ricardo was very worried. He told me not to tell anyone that I had picked him up. He asked me to drive to your apartment and wait for him."

"Where did you take him after he saw me?"

"To Panama City."

"To the airport?"

"Not directly, señor. First, we went to an all-night cafeteria... Well, no... First, I needed to get gas. Señor Ricardo told me to stop at the Delta station in El Espino. He got out there and talked with a man in another car while I got gas. Then we drove to Panama City. He had me take him to this cafeteria that was open near the airport."

"Who was he talking to at the gas station?"

"I do not know, señor. When I told him I needed to get gas, he asked me if I had enough to get to El Espino. I said yes, and then he called someone on his cell phone and told them to meet him at the Delta gas station there. But I did not see who he was talking to."

"And then you drove him to this cafeteria?"

Minor nodded.

"Which airport, Tocumen or Gelabert?" Dan asked.

"Near the Tocumen airport, señor. There's an all-night cafeteria on the other side of the highway. He wanted to eat, and he asked me to stay with him. We waited there for almost two hours. He ate, and then he was on his phone the whole time."

"Talking to someone?"

"No, señor. I think he was trying to buy a ticket. I could tell he was checking different airlines. Finally, I saw him get his credit card out and enter the numbers into the phone. I think he bought a ticket. Then he asked me to take him to the airport."

"Did he say where he was going?"

"No, señor. He only said he had a 6 a.m. flight he wanted to make."

"Did he say anything else about where he might be going?"

"No señor. He just repeated that I should not tell anyone that I had seen him or that I had taken him to the airport."

"Okay, Minor. Thank you. I think he would have wanted me to know. But I agree with him. If anyone else asks you, you don't know anything. You didn't pick him up last week, and you and I never had this conversation. Okay?"

"Sí, señor."

Dan looked around. Minor had basically made a huge circle around the side streets just outside the Parque Central. He was not that far from Matzel's bookstore.

"You can let me off here, Minor. How much do I owe you?"

Minor looked at his watch. Like most pirate taxi drivers, he priced his fares on time spent, rather than any type of meter. None of them even had meters because, after all, they were pirate taxis, not legal ones.

"Three bilboas, señor."

Dan handed him a twenty-dollar bill. "That's fine, Minor. Keep the change. And thank you."

"Thank *you*, señor."

Dan got out of the car and started walking down the street. He checked his watch: 12:10, right on time. After he talked to Matzel, he thought, he would go back to his apartment and look up the plane schedules of what planes had departed from Tocumen airport. Dan had to think back to what night Ricardo had come to his house. It was last Tuesday. No wait, it was after midnight, so that would have been early Wednesday morning, ten days ago. Yes, he would check what planes flew out of the Tocumen airport at 6 a.m. on Wednesday morning, ten days ago. That would tell him— maybe—where Ricardo had flown to. In the meantime, he wanted to talk more with Matzel.

But when he got to Matzel's shop, something was clearly amiss. The shop was dark, and there was a sign on the door, saying the business was closed.

"What the fuck?" Dan said out loud. He peered through the glass window of the front door. He could see the counter where he had stood the day before and talked with Matzel. It was too dark to see if any of the coins were still in the display cases. He took out his cellphone and turned on the flashlight and tried to shine it through the front door window at the counter, but it wasn't powerful enough to illuminate anything. He looked at the hand-printed sign on the front door: it only read "Closed for Renovation." Yet Matzel had clearly said yesterday that he would be open today and had invited Dan to come back. This made no sense.

He turned to leave, but out of his old detective habits, Dan tried the doorknob. To his surprise, it turned, and the front door opened. Dan froze for a second, as adrenalin pumped into his system. He pushed the door with his finger, and it swung open.

His cell phone was still in his hand. He had don Fernando's cell phone number on speed dial. In fact, it was the only number he had on speed dial. He hit it. After two rings, don Fernando answered.

"Hola, Dani," don Fernando's voice answered. "Qué tal?"

"Are you at your office?"

"No, Dani. I am taking the day off, you know, to be with my family. These days, I am easing toward retirement, so I only work part-time. It's good to spend time with my family. Why do you ask?"

"I'm sorry, don Fernando. I did not mean to disturb you."

"It's okay, Dani. What's up?"

"Well, it's just that Matzel Davis asked me to come and visit him at his bookstore today. I'm here at his bookstore, but there's a sign on the door saying it's closed for renovation, but the front door is unlocked. I don't know, but it just seems suspicious to me. I want to go in and look around, but I thought I'd better call you first."

There was a pause on the line, then don Fernando said, "Wait there, Dani. I'll be right over."

"No, no, don Fernando. I don't want to take you away from your family..."

Don Fernando lowered his voice. "Are you kidding, Dani? I'm dying of boredom here. I'll be right there."

CHAPTER NINE

A few minutes later, don Fernando pulled up in front of Matzel Davis's shop. Dan was standing on the steps, waiting for him.

"Listen, don Fernando, I'm sorry for..." Dan started to say.

But don Fernando waved him off. "No, I appreciate it, Dani. I needed an excuse to get away from the house. I'm really beginning to have second thoughts about this retirement thing. My wife thinks I am some kind of servant for home remodeling now... So, what's going on here?"

"Well, I was here yesterday, and Matzel told me to come back today. He said he would be open at noon, and I should come by at twelve-fifteen, so we could talk some more. But when I got here, all the lights were off, and there was this sign on the door," Dan explained, and pointed at the sign. "I can't see if the coins in his display case have been disturbed. But the clincher was that the front door is unlocked. I tried the handle. It wasn't locked."

"Okay, Dani. It's probably nothing, but let's go have a look."

Don Fernando opened the front door and examined the doorjamb and door frame. He stepped inside and looked at the back of the door. "Doesn't appear to be forced," he said and took a few steps inside. Dan followed him into the store.

"Hola, Hola," don Fernando said loudly into the dark shop. "Policía, policía. Señor Davis, are you here?"

There was only silence in the store.

Dan reached over to the light switch on the wall and flipped it on. Light illuminated the store. Dan could now see that the display case was still full of coins. He stepped up to the case and looked closer. There was no broken glass, no open panels. Nothing had been disturbed. He looked around the lobby. Everything looked normal. Don Fernando stepped into doorway of the room to the right of the lobby and called Matzel's name out again. He must have found the light switch because Dan saw a light come on from the room. Dan listened as don Fernando wandered down the hallway. Dan stared at the display case and felt foolish. Matzel was just an old man, who had invited him to return today to chat and had forgotten that he had previously arranged to have some restoration work done. Or maybe he had forgotten that he had invited Dan to return at all. After all, don Fernando had said he was loco. He also probably forgot to lock his own door. Dan had called don Fernando away from home for nothing.

Dan turned away from the display case. He started to go find don Fernando, to apologize again for disturbing his Saturday, when he heard don Fernando calling out to him from a room down the hallway.

"Dani. Come here!"

Dan stepped through the side room, down a short hallway, and into the doorway of another room. Don Fernando was in the middle of the room, kneeling down. Dan's eyes blinked and focused on what he was kneeling over. It was a body, a man's body, crumpled up on the floor. Around the body were heaps of papers and file folders. It took Dan another second to realize that the room contained at least eight full-size filing cabinets. Some of their drawers had been pulled out and the contents dumped around the body.

The body was lying halfway on its stomach, its legs pulled up, its face turned away from Dan. Don Fernando was gently lifting up the man's shoulder and looking underneath.

"Is it Matzel?" Dan asked.

"No," said don Fernando. "I don't recognize this man. It looks like he was shot once in the chest. The body is cold. He's been dead for a number of hours."

Don Fernando lifted up the side of the man's shirt and looked underneath. Dan saw a holstered gun on the man's belt. Don Fernando patted the man's backside and removed a wallet from his back pocket. He then stood up and opened the wallet.

"Let's see who we have here," don Fernando said, and pulled out a credit card. "Álvaro Renaldo... obviously not a local... ah, and here's a Colombiano driver's license... definitely not a local."

Dan stepped into the room, and carefully made his way around the piles of papers on the floor to look at the man's face. Thin nose, dark skin, mouth agape. Dan had never seen him before. He could see blood had seeped out from underneath the body and had soaked into the wood floorboards and dried. Dan looked around at the filing cabinets. Only half seemed to have been opened, their drawers emptied. The other filing cabinets were undisturbed.

"He must have been interrupted," Dan said out loud. "He was looking for something and got interrupted."

Don Fernando looked around at the file cabinets and nodded. He stooped back down, put the wallet back in the man's rear pocket, straightened up and pulled out his cell phone. Dan heard him call the police station and order a forensic team to come over pronto, along with several other officers. Then he dialed another number and talked to someone.

Dan stepped back into the hallway and looked up and down it. He had not realized on his first visit to the shop yesterday how far back the building went. He took a few steps down the hallway and peered into the next room.

"Uh, don Fernando," he called out.

"Yes, Dani?"

"There's another body here."

Don Fernando quickly joined Dan at the doorway to this other room. There, lying face down on the floor, was another man. Dan could see what looked like a bullet wound in the man's back surrounded by dried blood.

"Madre de Dios!" don Fernando said and stepped into the room to examine the body. Dan remained in the doorway.

"He's dead," don Fernando said. Don Fernando rolled the body on its side and looked at the man's chest. "He was shot in the back, Dani. There were no wounds in the front." Don Fernando reached into the man's jacket and removed a passport. Dan looked warily up and down the hallway. He wondered if there were more bodies.

"Another extranjero, Dani, but this one's from Francia," don Fernando said as he read the man's passport.

"France?" exclaimed Dan and stepped into the room. Don Fernando handed him the dead man's passport. Dan looked at the man's contorted face on the floor and then at the photograph in the passport. It was the same man, one Romain Martin Groslot, from Lille, France.

"This one's also been dead a number of hours," don Fernando said. Nonetheless, he drew his pistol and said, "You wait here, Dani. I'm going to check the other rooms."

Dan nodded. Don Fernando stepped down the hallway. Dan looked at the body again. This man was wearing a dark suit. Most unusual in this climate. Dan glanced around the room. This room was also filled with filing cabinets, but none of them were open. Strange, Dan thought. That's two rooms full of filing cabinets. He had assumed yesterday that each room would be full of books. There were shelves on the walls behind the filing cabinets, but they were bare. A small table and wooden chair were in the corner. This room, like the other, was clearly meant for storing documents.

Don Fernando came back into the room. "No more bodies," he said.

"Were any of the other rooms disturbed?" Dan asked.

"No, just that first room."

Dan still had the dead man's passport in his hand. He flipped through it and looked at the stamped pages.

"He came here directly from France," Dan said to don Fernando. "I'd like to know the other man's travel history."

"We can get that information," said don Fernando. "It looks like they both came here to search, and someone surprised them."

Dan nodded, looked around the room one more time, and then scanned the dead man again. Nothing else caught his eye. He handed the passport back to don Fernando.

"Come on, Dani. Let's wait outside," don Fernando said. "We don't want to contaminate this crime scene any more than we already have. I'll have my men photograph everything."

Dan looked at don Fernando and nodded. He thought to himself how much don Fernando had learned and changed over the years he had known him. The phrase "contaminate a crime scene" would never have escaped don Fernando's lips five years ago.

Dan and don Fernando stepped outside Matzel's shop. Three police cars pulled up almost immediately, followed by an ambulance. Don Fernando went over to them and barked out orders to the first car of officers for fingerprints and photos; he told his forensics officer to do paraffin tests on the hands of both men; he gave them special instructions for inventorying and removing the bodies; and he ordered immediate autopsies. Then he sent the officers in the second car scurrying to interview all the neighbors to learn if they had seen anything. He then said something to third car of officers, and they drove off.

"Where are they going?" Dan asked when don Fernando walked back over to him.

"I sent them over to Matzel Davis's house."

"Oh? Where does he live?"

"North of town, in Santa Rita, in the Ribera area."

"Ribera?" Dan asked. "That ritzy area?"

"I never said he was poor, Dani. I just said he was loco."

It wasn't that the Ribera area of Santa Rita was an affluent neighborhood, but relative to Villa Rosario, it was the nicest area in town. In fact, it was the nicest area until one got past La Chorrera, all the way to the suburbs of Panama City, meaning that all the houses in the Ribera neighborhood had paved roads, sidewalks, electricity, indoor toilets, and good water pressure. Dan thought about Matzel for a moment: Here was a man from North Africa with a German accent who lived in the nicest area in town but ran a bookstore that did not appear to do much book business but dealt in gold and rare coins. Nothing really fit. And now his shop is unexpectedly closed with two bodies inside.

He looked at don Fernando and asked, "What do you think is going on?"

"I have no idea, Dani. We'll just have to wait and see. Let's hope we can find Matzel Davis."

Dan nodded, and both men sat down on the front steps to the bookstore.

A few minutes later a police car bearing the name La Chorrera Policía pulled up. Jorge Manuel, don Fernando's nephew, was driving. Dan had wondered who the other person was that don Fernando had called. Now he knew.

"Hola, Koke," don Fernando called out, using Jorge Manuel's family nickname. "Thank you for coming."

Jorge Manuel stepped out of the car and greeted both men. Don Fernando told him about the two bodies on the floor of the unlocked bookstore, and then said, "But the reason I asked you to come by, Koke, was because Dani was here, and I wanted him to tell you what he told me about his friend Ricardo Mendes. You remember señor Mendes? He helped us catch that crazy man who murdered the poor blind boy in that gay bathhouse in La Chorrera about eight years ago?"

"Yes, of course, uncle. I remember señor Mendes well."

"Well, he's gone missing, and Dani thinks that he is somehow connected to Matzel Davis, who is the owner of this bookstore. At the very least, they were friends, but I will let Dani tell you what he knows."

So much for keeping Ricardo's secrets, Dan thought to himself. But he realized that it was logical that if don Fernando should know about Ricardo's disappearance, then Jorge Manuel should know too. So, Dan repeated the same story to Jorge Manuel that he had told don Fernando the day before. He decided to leave out his conversation with Minor, so he just indicated that he was certain that Ricardo went to the airport after he left his apartment. He asked that Jorge Manuel not share this information with anyone else, unless it was absolutely necessary.

As Dan was explaining the story, the police car that don Fernando had sent to Santa Rita returned. Don Fernando went up to the car and listened to the officers for a minute, then told them something and they drove off again. Don Fernando stepped back to front of the bookstore as Dan was finishing his story.

"So, I really have no idea why Ricardo's left," Dan was saying to Jorge Manuel. "It could just be a disagreement with his agent, or anything else. And I have no idea if it is connected to this guy Matzel Davis."

"Well," don Fernando interrupted, "*something* is clearly going on with Matzel Davis. His house has been completely ransacked, and he's not there. But someone broke in and tore the place apart looking for something. Every room was completely ripped apart. Some of the floorboards were even pulled up. My men are securing it and talking to the neighbors now."

Dan's heart sank. Not only for Matzel, but for the first time, he began to really worry about Ricardo's safety. Ricardo had been his friend for more than a decade. It was impossible to imagine Villa Rosario without him.

Don Fernando saw the look on Dan's face. "Dani, do not worry. We'll get to the bottom of this."

Dan just nodded.

The ambulance attendants came out of the shop with one of the two dead men on a stretcher covered by a white sheet. They placed him in the ambulance and went back inside for the other body. The police photographer came out and said something to don Fernando. Three forensic officers emerged carrying a box of files. Don Fernando spoke with them. Two of them left with the photographer. The third police officer remained by the door. The ambulance attendants emerged with the second body and placed it in the ambulance. Don Fernando gave them instructions, and then the ambulance took off, sirens wailing. and left. The officer who stayed behind started putting police tape over the front door.

"Since I don't have a key to this door, I'm having a locksmith come and put a new lock on it. I'm going to post a guard here until the locksmith gets here," don Fernando said to Dan. "They found lots of fingerprints inside, of course, but that doesn't tell us anything. We've got samples of the blood and photos…"

"How was Matzel's house broken into?" Dan interrupted.

"The back door was kicked in."

"The house was gated and had a fence?"

"Of course, a wall with concertina wire."

Dan looked at the wooden door and doorframe, then said, "You know, don Fernando, we don't know how many people are involved in this. Maybe the Colombian guy shot the French guy, and then someone shot the Colombian guy. Or maybe someone else shot both of them, we don't know. Maybe they both got surprised, or maybe they surprised someone else. Maybe someone else was starting to search the bookstore when these two guys showed up. And maybe that person then left and went to Matzel's house. And if that's true, and if he didn't find what he wanted there, he might just come back here to finish searching. And if *that's* true, then I don't think a new lock and police tape would keep him out."

Don Fernando glanced over at the front door to the bookstore and nodded his head.

"You have a point, Dani." Then he called out to the young officer putting up the police tape on the front door, "Eduardo, you want some overtime?"

"Sí, Capitán," the man replied eagerly.

"Okay, tell Sergeant Arias that I want this bookstore guarded even after the locksmith comes, and tell him I said that you can work extra hours."

"Gracias, Capitán."

Don Fernando turned back to Dan. "Come on, Dani, I'll give you a ride home."

"'But we still don't know what happened," Dan said.

"Of course not, Dani, but we will... we will. But there's nothing more we can do here now. My officers in Ribera are still interviewing Matzel's neighbors. We've radioed out his description, and we're searching for him. Koke notified all his men in La Chorrera to pull over anyone who they don't recognize and question them, especially any extranjeros. We've notified the Panama City police. We'll send the names of the two dead men to Interpol to find out who they are. We'll have their autopsy reports by Monday or Tuesday. But right now, there's nothing we can do but wait. We especially have to wait until find Matzel. He's the only one who knows what these dead men were looking for. My men took some of his files back to the office to read through them, hoping to find some clue, but we really need to talk to Matzel. Until we find him, we just have to wait. Come on, I'll drive you home."

Don Fernando looked at Dan's worried face, and then glanced at his watch.

"Actually, Dani, I don't want to go home quite yet. Come on, let's to El Balcón. I'll buy you a drink."

Dan looked up at the front of Matzel's bookstore, took a breath, then nodded okay, and they walked towards don Fernando's car.

CHAPTER TEN

El Balcón was the oldest bar in Villa Rosario, located on the second floor of an ancient wood-frame building. The building itself was probably more than a hundred years old, but it had survived because it had been constructed in the old style, made of wood from the gauyacán real, or ironwood tree. The old style was to construct a building with ironwood trees that had just been cut and milled. Fresh ironwood lumber had enough moisture in it that it was possible to cut it and hammer nails into it. But once a few months passed, the wood dried and hardened, and became impervious to insects, moisture, and nails. It became almost impossible to build with it. The advantage of the old style was that structures built with ironwood lasted forever, and never needed painting. But modern construction companies no longer milled their own timber. They simply bought cheap two-by-fours from large warehouses in Panama City and built houses in the new style: cheaply and poorly. But El Balcón had the old unpainted rough-hewn eight-by-eight beams of ironwood, and would probably last another hundred years.

One of the other characteristics of ironwood was that it darkened as it aged, going from yellow wood to dark brown and then to black. The inside of El Balcón was entirely black and gloomy because it was entirely ironwood, and it was the type of black that did not reflect light well. The original owners of the bar built a covered balcony that wrapped around the entire second floor, where all the patrons could sit and drink and watch the street scene below or enjoy the sunsets. It proved so popular that the bar simply became known as El Balcón. No one could even remember the original name.

Dan and don Fernando found a table out on the balcony. The waiter knew them both, and knew their drink preferences. All it took was a nod from don Fernando and the waiter went scurrying off to the bar. The fact that it was don Fernando meant that the bartender would give their drinks priority.

Dan was gazing out at the mountains that surrounded Villa Rosario. Don Fernando sat quietly and just watched his friend.

The waiter hurried back with their drinks. Dan's glass held two fingers worth of whisky and four ice cubes. Don Fernando's was just whisky without the ice.

Dan turned to the table, picked up his drink and said, "I'm too old for this, don Fernando."

"What? Too old for whisky? Dani, this is good stuff."

Dan smiled. "No, I meant too old for this detective stuff. One is never too old for whisky." Dan lifted his glass up against the light reflecting off the distant hills and said, "Now this is a gentleman's drink."

Don Fernando looked at him quizzically.

"Sorry," Dan said taking a sip of his drink. "That's an old Frank Sinatra line."

"The Italiano singer?"

"Yeah... what I meant was that there was a time back in California when I would get totally involved in every new case. They were like puzzles to me, and my brain seemed to be addicted to solving them. There was always a logic, a motivation, a secret pattern to every crime, and once I figured that pattern out, all the pieces would fall into place. And I wouldn't stop until I had solved that pattern. I was like a man possessed. But now... I don't know... I just saw two dead men, and I don't even care why they died. I just want Ricardo to be safe. I want to help him. But I don't know if have the energy any more to figure out what's going on... Maybe I'm jaded, or just worn out."

"Oh, I think you are still addicted, Dani. It's how your brain works," don Fernando said.

"It used to be interesting, but now, I don't know... The motives are always the same... power, greed, revenge, somebody always wanting something for nothing..."

"Corruptible seed," don Fernando said. "That's what Father Lopez always used to call it. He would say we're all conceived from Adam's rib, and so we're all corruptible."

"Yeah..." Dan said, then added, "I miss him."

"I do too, Dani. He was more than just my *consejero*. He was my best friend. Villa Rosario is just not the same without him. *I'm* not the same without him." Don Fernando paused, then said, "The Church was stronger when he was in charge. He had a certain moral authority. People knew that when they confessed to him, they were confessing to God. And he always shaped their absolutions so that they had to do something to atone for their sins... Did you know that the priests at the Church now, that they take confessions over the phone?"

Dan gave a laugh. "No, I didn't know that. Really?"

"What a joke, right? Confess over the phone because you are too busy to come to church and get down on your knees. It won't be long until confession will just be an app on people's phones."

Dan nodded. "It's probably already available."

"I remember Father Lopez telling me once that good never triumphs over evil," don Fernando said. "It stunned me when he said that. He said that the best good can do is to coexist with evil."

"I don't know if I buy that," Dan said. "It seems to me that he spent all his life fighting evil. He always seemed to act as if evil was a real force in the world that had to be confronted."

The two men sat silent for a moment, each sipping their drinks. Then Dan spoke. "Do you remember that time, about eight or nine years ago, when he came to us with the plan to use Ricardo as bait to lure that brujo out of hiding? Man, I was never so scared about doing something in my whole life. Ricardo was my friend, and I had to pretend that I didn't know that he was walking into a trap, a potentially deadly trap."

"Ah, yes. I remember that," don Fernando said.

"I didn't want to do it, but Father Lopez kept insisting it was the only way to catch the brujo in his true form, when he would be at his weakest," Dan said.

"Yes, yes. I remember Father Lopez reassuring you that Ricardo would be safe, that we would follow him very carefully, day and night, and protect him from the brujo," don Fernando said.

"Yeah," Dan said. "He kept telling me: 'Follow Ricardo, that's all we have to do, follow Ricardo.' He convinced me it would be that simple..." Dan's voice trailed off. Then something in Dan's brain clicked. Maybe it was the whisky, or maybe it was just thinking about Ricardo, or something else falling into place, but he suddenly turned to don Fernando and asked, "How far is El Espino from Santa Rita?"

"Hmm... not far, maybe four kilometers. Why?"

"Fuck! I don't know why I didn't see it sooner. The man at the gas station was Matzel!"

Dan pulled out his cellphone and started punching buttons.

"What? I don't understand, Dani," don Fernando said.

"After Ricardo left my apartment last week, he went to the airport in Panama City. But before he got there, he stopped in El Espino at a gas station and met with someone. I bet that someone was Matzel! Then, he went to the airport and caught a flight that left at six a.m."

"How do you know this, Dani?"

Dan was tapping furiously on his phone now. "Before I got to Matzel's shop this afternoon, I tracked down the taxi driver who brought him to my apartment. He told me... Avianca, Copa, no, no, Iberia... ah, yes. Here it is: there's a six a.m. flight that leaves Panama City for Madrid on Iberia Airlines. Ricardo flew to Madrid. Toledo's about an hour south of Madrid."

Don Fernando just stared at Dan. Finally, he asked, "Okay... and?"

"Well, that's where Matzel's gone, too... or that's where he's on his way to go," said Dan. "Don't you see? Something happened a week ago that scared Ricardo. Clearly, it was something that involved Matzel... somehow. And somehow it involves his New York agent, too. Ricardo had to get out of town quickly. He told me to lie to his agent. He leaves my apartment, meets with Matzel, then heads to the airport and catches a flight to Madrid. But he deliberately leaves these maps behind that his agent is very interested in—the same maps that Matzel tells me to guard carefully. Then, a week after Ricardo leaves, strangers start showing up. Someone ransacks Matzel's house. Two guys start to search Matzel's bookstore, but they get shot. And now, Matzel's disappeared. The two dead guys are foreigners. Maybe there's two competing gangs."

Don Fernando continued to stare at Dan.

"Don't you see?" Dan blurted out. "Matzel's gone to Toledo."

"Why do you say that, Dani?"

"Because he's following Ricardo," Dan said quickly. Dan paused for a second to make sense out of what he had just said, then the words rushed out of him. "It's just an intuition, don Fernando. I'm not sure I can explain why, but it was obvious to me yesterday that Ricardo was more than just a client of Matzel's—he was a friend, a good friend. Matzel said that Ricardo used to come over to his shop to visit two or three times a week. They had spent enough time together that Ricardo had told him about me. Matzel even knew me by sight. He had said that Ricardo pointed me out to him one time, which means that maybe they spent time together outside of the shop as well, maybe walking around town, somewhere where he and Ricardo might have seen me walking. And what was it Matzel said? That Ricardo would study up on the history of Toledo and try and come up with questions to stump Matzel. That's something only a friend does... or, maybe a business partner... someone who's interested enough in either you, or the subject, to invest time studying it. I never knew Ricardo to be a history buff, so there was something about either Matzel or Toledo that interested him. And then, clearly, Matzel was encouraging me to learn about Toledo. Why would he insist I do that first, and then come back to talk to him?"

"Maybe he used to live there, Dani," don Fernando said. "Maybe he is just a lonely old man who wants someone to chat with about the home of his youth. Or maybe he had some old books on Toledo he wanted to sell you."

"No, he was trying to draw me in, I can feel it."

"Dani, slow down," don Fernando said. "It's also possible that someone was just trying to rob Matzel. Everyone knows he deals in coins, and that he used to deal in gold. Maybe it's just a simple robbery. Those two guys go to his house and tear it apart looking for gold. They don't find anything. So, they go to his office. Maybe Matzel surprised them there. Maybe *he* shot them. And maybe he's gone into hiding now. We just don't know. Maybe your friend Ricardo and his problem with his agent have nothing to do with Matzel."

"No, they're connected. I can feel it," Dan said.

"Maybe yes, and maybe no. But we just don't know, Dani. Without more evidence, all we have are two dead men, and one missing loco." Don Fernando paused, then asked, "Do you know *why* Matzel has a reputation for being crazy, Dani?"

"No. He seemed pretty sane to me."

"Yes, he always *appears* very relaxed, very calm. But he's killed people before, Dani. There was a situation one time, back when he used to buy gold from the oreros, when these three Colombianos ambushed one of Matzel's favorite miners, a poor man who panned for gold illegally in creeks in the Paramillo National Park, just over the Colombian border. Anyway, he had a month's worth of gold, and he was bringing it back to see Matzel. They were supposed to meet in this hotel in Panama City where Matzel was going to buy the man's gold. But these punks had followed him from Colombia and attacked him in the hotel room before Matzel got there, beat him mercilessly and stole all his gold. When Matzel showed up the guy was almost dead, but he knew who the men were who had attacked him, and he told Matzel with his dying breath who they were. Well, Matzel tracked them down back in Colombia and killed all three of them. Found out where each of them lived, went to their houses, and shot each one dead."

"Really?" said Dan. "Did he get arrested?"

"What? For killing the robbers who killed his friend? Of course not. He was just settling the account. Nothing to arrest him for. My point is, Dani, that nothing and no one is as they appear. Your friend Ricardo is missing, but he clearly *wanted* to go missing. So, we just have to wait until he reappears. We have two dead men, but they were burglarizing a store. And we have a missing Matzel. We just have to wait until we find Matzel. He's the key to this. We've got all the police from here to Panama City notified to detain him if they see him. We just have to wait until we find him, or he reappears. For the moment Dani, that's all we can do. We have to wait."

CHAPTER ELEVEN

The next day was Sunday, and Dan slept in, not because it was Sunday, but because he had had several more whiskies with don Fernando at el Balcón the night before. Then he came home to his apartment and had a few more. At some point he had stumbled off to bed.

It was almost ten when he got up. He had no plans for the day. Don Fernando had told him that it would take at least thirty-six hours to get the autopsy reports and the response from Interpol. Don Fernando promised to call Dan if the police found Matzel. Otherwise, Dan was to come over to the police station around eleven Monday morning, and they would see what reports had come in and talk about the case. So, Dan had Sunday free. He showered and shaved and thought about making breakfast. Maybe it was the hangover he was feeling, but he decided to go have breakfast out. There was a row of tiny fast-food stalls called *fondas* about two blocks away that would cook a US-style breakfast for expats, with bacon, scrambled eggs, and hash browns, so he decided to eat there. He got dressed and headed out the door.

Whisky had a way of clearing his mind—in a sense— much the way a bulldozer clears a field of overgrown bushes and undergrowth, leaving the bare earth exposed. As he walked down to the fonda, Dan considered don Fernando's theory that maybe Matzel shot the two burglars in his shop and then fled but disregarded that theory. Matzel would be well within his rights to shoot burglars in his own shop, so he could have just called the police. There had to be something else, something bigger, going on to all this. Don Fernando had said that Matzel's house was completely torn apart.

That would have taken time. A normal burglar doesn't want to spend time—he wants to get in, grab anything of value, and get out. No, whoever it was that ransacked Matzel's house was looking for something specific. Dan thought about the coins that were in the display case. He added up the value of all those coins he had seen in the case... probably two or three thousand dollars... a lot of money to the average Panamanian. Did Matzel have more coins at his house? Enough coins to warrant the kind of complete ransacking of the house that don Fernando had described.

Dan got to the fonda, ordered breakfast, poured himself a cup of coffee from the sideboard coffee pot, sat down at one of the outside tables, and continued to think. Don Fernando had suggested that Ricardo's disappearance had nothing to do with Matzel, but Dan didn't buy that. The recent events had too many interconnections. Ricardo had met with Matzel in the middle of the night before going to the airport. When Dan told Matzel that Ricardo had disappeared, Matzel seemed unconcerned, and yet obviously they were good friends. That implied that Matzel already knew that Ricardo had left. Then there was the fact that both men had disappeared during the same week. That alone connected them. But what was their connection? Matzel had not denied it when Dan had guessed that Ricardo had an appointment to talk with him about coins. In fact, Matzel had said that they would talk about coins during Ricardo's many visits. But Ricardo had never mentioned coins to Dan.

Dan's food arrived. His brain continued to obsess about Matzel and coins while he ate. If Ricardo was not interested in coins, why would he spend time talking to a coin dealer about coins? Dan tried to remember what types of coins were in Matzel's display case. They weren't old Panamanian coins, and they weren't old US coins. Dan remembered the pictures of the various Spanish coins he had seen when he was researching Toledo. He pulled out his cell phone and started scrolling through images of old Spanish coins. Yes, he thought, those pictures looked a lot like the coins that he had seen in Matzel's display case. That would make some sense out of Ricardo's interest. Ricardo had spent his twenties in Spain. Maybe he had some old coins he wanted to sell. Maybe he just enjoyed talking to Matzel about Spain. Maybe Matzel had lived in Spain in his youth as well.

Dan was almost finished with his breakfast when his cell phone rang. His caller ID identified it as a local number, but not one of his contacts.

"Hello."

"Is this Dan Landes?"

"Yes."

"Mr. Landes, this is Silas Edwards. I hope I didn't wake you."

Dan's heart skipped a beat. This did not sound like the same person he had spoken to a few days ago. There was no British accent."

"Oh?" Dan said cautiously. "Um, no, I'm awake. What can I do for you?"

"Have you shipped Ricardo's items to us yet?"

Dan's mind was racing. This was a local call. And this was *not* Silas Edwards. But he knew about Ricardo, and he knew about the shipment.

"No," Dan said. "As I told you, I am going to ship them Monday, tomorrow."

"Excellent," the voice said. "Then I arrived in time. I was explaining the situation to Ricardo, and he asked me to come down to Panama and... well, *expedite* the process. So, I flew down late last night. I was wondering if we could meet today so that I could pick up Ricardo's files. I have a flight back to New York tonight."

Dan's brain was in overdrive now. He had to stall this guy until he knew what the fuck was going on.

"Where are you calling from?" Dan asked.

"I'm in Panama City," the voice said. "I booked a hotel near the airport."

"Ah, said Dan. "That explains why my caller ID showed a local call."

"Yes, I bought one of those prepaid Panamanian chips for my cell phone at the airport. I figured that would be the most convenient way to have phone service down here."

Yes, Dan thought to himself, and also the best way to not be traceable.

Dan decided to be a bit difficult. "Let me get this straight, Silas. You flew all the way down here simply to look at Ricardo's files? The same files I told you I was going to ship to you tomorrow? That seems like a huge waste of money."

The voice laughed. "Well, Ricardo asked me to. And I can never refuse a client. He was very anxious to have his files. I rented a car at the airport last night. I can drive down this morning, if that's convenient."

Dan remembered one of his old interviewing tricks: When trying to determine whether a suspect is telling the truth, throw him a lie and see how he reacts.

"Did Ricardo say he wanted his box of computer disks?" Dan asked, making it up on the spot. "The ones labeled *maps?* You know, the disks we talked about?"

"Oh yes, Mr. Landes. He said he especially needed those for his work."

That clinched it for Dan.

"Okay, Silas. Well, if you want to drive down, why don't you come by at one o'clock? That'll get you plenty of time to get back to the airport."

"Excellent, Mr. Landes. Can you give me your address?"

"Well, Silas, there really aren't street addresses down in Villa Rosario. If you have GPS or a map, just come to the front gate of the Catholic Church. It's in the center of town and near my apartment. You can't miss it. It's the only church in town. I'll meet you there at one o'clock. You'll need about an hour to drive down here from Panama City."

"Excellent, Mr. Landes. I'll come to the main gate of the Catholic Church. See you at one."

And the phone clicked off.

Well, fuck, Dan thought to himself. He hit don Fernando's number on his speed dial.

"Hello, Dani."

"Don Fernando, I'm sorry to disturb you at home two days in a row, but I just got a call from someone claiming to be Silas Edwards. And he says he flew into Panama City last night and he's driving down to meet me here at one o'clock to pick up Ricardo's things."

"Ah, gringos... always in a hurry, always in a rush."

"No, you don't understand, don Fernando. This *wasn't* Silas Edwards. This was some impostor claiming to be Silas Edwards."

"Really? How do you know?"

"Because I spoke with Silas last week, and I remember what he sounded like! Plus, I tested this guy. I made up a story that he and I had talked about some computer disks last week when in fact the real Silas and I had *never* talked about any disks, and this guy took the bait and acted like we had talked about them. No, this guy's a fraud."

"Hmm, this is not good, Dani," don Fernando said. "Is he meeting you at your apartment?"

"No, I told him to meet me at the front gate to the church. We're supposed to meet at one o'clock."

"Ah, that was a good move. I'll meet you there at 12:45. And I'll bring some men. Maybe we need to have a little chat with this man, eh?"

Dan knew that "having a little chat" with don Fernando meant being arrested.

"I think that's a good idea, amigo," Dan said. "See you at 12:45."

CHAPTER TWELVE

At a quarter to one, Dan was standing in front of the Catholic Church. Don Fernando was sitting in his car parked a few feet away, pretending to read the paper. Two other Villa Rosario policemen, dressed in plain clothes, were pretending to buy lottery tickets from one of the local freelance lottery vendors who worked that block. Actually, they weren't pretending. Each of the two policemen actually bought a ticket for luck and were chatting with the vendor. Dan stood by the front gate of the church, as if he was waiting for someone... which he was.

Five minutes later, a portly white man came walking up the street. Dan noticed him right away. Not only was he an unfamiliar face, but he was dressed in a suit, complete with necktie, which made him stand out in the tropical climate. It was a cream-colored suit, but it was still a suit. Dan thought again of the dead Frenchman who was also in a suit.

He walked straight up to Dan and said, "Dan Landes, I presume?"

"Yes. Silas Edwards?"

"Yes."

The two men shook hands. Don Fernando casually stepped out of his car, folded his newspaper and strolled just past the two men, and took a position a few feet behind the man in the suit, and pretended to look at the posted schedule of church services on the gate.

"Did you have any trouble finding our town?" Dan asked.

"No, not at all. The GPS took me right here. However, my flight out is a bit earlier than I thought, so I am in a bit of a hurry. So, I was wondering if we could go pick up Ricardo's files right away... Is your place nearby?"

"Of course. It's very near," Dan said. "But before we go—just as a formality—could I see some identification?"

Dan thought he detected a tiny blanching in the man's skin tone. But the man retained his composure and reached inside his jacket.

"I think I have a business card here," he said.

"No, Mr. Edwards, I mean something more official, a passport, a driver's license, some type of photo ID."

The man produced a business card from his inside pocket and held it out. Dan looked down at it but did not take it.

"Is this really necessary?" the man said in a huff. "I've told you who I am. Here's my card. *I* was the one who called *you*, remember? I flew all the way down here to retrieve these papers. I don't have to prove who I am to you!"

"You don't have your passport?" Dan asked calmly.

"It's at my hotel," said the man. "Come on, I don't have a lot of time. Just take me to your apartment and show me these files!"

"You don't have your passport?" Dan asked again.

"Not on me! I just told you, I left it at my hotel!"

"Well, that's a shame, Mr. Edwards, because the law in this country is that any tourist has to carry their passport on them. Failure to do so is an arrestable offense."

"I don't have time for this nonsense!" the man shouted.

On a signal from don Fernando, the two police officers casually walked away from the lottery vendor. One stepped to the man's side. The other stood behind the man. Don Fernando then stepped up to the man's other side and held out his police ID.

Dan said, "Let me introduce you to José Fernandez, our chief of police. We'd like you to come with us down to the police station, please."

For a microsecond, Dan thought the man was going to bolt. But one policeman grabbed his right wrist, and the other policeman reached around from behind the man and grabbed his left arm. Both officers pulled the man's arms behind him and placed him in handcuffs.

"This is ridiculous!" the man shouted.

Don Fernando reached inside the man's jacket and removed a wallet from the jacket's left breast pocket. He opened the wallet and pulled out a driver's license.

"Jacques Foucher," don Fernando said, reading the name on the license. "From New York City. Interesting. Señor Foucher, you are under arrest for failing to carry your passport on your person as required by Panamanian law."

"I have my passport!" the man shouted. "It's in my other pocket!"

Don Fernando reached into the man's right jacket pocket and retrieved a US passport. He opened it and examined the photograph.

"Interesting. A French name and a US passport. Well, señor, you are still under arrest."

"What is the charge?" demanded the man.

"Suspicion."

"Suspicion of what?!"

"Suspicion of being suspicious."

Don Fernando nodded to one of the two policemen, who began patting the man down.

"Well, Dani..." don Fernando started to say.

"Capitán," said the officer, interrupting don Fernando. The officer was holding open the man's jacket.

Don Fernando reached in and pulled out a small pistol.

"And under arrest for carrying a weapon," said don Fernando to the man.

"I have a concealed weapons permit!" the man shouted.

"Not valid in Panama," don Fernando said calmly as he examined the pistol.

Dan looked at the gun that was in don Fernando's hands. It was a Sig P365, a very easily concealable 9mm pistol. Then he looked at Jacques Foucher. The man just glared at Dan with hatred in his eyes.

The two officers finished patting him down.

"I want a lawyer!" the man demanded.

"Yeah, yeah, take him away," don Fernando said.

The two police officers yanked the man towards a police car that had pulled up. They stuffed him in the back seat and took off.

"Well, Dani, as I was starting to say, your hunch was right. This señor Foucher was up to no good. I wonder if this gun will match the bullets in the two corpses."

Dan nodded. But he was wondering more to himself if this Jacques Foucher had intended to use the gun on *him*.

"Come on Dani, my car is right here. Let's go to my office. We'll let this man sit in a cell for an hour while we have some coffee and examine his possessions. Then we can interview him."

"He told me he drove a rental car here," Dan said. "I imagine it's parked somewhere nearby."

"Ah, I will have my men look for it. If we find it, we will tow it away. Come."

CHAPTER THIRTEEN

As soon as they got to his office, don Fernando placed Jacques Foucher's gun in an evidence envelope. "That reminds me," he said out loud, and then pressed a button on the intercom on his desk.

"Sí, Capitán," came the response over the intercom.

"Carlos," said don Fernando, "could you have the lab technician swab our new prisoner's hands for gunpowder residue and send those swabs to the lab in Panama City? The prisoner might resist, so send an extra officer, and tell the lab technician he has my permission to be firm."

"Sí, Capitán."

Then don Fernando started a fresh pot of coffee.

"After the coroner finishes the autopsies, we'll have the bullets from the two bodies," he told Dan. "Then we can send the bullets and this gun to the ballistics lab along with the gun from the Colombiano and see if either one matches. We should have that report by Tuesday."

"If Jacques Foucher's gun matches the bullets," Dan said, "that would mean that he was already here yesterday during the day—that he didn't fly in late last night like he had told me."

"Well, at this point," said don Fernando, "it would certainly be a break if we could connect *either* one of the guns to the two murders."

Don Fernando pulled out two evidence envelopes from a filing cabinet. He carefully emptied them out into two piles on his desk. One pile contained the passport and wallet of Romain Martin Groslot. The other was just the wallet of Álvaro Renaldo. He started a third pile with the wallet and passport of Jacques Foucher.

"Let me take a look at Foucher's passport," Dan said.

Don Fernando handed Dan the passport. Dan opened it to the photo page. "Born in Baton Rouge. Well, maybe that explains the French name." He started flipping through the visa pages. "I'm looking for... ah, here it is... fuck, he's been in Panama for four weeks!"

Dan looked at the calendar on don Fernando's wall. "He arrived two and a half weeks before Ricardo came to my apartment... I wonder if he's the reason that Ricardo left..." Dan turned a few more pages of the passport. "This guy basically travels back and forth from New York to Madrid about three times a year," Dan said aloud as he flipped through the pages. "Of course, with the EU, we can't tell if he travels about in Europe once he enters Spain. But he always departs from Madrid back to New York City."

"How long does he stay in Europe?"

"About a week each trip... too short to be a vacation," Dan said as don Fernando placed a cup of coffee in front of him. "Oh, thanks."

Dan took a sip of his coffee and then picked up the passports of the dead Frenchman, and then the Colombian. His brow furrowed as he scanned the visa pages of each passport.

"Shit, don Fernando. These three guys all arrived here in Panama on the same day. And they all flew in from Madrid! That can't be coincidence. They must have known each other."

"Bad news travels in threes," don Fernando said.

Dan picked up Jacques Foucher's wallet and looked through it until he found a driver's license.

"Yup. He lives in New York City. Okay... interesting, but not enlightening. What else? Oh, hello..." Dan pulled a business card from the wallet. "Jacques Foucher, Esq. He's a fucking lawyer. With the firm Foucher and Ortega, LLC. Don Fernando! I bet that his Ortega partner is *David Ortega*. That's the lawyer that the real Silas Edwards said was Ricardo's lawyer!"

"Ricardo has a lawyer?" don Fernando asked.

"Who the fuck knows? Silas may have been lying, but David Ortega was the name of the guy that Silas said would be in touch with me about paying Ricardo's rent while he was gone. Jesus Palomino! This case is getting more convoluted by the minute."

Dan started going through all the pockets and folds in the wallet. "Looks like about a thousand dollars in cash... lots of credit cards... hello?"

He pulled out a black Todo Visa debit card.

"What's that?" don Fernando asked.

"It's a debit card from this new company I saw in the Parque Central last week. They rent electric bicycles." Dan showed it to don Fernando. Don Fernando looked at it and just shrugged.

A uniformed policeman appeared at don Fernando's door holding a small manila envelope and said "Las posesiones personales del gringo, Capitán."

"Thank you, Carlos," don Fernando said, and took the envelope from the policeman and poured the contents on the desk: some coins, a hotel keycard with a big H on it, three business cards with Silas Edwards' name on them, and a set of car keys. "Ah yes... the car," said don Fernando. "Carlos, somewhere near the church is a parked rental car that goes with this key. Take Marcelo and go find it. Bring it back here and search it."

"Sí, Capitán," said the policeman, taking the keys from don Fernando.

"And ask Sergeant Arias to step in here."

"Sí, Capitán."

Don Fernando picked up the hotel keycard and held it up for Dan to see.

"I recognize this brand, Dani. It is from the Hilton, the most expensive hotel in Panama City."

A minute later, Sergeant Arias appeared in the doorway. Don Fernando handed the hotel keycard to the officer.

"Marcelo, this is a keycard to a room in the Hilton Hotel in Panama City. I don't know which room, but we need to find it and search it. I'm not sure what we're looking for, so seize anything suspicious. We need to act fast, so this has to be done *informally*."

Sergeant Arias gave a knowing nod.

Don Fernando continued, "Call Jorge Manuel and explain the situation. Ask him to call Captain Garcia in Panama City to coordinate this."

Sergeant Arias gave a quick salute and left.

Dan looked quizzically at don Fernando.

"Captain Garcia is the chief of police in Panama City. His sister is also Koke's wife. I can hold this Jacques guy in jail without any problem until we get the ballistic report. We've got two dead foreigners and he's a foreigner with a gun. That's enough probable cause for me. I don't care if he's a lawyer or how much money he has. But if his gun does not match the bullets in either of those two bodies, then at some point, I'm going to have to charge him with something else in order to hold him, or let him go. So, I don't have time to go through all the red tape in Panama City to get a search warrant to search his hotel room. It's easier to have Koke call his brother-in-law, and we can just search. The hotel will cooperate."

"Ah, yes," Dan said with a smile. "The strength of family ties is the fabric of society."

"Well," said don Fernando, "it's always faster to do things informally."

Dan put all the credit cards and the slip of paper back into the wallet and placed it on the desk. Then he picked up one of the Silas Edwards's business cards, examined it, and wondered: How did Jacques get his cards? Why did he carry them in his pocket, and not his wallet? How did Jacques know about Ricardo and the notebooks?

Dan placed the business card back on Foucher's pile. Then he picked up the wallet of Álvaro Renaldo.

"Let's see what we've got here," he said. "A couple of dollars, his Colombian driver's license, and..." Dan stopped as he pulled out a Todo Visa debit card. He quickly picked up the wallet of Romain Martin Groslot, thumbed through it, and also pulled out a black Todo Visa debit card. He turned it to show don Fernando the two cards.

"Okay, don Fernando, all three of these men have the same debit card."

Don Fernando just shrugged. "They are just Visa cards, Dani."

"Maybe," said Dan. "Maybe so... but it strikes me as odd that all three men have cards from what I think is a brand-new company. Maybe I'm wrong. Maybe Todo has been around for a long time. I'll have to research it."

Don Fernando nodded and sipped his coffee.

"Do we have anything new since yesterday?" Dan asked.

Don Fernando shook his head. "No trace of Matzel. No other suspicious extranjeros except this Foucher guy. No hint of Ricardo. We'll hear something back from Interpol by tomorrow. We interviewed the neighbors around both Matzel's house and his store. They either didn't see anything or didn't want to say anything. People love to gossip, but they never want to talk to the police. We'll have the autopsy reports later today or tomorrow, and we'll have the ballistics by Tuesday. So right now, all we can do is wait."

"Do you want to go interview Foucher?" Dan asked.

Don Fernando looked at his watch. "Nah, let's let him wait some more. In fact, I'll have some sandwiches brought in. Are you hungry?"

"A bit, yes."

Don Fernando got on his intercom and asked the desk sergeant to have someone pick up some empanadas from the fonda down the block. Dan refilled both their coffee cups, and the waited for the food to arrive.

Dan mused aloud. "What have we got so far? Two missing men, and two dead men... what are the commonalities? Everybody's from a different country? I guess that's a commonality. A Frenchman, a Colombian... I think we can count Jacques Foucher as from the US. His French name is just coincidental... Matzel's from North Africa... but he's lived here for how long?"

"Oh, about ten years, Dani."

"Then, we have the real Silas, who has a slight British accent... at least I think it was British..."

"Well, Panama is an international country, Dani. Ever since the canal was built, we've traded with the world, so it's not unusual to have many extranjeros in any group of people here."

"True," said Dan. "But something connected them. Something made both the Frenchman and the Colombian break into Matzel's bookstore. Something made Ricardo flee town. Something caused Matzel to disappear. And something caused this Jacques guy to impersonate Silas Edwards, and come down here. To do what? It can't be Ricardo's notebooks, so it has to be the maps. Jacques had to have come down here for the maps. Maybe the real Silas sent him... No, that makes no sense. The real Silas could have just said he was sending a courier to pick up Ricardo's notebooks... I think I'll call Silas tomorrow. I'll tell him the truth: that someone came down here impersonating him, and see how he reacts. What do you think?"

"Why not?" agreed don Fernando.

"None of it makes any sense, don Fernando. Those maps were just crude drawings. They can't be valuable. And the two dead men weren't looking for the maps. They were searching for something else in Matzel's bookstore... Whatever connects these people has to be worth a lot of money..."

"The world is a crazy place, Dani," don Fernando said. "I've been the police chief here for almost four decades, and I've seen some strange crimes. But it almost always comes down to money... money or women. Men will do crazy shit for either money or women."

Just then, the desk sergeant arrived with two take-out paper bags of food and placed the bags on a side table.

"Ah, good," said don Fernando. "I'm starved."

"Will the guards feed Foucher some lunch?" Dan asked.

"No, I'm afraid he missed the jail lunch. He'll just have to wait until dinner."

CHAPTER FOURTEEN

After they had eaten some lunch, don Fernando arranged to have Jacques Foucher taken to an interrogation room. When Dan and don Fernando walked into the room, Jacques was seated at a small table, his hands cuffed behind his back. A police officer stood guard over him. Dan and don Fernando pulled up chairs and sat down opposite Jacques.

Dan spoke first. "Let me describe your situation, Mr. Foucher. In Panama, only a legal resident can carry a gun, and then, only with a permit. You are not a resident. The penalty for illegal possession of a firearm is enhanced depending on any crimes the gun is connected with."

"You haven't read me my rights!" Jacques spat out.

"I assume you're referring to your Miranda Rights," Dan said, "but unfortunately, they only apply in the States. You are in Panama now."

"I'm not answering any questions. I want a lawyer."

"I haven't asked you any questions," Dan stately flatly. "As I was saying, the penalty for illegal possession of a gun is enhanced depending on any crimes the gun is connected with. At the present time, the police are investigating two murders—"

"I want an attorney!"

Dan sighed. "You do have the right to the timely advice of an attorney. Even in Panama. But the word 'timely' is open to interpretation; and today is Sunday. And nothing is timely on Sunday."

"I want to call the American Embassy!"

"Again, Mr. Foucher, today is Sunday, and the Embassy is closed. Now, as I was saying, the police are investigating two murders that occurred—"

"I'm a lawyer!" Jacques shouted. "I know my rights! I don't have to submit to police questioning without my attorney present! I don't have to answer any questions!"

Dan sighed again. "Mr. Foucher, I am not the police. I am not questioning you on behalf on the police. So, I can ask you anything I want. Now, as I was saying, the police are investigating two murders that occurred yesterday. But I am not concerned with that. What I want to know is, why did you tell me you were Silas Edwards?"

"Fuck you!"

"Well, that's not very hospitable, Mr. Foucher. I would have thought that a man of your education would appreciate the difficult situation he was in. Did I mention that the police here are investigating two murders?"

"I told you. I'm not answering any questions."

Dan decided to take a chance and lie. "Mr. Foucher, are you familiar with the term 'prisoner's dilemma'? It describes your situation, because at this very moment, David Ortega is also being questioned."

Dan saw Jacques' eyes dart down and to the right. Dan knew that his guess about David Ortega was correct.

"So, tell me, why did you pretend to be Silas Edwards?"

Jacques paused. His eyes flitted left and right. Dan knew he was thinking.

Finally, he lifted his head and said, "I told you, I'm not answering any questions."

"Suit yourself," Dan said, and looked at don Fernando. Don Fernando just shrugged. Both Dan and don Fernando stood up and both men started to walk out of the room

"I want access to a telephone! I want to call my attorney back in the States! I want to call the Embassy!" Jacques shouted.

"Mr. Foucher," Dan said, shaking his head, "you're in Panama. Things are different here. The police can keep you as long as they want."

And both men walked out.

As they walked down the hall, don Fernando said, "That wasn't very productive."

"Well, we did learn that Jacques is hiding something,

and that David Ortega is involved... How long *can* you keep him here?"

"Well... as long as I'm 'investigating' the case, I can hold him here for a few weeks. If the ballistics tie his gun to the murders, I can keep him a year before we press charges. But if I can't connect him to the murders, then after a few weeks, I'd have to refer the case to the prosecutor in Panama City just on the gun charge. Then they would have jurisdiction. They'd probably just give him a fine and cut him loose. They're got bigger fish to fry."

"Okay. Let's let him stew overnight. I'm going to head on home. Are we still on for tomorrow at eleven?"

"Let's make it Tuesday morning, Dani. We'll have the ballistics from both guns and all the reports by then."

"Sounds good. Tuesday at eleven."

Dan said his goodbyes and walked out of the police station into the mid-afternoon heat.

He cut through the Parque Central as usual on his walk home and glanced over to the side of the park where the electric bicycle display had been on Friday. They were back, but this time, they had erected a large tent with a huge banner that read *Todo*. A crowd of people were gathered underneath the tent. Don Fernando had thought it was just a coincidence that Jacques and the two dead men all had the same type of Todo debit card in their wallets. But Dan didn't believe in coincidences. There had to be some connection. He decided to do some online research on Todo when he got home.

But as Dan got to his apartment building, he sensed that something was wrong. He approached the stairway that led to his second-floor apartment and paused. He couldn't put his finger on why, but he suddenly felt hyper-alert. He sniffed the air. He listened carefully. Neither sense told him anything. He stepped carefully up the stairs and peered around the corner at his door. It was opened about an inch. The wood around the lock was splintered apart.

Dan's immediate impulse was to kick the door open and confront anyone who might be inside. But they might be armed, and he didn't own a gun. So, he quietly eased his way back down the stairs. He pulled his cell phone from his pocket and, for the third time in two days, hit speed dial for don Fernando.

When don Fernando answer, Dan whispered, "My apartment's been broken into."

"I'll be right there, Dani."

Dan looked around the base of the stairway. A broom was leaning against the wall. He grabbed it, unscrewed the brush, held the stick, and stepped behind the stairwell. This stairway was the only exit from the second floor. If anyone was upstairs, they had to come down the stairs.

Ten seconds later, he heard sirens. After a screech of tires, two uniformed policemen came running up the path that led to his stairs. Don Fernando lumbered behind them. Dan leaned the stick against the back of the stairwell. The two policemen, whom he recognized, ran up to him. He pointed up the stairs, and they ran up, with their guns drawn. He heard them shouting "Policía" several times, and the sound of a door being kicked open. Don Fernando made it to the stairwell, breathing heavily.

"I'm too old for this, Dani," he grunted.

"Tell me about it, amigo," Dan replied.

And both men walked up the stairs.

The two police officers were standing on the balcony, their guns holstered.

"There's no one inside, Capitán."

Dan and don Fernando looked at the doorframe.

"Crowbar," Dan said, looking at the scrape marks on the wood. Don Fernando nodded in agreement.

Dan looked inside the apartment. Everything looked normal. Nothing seemed to be disturbed. All the drawers to his dresser and cabinets were still closed. Nothing was on the floor except the five neat stacks of Ricardo's notebooks on the floor by his desk. Nothing seemed out of place. He looked at his desktop. His laptop was still there, in exactly the same position as when he left it this morning...

Then, he saw what was missing.

"I'll have my fingerprint man come over," don Fernando said. "Then you will have to do a careful inventory to see if anything was stolen."

"I already know," Dan said.

Don Fernando looked at Dan.

"They just took the notebook with the maps. It was there, on my desk. That's the only thing that's missing. See? Even my spare change jar on the desk is untouched. They busted in, looked around, saw the notebooks stacked on the floor, but then saw the two notebooks on the desk. They opened both of them, but only took the one with the maps. That other notebook—there by the computer—has some essays by Ricardo. It was closed when I left. Now it's open. They flipped through both notebooks and then took the one with the maps. That's what they were after. You can have the fingerprint guy come over, but the only thing he needs to dust is the doorknob and that open notebook on the desk."

Don Fernando took out his cell phone and made two calls.

"A forensic officer is on his way with the fingerprint kit," don Fernando said. "And I'm having a locksmith I know who also does carpentry come over as well. After we get photos of the doorframe and the crowbar marks, he can repair your door and give you a new lock."

"Thank you, amigo," Dan said. "I just want to check one thing..."

Dan stepped inside his apartment, took out a handkerchief, and carefully opened the door to his liquor cabinet. The whisky bottles had not been moved. More importantly, the secret compartment behind the whisky bottles was undisturbed. He closed the door and stepped back outside.

"Checking your whisky?" don Fernando asked incredulously.

"Well, a man's gotta protect the important things," Dan said and smiled.

Don Fernando just shook his head, then offered, "I can post an officer here tonight, Dani."

"No, no thanks, amigo. Whoever it was, he got what he wanted. I don't think he'll be back."

Dan stepped back out onto his balcony and sat down

on one of his balcony chairs. There was nothing to do now but wait for the forensics team and locksmith to arrive.

Don Fernando pulled up a chair beside Dan.

"I'm sorry this happened, Dani."

"Me too… I'm just trying to figure out how it's connected to Foucher. My first thought was that he might have had an accomplice, maybe someone who was going to meet him here. But how would he have known my address?"

"It's a small town, Dani. All the locals know where the gringos live. A visitor would just have to ask. But we will check around. If it was a gringo who was asking where you live, people would remember that."

Dan nodded and thought some more, then said, "I wonder if David Ortega came down to Panama *with* Jacques… maybe he was on the same flight. We know from his passport what day Jacques arrived. Can you find out what flights came in from New York City that day? Maybe there was a David Ortega on that same flight… Shit, if that's true, he would be staying at the same Hilton Hotel in Panama City as Jacques!"

Dan looked at don Fernando, but don Fernando had already dialed the station and was barking out orders to the desk sergeant to tell Sergeant Arias to call Jorge Manuel and have him ask Captain Garcia in Panama City to allow them to go to the Hilton Hotel and search for one David Ortega this afternoon, and arrest him if he was there.

Dan opened his mouth to say something else, but then decided not to. Instead, he sat and speculated some more. If it wasn't David Ortega, then who *did* break into his apartment? The thought occurred to him that it might have been someone not affiliated with Jacques Foucher. Maybe there were two different groups involved. After all, someone shot the two men inside Matzel's bookstore. Maybe that's why Jacques was so pressed for time. Maybe he wanted to get the maps before someone else did… There were too many possibilities. It all made Dan's head hurt.

Two police officers showed up with cameras and a fingerprint kit and started getting busy. One of them took Dan's fingerprints so they could eliminate any of his prints they might find inside. Then he started dusting the front doorknob, Dan's desk, and the notebooks. The other one started taking close-up photographs of the doorframe and the scrape marks on the wood where the strike plate used to be. A few minutes later, a man with a large toolbox showed up. This was the locksmith whom don Fernando had called. He nodded toward don Fernando, then looked at the doorframe and went back to his truck to get some wood, metal brackets, and a new strike plate. When he came back, don Fernando got up to talk with him.

Dan looked at his watch. It was only three in the afternoon. Too early to drink. He sat and waited... and thought.

CHAPTER FIFTEEN

Hours later, the locksmith finished his work and left. All the police technicians also finished up and left. Don Fernando remained behind to ask again if Dan wanted a police guard. Dan said no, and promised don Fernando he would call if anything happened. Don Fernando nodded and said his goodbyes. Dan was finally alone. He inspected the door. Don Fernando had told the locksmith to make it burglar-proof, so the locksmith had screwed in a length of metal framing around the wooden door jamb and then installed an extra-long deadbolt with a special deep door strike. If someone tried to break in again, they would have to tear out the entire door and door casing.

Dan went inside and closed the door. Even though he did not believe that the burglar—or burglars—would return, he locked the deadbolt. He went to his liquor cabinet and took out all the bottles and then opened the secret compartment in the back, and then dialed the combination to the safe. The photocopies of the maps, along with his passport and an envelope of extra cash, were all there. He closed the safe and replaced the fake wall panel and whisky bottles.

He realized he was hungry. It had been many hours since his lunch in don Fernando's office. He looked through the refrigerator, but there was nothing to eat there. So, he grabbed a can of tuna from his shelf and started preparing a tuna fish salad mixture for some sandwiches. He just wanted something fast. He cut up some olives and celery and mixed that with the tuna and mayonnaise and red pepper flakes. Then he toasted some bread and made himself two large tuna fish sandwiches.

He sat at his desk and devoured the sandwiches, washing them down with a beer. As he was eating, he thought about the three Todo debit cards. He switched on his computer and started searching for anything on Todo. It didn't take him more than a few seconds to find something. The first thing he read on Wikipedia was that Todo was a "fintech" company. Dan had never heard that phrase before, so he had to look it up. "A technology company to enable banking or financial services." That seemed vague. But as he read about Todo, it because clearer... much clearer.

Todo was not a bicycle company; it was a bank, or rather, it was a wannabe bank. It was incorporated in Spain in 2014, but its website was domiciled in Bulgaria, and its corporate headquarters was located in the Cayman Islands. Todo claimed it had banking branches in six countries: the Cayman Islands, Ireland, Croatia, Malaysia, El Salvador, and Panama. After about ten minutes of internet searching, Dan understood that their "banking branches" were just licenses from those six countries to operate as a "foreign exchange and processing bank," meaning that they could not accept deposits or do any banking business *inside* those host countries, but they *could* issue debit cards from those countries, and they could process payments, transfers, credits, and debits on those cards. And once being lawfully issued, those debit cards could be used all over the world. Originally, Todo was only connected to one bank—a bank called "You-Bank" in Belize. But the You-Bank was closed by the Belize government five years ago amidst allegations of money laundering and a missing five million dollars' worth of debit card deposits. Todo had to scramble to set up a replacement foreign exchange and processing bank in Ireland and to cover the missing money. Now, Todo boasted banking branches in six countries and over two hundred "transfer offices" in twenty-three other countries, including the US. Those transfer offices existed to help customers apply for the debit cards that were actually being issued from their "banks" in those six other countries. The transfer offices also sold credit card readers that plugged into clients' cell phones to take credit card payments that would be automatically credited to their Todo debit cards. And those offices also helped clients set up digital payment systems to transfer money. Todo advertised their debit cards as an "alternative bank," a place to receive and maintain funds, and a way to spend funds. To Dan's white-collar detective brain, it screamed money laundering. Customers could use the debit cards to pay bills just like any other credit/debit card, of course. But they could also go to Todo's transfer office and load their debit cards with money in whatever currency was used in the country they were in, and then use the Todo App on their cell phone to transfer that money anywhere in the world to anyone who also had a Todo debit card. Then that second person could go to any ATM and withdraw those funds in the currency of their own country. Completely anonymously—no oversight, no records, no taxes, no accountability.

Dan understood that there were legitimate groups of people who might need alternative banks: Women who worked as webcam girls—modeling nude online for money—needed a way to receive credit card payments from customers. Traditional banks often refused to open accounts for women doing such work, so Todo's debit card would allow them to make a living. They could give customers a special passcode that would allow the customer to pay the girls through an encrypted page on the Todo website, and the money would be deposited to the girls' debit cards. Traveling salesmen could plug a Todo credit card reader directly into their cell phone, take a client's credit card and deposit that money directly into their Todo debit card. They could use that same Todo debit card to pay for their hotel room each night. It was convenient. Other groups, for various reasons, might not trust traditional banks, or might not want spouses knowing about their financial activities. Dan understood this. But he also knew how drug traffickers, arms dealers, and human traffickers would also find a digital bank very attractive.

Dan thought about don Fernando's explanation of how the Colombian cartels laundered money into gold through offshore banks. The Todo debit card and money transfer system made all of that unnecessary. To Dan's ex-detective brain, it was clear that any drug dealer in the US could take US dollars to a Todo transfer office, load them onto his debit card, then either go home to his computer or use the convenient computers in the Todo transfer office to wire money from his debit card to someone in Colombia with a Todo debit card. The person in Colombia could then transfer those funds anywhere in the world or simply go to any ATM and withdraw the money as Colombian pesos. Because Todo's "banks" were outside the US, they were outside the jurisdiction of US law enforcement, courts, and laws. They didn't have to report to the IRS or the FBI or anyone.

The more Dan read, the more incredulous he became. He hated that he was always so suspicious, but it sure seemed like the perfect money laundering system to him.

He wondered how the electric bicycles fit in to all of this, so he went to Todo's website and analyzed it carefully. Electric bicycles were just a tiny part of Todo's business model. The model was actually based on the Todo debit card. Todo pitched convenience and one-stop shopping. Todo had set up relationships with Uber, Airbnb, and even dating services. You could order a taxi or Uber on the Todo card; you could order a pizza on the Todo card and have it delivered by Uber Eats or any other food delivery service; you could find lodging for the night; you could even find a romantic partner using Todo's link to Tinder, Match.com, Grindr, and several other dating services. Their stated mission at the top of their website was "to digitalize the world." But Dan viewed it as Todo wanting to become completely indispensable to any financial decision. Todo was trying to position itself as the one app that its clients would use for *everything*. Not mentioned in any of the breezy website language was the fact that Todo took a small commission from every transaction. So not only were you paying Uber for transportation—you were also giving a few pennies to Todo. Book a hotel through Todo's link to Booking.com, and you were also paying a tiny commission to Todo. Todo didn't provide any services; they just hooked you into another company that provided the service, and Todo took a small percentage for helping you connect.

The only two services that Todo did offer were money transfers and bicycles. At first, this seemed like an odd combination to Dan. But the more he thought about it, the more it made sense. Todo was trying to appeal to the young hip urban dwellers. Finally, Dan understood how they could rent electric bicycles for a dollar an hour. Todo had no intention of making money on the rentals. The bicycles were simply a way to hook people into opening an account with them, and being exposed to their debit card. The electric bicycles were just a loss-leader to get people to apply for the debit card. Once someone opened up a bicycle-rental account with Todo, they would be deluged with offers and suggestions to let Todo "manage" their digital world: order their food, set up meetings, book their vacations, manage their phone calls, arrange dates, and organize their time. Dan thought that Todo's real mission wasn't to digitalize the world but rather, to put their digital fingers into every aspect of your life.

Dan leaned back in his chair and stared at the ceiling. He felt depressed at how technology was making the world so small, so controlled. He wondered if that was always the price of progress. Panama used to feel beyond the reach of such progress. Not anymore. Maybe Todo just symbolized what the world was becoming; maybe Todo was just one of many multinational companies all competing to turn people into total consumers. Dan wondered what happened to all the consumer data that was being generated by these accounts, by these debit cards? After all, Todo had its website domiciled in Bulgaria, a Russian satellite. What better way to spy on the western world than by putting a debit card into everyone's pocket? It was depressing to think about.

He wondered what—if any—connection all this had to the two dead men in Matzel's bookstore. Maybe it was just coincidence that they both had Todo debit cards in their wallets. And Jacques Foucher, too. After all, as don Fernando had said, they were just debit cards. Maybe those debit cards were just the easiest way those guys had for moving money around. Dan just didn't know. It was just another piece of a puzzle that made no sense to him.

He checked the time. It was almost eight o'clock. He opened another beer and keep looking for other articles on Todo.

CHAPTER SIXTEEN

Dan did not sleep well that night. No one ever does after a burglary. Even though the doorframe had been reinforced with a metal frame that would withstand a battering ram, his brain remained on alert and would simply not turn off. Finally, after several hours of tossing and turning, he got up and wedged a chair against the door. That small act seemed to satisfy some psychological need to do something, and he was finally able to fall asleep.

He awoke the next morning feeling ragged. But then he thought that Jacques Foucher probably had a worse night's sleep. That thought made him feel better. So he got up and made some coffee.

After breakfast, he checked the time. Nine a.m. Panama was in the same time zone as New York, so Dan figured that Silas would be in his office by now. He decided to call him and see how he reacted to the news that someone had been impersonating him.

He recognized the receptionist's voice when she answered. It was the same woman who had been so haughty to him on the previous two phone calls. But her voice seemed quiet, almost timid, this morning.

"This is Dan Landes, calling from Panama," he said.

"Yes... yes, sir, Mr. Landes," she said.

"Is Silas Edwards there?"

There was a long pause. Dan waited. She hadn't put him on hold. He thought maybe she hadn't understood him, so he asked again.

"Could I talk with Silas Edwards please?"

He thought he heard a muffled sob on the line.

"No," she finally said. "I mean, no that's not possible.

He's not..." and her voice trailed off.

"When do you expect him?" Dan asked.

There was another long pause. Finally, she said, "I'm sorry, Mr. Landes. I mean it's not possible. Mr. Edwards... passed away over the weekend."

"What?"

"I'm not sure what I'm supposed to say," she blurted out. "No one has told me what I'm supposed to say."

Dan could hear her voice breaking.

"It was in the newspapers. He was murdered in his parking garage. The police don't know who did it."

Dan could hear her crying now.

"I've worked here for twelve years," she said between sobs. "Mr. Edwards gave me this job right out of college. I've never worked anywhere else." She was sobbing hard now.

Dan's mind was racing. But there was no point in asking this woman anything.

"I'm sorry, Miss..." he said.

"Meyers... Susan Meyers... I'm sorry, but I... I don't know what I'm supposed to tell people when they call."

"I understand, Susan," Dan said. It was all he could think to say. "Thanks for letting me know." And he hung up.

Dan leaned back in his chair. *Fuck*, he thought, *this complicated things.* He was hoping that he could somehow squeeze some information out of Silas, some clue about who Jacques Foucher was, and how he knew about Silas and about Ricardo's files.

He opened his laptop and started searching for news in New York City. He found short two articles about the murder, but they didn't tell him anything more than what Susan had said. "Literary Agent found Murdered" read one headline. "Possible Carjacking Attempt Ends in Death" read the other. Both articles mentioned that Silas was a well-known literary agent in New York's publishing world, but neither article had any details about what had happened. No suspects, no parking garage video. No leads.

He picked up his cell phone and called don Fernando.

"Hola, Dani, qué tal?" Don Fernando sounded chipper.

"Listen, don Fernando, I just called New York City.

Remember the guy that Jacques Foucher was impersonating? Silas Edwards? Ricardo's agent in New York? Well, he's dead. Someone murdered him over the weekend."

There was an audible sigh over the phone. "Ah Dani, just when this case was starting to make sense to me... What happened to him?"

"I don't have any details," Dan said. "Evidently, someone, or maybe more than one person, shot him in a parking garage. The police have no suspects."

"Well, it wasn't this Foucher guy, because he was already down here, as were the two dead men in Matzel's bookstore," said don Fernando. "Speaking of which," he continued, "I got some interesting news from Immigration today."

"Oh?"

"Yes. It turns out that the two dead men and Jacques Foucher all arrived in Panama together. In fact, they all arrived on the same flight from Madrid. Now the Colombiano—what was his name? I had it right here... here it is: Álvaro Renaldo. He flew to Madrid from Bulgaria. He had been in Bulgaria two months. He flew to Madrid for one day and then joined the other two on the flight to Panama. The Frenchman, Romain Martin Groslot, he flew to Madrid from Paris, and stayed exactly six days before taking the flight to Panama. And Jacques Foucher, he flew from New York City to Madrid for the exact same six days before boarding the same flight to Panama with the other two men. In fact, he stayed at the same hotel in Madrid as the Frenchman Groslot."

"So they all *did* know each other!" Dan exclaimed. "What about David Ortega?"

"No sign of anyone by that name. Without a passport number or other identification, Immigration can only look by name, and no one by that name has flown into Panama in the past four weeks."

"Okay," Dan said.

"Nor was there anyone by that name at the Hilton Hotel in Panama City. It looks like Foucher stayed there alone. We don't know where the Colombiano and the Frenchman stayed, but they didn't stay at the Hilton. Evidently, the split up at the airport after they arrived. But they clearly arrived together. Immigration said that they processed their passports all in a row, which means they were standing in line together, but they each indicated on their forms they were traveling alone, yet they were processed through Immigration one after the other. That's no coincidence."

"I agree."

"I've got rap sheets on the Colombiano and the Frenchman from Interpol, but I'm still waiting on them to reply on Foucher. The Frenchman, Groslot, has several arrests for money laundering, but no convictions. The Colombiano has a long rap sheet of various crimes, mostly involving violence. You can look at it tomorrow when you come over. By then we should have the Interpol results on Foucher and, most importantly, the ballistic reports on the two guns."

"Okay... And how is Foucher doing?"

"Ha! Oh, Dani, he's a whiny bastard! Every time one of my officers walks by his cell, he yells out that he wants a lawyer. I did go ahead and notify the US Embassy that we had arrested him, but of course, they're not coming to see him. There's nothing they can do."

"Right. Any other news?"

"Not really. Still no trace of Matzel. My officers are searching the woods near his house now."

"Oh?" Dan said.

"Well, just in case he was murdered, and they buried him nearby. Leave no stone unturned—that's what they say in the online police course I've been taking."

"What? You're taking a police course online?!"

"Oh yes, I use Zoom now. I quite like it."

"But, don Fernando, you're going to retire in six months!" Dan exclaimed.

"Well, yes and no. I want to retire, but I decided that it would be better for my marriage—and my mental health—if I wasn't home all that much. So, the city council has agreed to create a new job for me. I'm going to be Villa Rosario's first *consulting detective*. I got the name from the Sherlock Holmes stories. That way, I'll be able to help Koke when he becomes police chief and get paid for it, too. I was so pleased when I thought of the idea. It... how do you say? It kills two birds with one rock? Koke is going to need some help, and I need an excuse *not* to remodel the kitchen. Koke showed me how to set up Zoom on my computer, so I can keep up to speed with new police methods."

Dan thought about it for a minute, and decided that despite the title, it did make some sense. Don Fernando had been the police chief of Villa Rosario forever. It would be a waste to let all his skills go unused.

"Speaking of police methods," Dan said, "I'm going to find out the name of whatever police chief is working this New York murder. I'll call you when I have it. Then, maybe you can email him and tell him you have someone in custody that is connected with his case. That way we can find out the latest on what's happening there."

"Ah, good idea, Dani. You know, if you weren't a gringo, I could get the city council to make you *my* consulting detective. Ha."

Dan smiled and shook his head. "That would be an honor, don Fernando," he said. "What time should I come by tomorrow?"

"We should have the ballistics in the morning. Why don't you come by after eleven? I'll have some lunch brought in and we can go over all the reports."

"Sounds good, amigo."

CHAPTER SEVENTEEN

It took Dan about thirty minutes of internet research to find the name and email of the police chief at the precinct that was investigating the murder of Silas Edwards. He also found the name and email of the district attorney's office that would have jurisdiction over the case if any suspect was arrested. He called don Fernando back with those contacts.

But now he had to wait. Wait until tomorrow. This was one aspect of detective work that always drove him crazy back in the States: the inevitable waiting on autopsies and ballistics reports.

So, he put on another pot of coffee, and decided to resurrect an old practice from his detective days: Meditative investigation, he called it—just emptying his mind and writing down words and questions about a case. He got out a legal pad and spent the next hour and a half just doodling and making notes, not actively trying to think about the case, but rather, posing questions and letting his subconscious chew on them. He wrote down the names of all the people involved in the case, including Ricardo and Matzel; he drew solid or dotted lines between the names to indicate connections; on another page, he wrote the words New York City and then the country names Colombia, France, Panama, and Spain; under the name Spain he wrote Toledo and then Ricardo. But something nagged him... Don Fernando had said that the Colombiano had flown to Madrid from Bulgaria, so he added the word Bulgaria to the page. Bulgaria... wasn't there something about Bulgaria in that Wikipedia article on Todo? He wrote Todo next to the word Bulgaria on the page, and then a big question mark. On another page, he wrote the names of the two dead burglars: Romain Martin

Groslot and Álvaro Renaldo. Underneath the names he wrote France and Colombia and drew a circle around the names. Underneath the circle, he wrote three notes:

"Frenchie wearing suit, shot in the back"

"Colombiano shot in chest, shot face to face"

"Matzel missing"

Obviously, Dan thought, there were three men in Matzel's bookstore, because some unknown person shot the Colombian and the Frenchman. Dan had already dismissed don Fernando's suggestion that it was Matzel who did that, because Matzel could have called the police after defending his property. The only other person whose identity was known was Jacques Foucher. Since Jacques knew both the Frenchman and the Colombian, he was automatically a suspect. They had all traveled to Panama together. The three of them could have burglarized Matzel's bookstore. But why would Jacques travel with these two and then kill them? Maybe there was a falling out. No, there had to be other people involved. Someone broke into his apartment while he was interrogating Jacques. Maybe Jacques and another person killed the Frenchman and the Colombian. Maybe they found something really valuable at the bookstore and then fought over it? Dan chewed on this for a bit. Did the four men go first to Matzel's house, ransack it, find nothing, and then go to the bookstore? Maybe that's why only one of the rooms was torn apart at the bookstore—because they found what they were looking for?... but then they fought over it?... but if they found what they were looking for, then why would Jacques pretend to be Silas and still want Ricardo's files? There were so many unanswered questions. Clearly, there was someone else involved. Someone, or maybe more than one person, broke into his apartment and stole the notebook with the maps. They had to know what they were looking for, so they must have known the real Silas Edwards. Silas was the only person besides him and Ricardo who knew that there was a notebook with maps. So, Silas must have known Jacques. How else would Jacques have known about Ricardo's files? But according to his passport, Jacques was already in Panama with the other two men when Dan told Silas about the maps...

Dan stopped doodling. He stood up and went over to the wall where a paper calendar hung. He took it down and brought it back to his desk and looked at it. Ricardo showed up at his house early Wednesday morning a week and a half ago. Jacques and other two men had landed in Panama two and a half weeks before that. So, they were in Panama City two and a half weeks before Ricardo felt he had to leave Villa Rosario. What was the connection? Had they contacted Ricardo? Or was there some history there? Did Ricardo know them from some earlier encounter? Ricardo must have known Silas was involved because of his specific instructions to lie to Silas about how long Ricardo had been gone.

Dan started tapping on his calendar with his pen as he was thinking. Maybe the maps were a ploy. Maybe Ricardo left the notebook with the maps on purpose, knowing that Silas would want them. Maybe they were a false clue, maps that led to nowhere. Maps of Spain... maps of a town called Toledo in Spain... the Tagus River that ran through Spain all the way to the Atlantic Ocean...

An image of a pirate ship with a jolly roger flag flashed across his brain. Were these treasure maps? Dan shook his head. No, he thought, that makes no sense. Yet, something valuable was at stake here.

There was so much he didn't know. And clearly, there were more people involved—unknown people who were still on the loose. How many more?

Nothing to do but wait.

CHAPTER EIGHTEEN

Dan arrived promptly at don Fernando's office at eleven o'clock the next morning.

"Ah Dani, you gringos are always right on time," don Fernando joked as Dan walked in. He gestured to the coffee pot and said, "I've made a fresh pot. There is much to discuss."

"I'm all ears," Dan said. He poured himself a cup of coffee and sat down in front of don Fernando's desk, a desk covered with papers.

"Well, first of all, Dani, the good news. The bullet in the Frenchman's back came from the gun we took from Jacques Foucher."

"Really!?" Dan exclaimed.

"Yes, the Forensic lab in Panama City did a test firing of his gun, and the rifling of the bullets is a match. Not only that, but the test swabs we took of Jacques Foucher's hands came back positive for gunpower residue. So now we can charge him with murder for shooting Groslot."

"And the bullet that killed the Colombiano?" Dan asked.

"It came from a forty-five. It doesn't match Foucher's gun."

"So, maybe there was a fourth person inside Matzel's bookstore?" Dan said.

"I think so, unless Foucher had another gun. But we didn't find one in his hotel room nor in his rental car. So, yes. I think it's likely there is another shooter involved. Anyway, here's the ballistics report," don Fernando said as he slid the report across the table to Dan. "We tested the hands of both the Frenchman and the Colombiano for gunpowder residue and found nothing. The Colombiano's gun still had a full magazine in it. Nonetheless, we did do a test firing from his gun so that we have a sample bullet to compare any other bullets we might find."

Dan flipped through the report and started thinking aloud. "Okay. So, either Foucher has two guns, or there were four people inside Matzel's bookstore. At some point, Foucher shoots the Frenchman. But then, somebody else shoots the Colombiano... or maybe it's just Foucher and the Colombiano working together to kill the Frenchman, but then someone else shows up and shoots the Colombiano and everyone flees... shit... something or someone else had to have interrupted them, because they never finished searching. There were all those unopened file cabinets..." Dan paused, rubbed his cheek, then said, "But they go to the bookstore because they're searching for something. But they don't find what they're looking for, because the next day Foucher calls me pretending to be Silas Edwards... And while he's talking with me, someone else is burglarizing my apartment, looking for... looking for whatever it was they were looking for... it *has* to be the maps. That's the only thing they took from my apartment. But those maps are just sketches, just simple drawings..."

Dan paused, and then said, "Besides, Foucher knew I had the maps, because Silas told him that... and if he knew I had the maps, then why burglarize Matzel's bookstore? Maybe they were looking for something else... Shit, don Fernando, this case still makes no fucking sense to me!"

"I know, Dani, but we are making progress. Now we have something we can pressure Foucher with. I can keep him in my jail for up to a year before turning him over to the prosecutor while we investigate this case," don Fernando said with a smile.

"What about the autopsy reports?" Dan asked.

"Yes, I have them here. The coroner thinks that the Colombiano and the Frenchman were killed around ten on Friday night. I sent my officers back to talk to the neighbors again as to whether they saw anything around the bookstore, at that hour of the night. But we still got no response."

"Jeez," Dan said, "you'd think they would have heard the gunshots... What about cars, don Fernando? How did they get to the bookstore? Are there any abandoned cars near the bookstore?"

"No, we've identified all the cars within three blocks of the bookstore. They all belong to various neighbors. If they arrived by car, then they left by car."

Dan tried to visualize the sequence of events. "There *has* to be four men, don Fernando. Four men arrive at the bookstore; Foucher shoots the Frenchman; the fourth man shoots the Colombiano; then Foucher and the fourth man leave."

"Maybe," don Fernando shrugged. "Who knows?"

"Well, if there *was* a fourth man, maybe he came with them from Madrid. Maybe he was on that same flight. You said they were all standing in line together at the airport to go through Immigration. Maybe the fourth man was standing with them. Can we check the names of the other passengers who passed through Immigration standing with or near these three?"

Don Fernando nodded. "Yes, that's a good idea. We'll do that."

"What else have we got?"

Don Fernando slid another sheet of paper towards Dan. "This is an Interpol report on Jacques Foucher. He has no convictions, but he's a person of interest in Belize for financial fraud."

"Oh?" said Dan, and picked up the report and started to read.

"Oh my God, don Fernando!" Dan exclaimed. "The financial fraud was with *You-Bank*! Foucher was on their board of directors!"

Don Fernando just shrugged. "What is that?"

"You-Bank was a bank in Belize, a fly-by-night bank, that provided Todo's first debit cards. Todo!—the company I was telling you about on Sunday? The company that rents those electric bikes here in town? That's the same company that issues those debit cards we found in Foucher's wallet and the two dead men's wallets. You-Bank was the bank that *used to* manage Todo's debit cards, but the Belize government closed them down five years ago, and Todo shifted its debit card business to another bank in Ireland."

"Ireland?" said don Fernando. "The Lucky Charms country?"

"Yeah, well, Ireland has some lax banking laws, not much regulation. Anyway, if Foucher was on the board of directors of You-Bank, that means he's involved with Todo."

Dan read through the rest of the Interpol report. Jacques Foucher was a "person of interest" but was never charged. However, the investigation was ongoing. Dan handed the report back to don Fernando, and just said, "Damn, that's so weird."

"There's more, Dani," don Fernando said. "We checked flights leaving Panama these past two weeks. You were right about your friend Ricardo. He caught a six a.m. flight to Madrid two Wednesday's ago, the same morning after he visited you. And you know what else?"

"What?"

"Matzel Davis also flew to Madrid three days ago. He took an Iberia airlines flight early Saturday morning, the same day he was supposed to meet you. And here's the interesting part: he flew one way. No return ticket, no luggage, not even a carry-on bag. That's a man in a hurry."

"Wow," Dan said. "So, he was probably landing in Madrid when we found the bodies in his bookstore—"

Just then the desk sergeant appeared in the doorway holding bags of food from the fonda down the street.

"Ah, yes sergeant. Come in," don Fernando said. "Dani, I took the liberty of ordering some lunch for us."

The sergeant placed the bags on the desk. Dan looked inside the bags. There were fresh empanadas and bowls of rice and beans. Dan reached in and pulled an empanada out and munched on it silently. He was deep in thought.

CHAPTER NINETEEN

Dan read the reports again while he ate his lunch. He asked don Fernando for a legal pad and jotted down key points: The Frenchman Groslot was shot in the back with a 9mm gun. There were powder burns on his suit, indicating he was shot at close range. The rifling marks on the bullets match the gun that Jacques Foucher was carrying. There was no gunpowder residue on neither the Colombian's nor the Frenchman's hands, but there was a trace amount of gunpowder residue on Jacques Foucher's hands.

The Colombian was killed by one bullet, a 45mm, to the chest. There were no powder burns on his clothes. The shot, however, was accurate: straight to the heart.

All of the neighbors around Matzel's office claimed they didn't see or hear anything. However, that's the norm. Neighbors in Panama never want to get involved and never want to talk to the police.

Don Fernando's officers had conducted an "informal" search of Jacques Foucher's hotel room at the Hilton in Panama City. No other gun was found there. They did find an open ticket for a flight to Spain along with several thousand dollars in both dollars and Euros in his hotel safe.

Don Fernando had talked with the precinct police chief in New York City where Silas Edwards was killed. Silas was also killed by 9mm bullets, five of them in fact. The police had no suspects but were reviewing surveillance tapes from nearby businesses. Jacques Foucher could not be a suspect, of course, because he was in Panama. But the police chief promised to keep don Fernando informed.

According to airport records, Matzel Davis had taken a five a.m. flight from Panama City to Madrid. He showed up at the airport at three a.m. and paid cash for a one-way ticket. As don Fernando had stated earlier, Matzel had no luggage, not even a carry-on bag.

The police found what they believed were Matzel Davis's fingerprints on all the common household items at his house—things that hadn't been moved by the burglars—so they assumed they were Matzel's fingerprints. But they found two additional sets of fingerprints on the ransacked items at his house—items that had been opened and thrown to the floor. The police assumed these were fingerprints of the burglars. They did not match the fingerprints of the two dead men—neither the Frenchman Groslot nor the Colombian Renaldo. Nor did they match Jacques Foucher's fingerprints. Given the time of death of the two men in Matzel's bookstore, and the nonmatching prints, the police ruled them out as the burglars of Matzel's house. That meant there were two different teams of burglars—one group at Matzel's house and one group at Matzel's bookstore.

However, there was one matching fingerprint: on the notebook of Ricardo's essays that was on Dan's desk—the notebook that Dan believed the burglar, or burglars, had opened before taking the notebook of maps. A single print on the cover of that notebook matched one of the prints found inside Matzel's house. Thus, the same person or persons who had ransacked Matzel's house had broken into Dan's apartment.

Dan finished the last empanada, wiped his mouth, and looked at his notes.

"Oh, there was one other thing, Dani," don Fernando said. "We took some of Matzel's files that were scattered on the floor by the dead Colombiano and looked through them. I was assuming they were going to be tax records, or something related to his inventory of books. But they were all ancient history."

"History?"

"Yes, you know, histories of Spain and France. Who the kings were, what battles happened, what the politics of the time were, etc. The files were organized by year, going back to 3000 AD."

"Really?"

"Yes, it was very strange. I sent my men back to go through all the file cabinets of all the rooms. They were all just all full of articles, research papers, and notes on ancient history."

"Well, he did tell me he was a history buff," Dan said.

"This was a bit more intense than just a history buff, Dani. These were files of an obsessive man. There were three rooms full of file cabinets, and each file cabinet was crammed with file folders of these articles."

"You did tell me he was loco, don Fernando."

"Yes, loco like a fox. Because all these articles had something to do, one way or another, with finance."

"What do you mean?" Dan asked.

"In all the articles and papers we looked at, he had underlined or highlighted anything to do with money: the rate of exchange, the price of gold, how gold was transported, who controlled what wealth... anything to do with money was marked somehow. That's what all the articles were about, really. They were all about money."

"Interesting, but I don't know what to make of it."

"Neither do I, Dani."

Dan looked down at his notes. The case was still a puzzle to him.

"Do you want to go have another chat with Mr. Foucher?" don Fernando asked. "I haven't told him yet that we've charged him with murder."

"Hmm, yes, in a minute. I'm thinking about something."

Dan thought about the notes he had made on the legal pad back at his apartment. "You know who's missing, don Fernando? David Ortega. We've learned a little bit more about each person, except David Ortega. Can I see Jacques's wallet?"

Don Fernando pulled a large evidence folder from his drawer and took out the wallet belonging to Jacques Foucher and handed it to Dan. Dan opened it and took out the business card with the name "Foucher and Ortega, LLC" on it.

"Let's give Mr. Ortega a call," Dan said.

"What are you going to say to him?" don Fernando asked.

"I don't know yet... but I'm going to call on a Skype line so that it won't show that I'm calling from Panama."

Dan opened his Skype application on his phone and typed in the number on the business card. There was a delay, and then a ringing. Then someone answered.

"Foucher and Ortega," said a female voice.

"David Ortega, please,"

"I'm sorry, Mr. Ortega is away on business this week. Would you like to talk with his secretary?"

"Yes, please."

There was a click on the line and then another female voice answered.

"David Ortega's office. Monica Jamison speaking, how may I help you?"

"I was calling for David," Dan said.

"I'm sorry. Mr. Ortega is away on business. May one of our associates help you?"

"Well, no. I need to speak directly with David," Dan said, trying to feign a tone of familiarity. "Do you know when he'll be back?"

"I don't have a definite date. He's out of the country on business. May I ask who's calling?"

"This is Dennis Wilson, a colleague of David's," Dan lied. "Is there any way I can get in touch with him? It's rather urgent."

"He does check in for his messages every few days. Would you like to leave a message?"

"Yes, please, just tell him Dennis Wilson called. He has my number." Then on an impulse, Dan added. "I bet he's gone back to Spain again, hasn't he? He always says he likes it there."

"Yes, sir. I believe that's where he is."

"Okay, thanks, just tell him I called."

"Yes, sir."

Dan pressed the OFF icon on his cell phone and looked at don Fernando.

"David Ortega's in Spain," he said, "and my guess is that he's in Toledo."

Don Fernando just nodded.

"Okay, let's go have another chat with Jacques Foucher," Dan said.

Don Fernando nodded again and was reaching for his phone when an officer appeared in his doorway.

"Capitán?"

"Yes, Marcelo."

"There is a man come to see you."

"Well, Marcelo, as you can see, I'm busy in a meeting."

"This man is a gringo, Capitán. He says he is the attorney for the prisoner with the foreign name."

Dan and don Fernando just looked at each other.

"Well, in that case, Marcelo, show him in," don Fernando said.

"Yes, Capitán." The officer turned to leave.

Dan leaned forward and said to don Fernando in a hushed voice, "Don't let him talk to Foucher."

"Oh, of course not, Dani," don Fernando laughed.

Dan slid his chair over to the corner of the room so that anyone who came to the doorway would not be able to get a good look at him. A minute later, the officer reappeared, escorting a young man with blond hair, wearing a suit. Another suit, Dan thought, how strange. The officer and the man stood in the threshold of don Fernando's office.

The officer spoke. "Éste es el gringo, Capitán. Dice que es abogado, y que el otro gringo es su cliente."

"Thank you, Marcelo," don Fernando said in Spanish. "Why don't you wait a minute until we know what this man wants."

"Sí, Capitán." The officer remained standing in the doorway.

Don Fernando looked at the fresh-faced man in the suit and said in English, "Señor, I am José Fernando, the chief of police of this town. What can I do for you?"

"My name is Eric Trout. I am an attorney. I spoke with the US Embassy in Panama City, and they say you are holding my client, Jacques Foucher, in your jail. May I ask what the charges are?"

Don Fernando leaned back in his chair, placed his hands behind his head, interlacing his fingers, and looked the young man up and down.

"With all due respect, señor, you don't look old enough to be an attorney."

The young man reached into his suit pocket and retrieved a business card carrying case. He stepped into don Fernando's office and handed him a business card. Don Fernando looked at it, and then read it aloud. Dan knew he was doing this for Dan's benefit.

"Eric Trout, attorney at law, with the firm Foucher and Ortega, LLC. Very interesting, Mr. Trout. So, you are representing your boss?"

Eric Trout shrugged acquiescence. "I am."

"Well, he is being charged with murder, burglary, carrying a firearm without a permit... so far. There may be other charges. The case is still under investigation."

Eric Trout seemed visibly stunned by the charges.

"Were you sent down here?" don Fernando asked.

"Yes, yes, I was."

"Who sent you?" don Fernando continued.

"Well... the firm did."

Don Fernando smiled. "Who in the firm?"

"My boss, David Ortega."

"But Mr. Ortega is in Spain, is he not?"

Now Eric Trout was on the defensive. He began to sputter. "Well, Mr. Ortega called the office from Spain, and said he hadn't heard from his partner, so we called the hotel, and they told us the police had been there, so we called the Embassy, and they said he was here."

"And tell me, Mr. Trout," don Fernando said, "why was Jacques Foucher here? What was his business in Panama?"

"I don't... I don't know exactly. He and Mr. Ortega had some investments in Spain, some kind of project. It was a surprise to us that Mr. Foucher was in Central America."

"Ah, they were in Spain together recently?"

"Yes."

"And Mr. Ortega called you from Spain and told you to come to Panama and see what was going on?"

"Well, yes..."

Eric Trout seemed to regain his composure. "Can I see Mr. Foucher?" he asked.

"Are you a licensed attorney in Panama?" don Fernando asked.

"No, but I'm licensed in New York, and I work for Mr. Foucher."

"Well, then, the answer is no, you cannot see him," don Fernando said and smiled.

Eric Trout stiffened up. "Well, I can just align with a local attorney and file a *pro hac vice* motion to practice here, and then get a court order to see my client," he said with a slight defiant tone in his voice.

"Yes, I guess you'll just have to do that," was don Fernando's response. "Thanks for stopping by."

Then don Fernando said to the officer in Spanish, "Marcelo, can you show this young man to the front door?"

"Sí, Capitán." And the officer grabbed Eric Trout by the arm and firmly guided him down the hallway. Eric Trout said something as he was being led out, but Dan could not make out what it was.

"Ah, gringo lawyers," sighed don Fernando, and picked up the phone and dialed. After a moment, he spoke to someone in Spanish.

"Ah, Elena, hello, it's José Fernando. How are you? Yes good. How is your husband? Excellent. And the children? Wonderful. Is Andrés busy? Could I speak with him? Thank you... Hello, Andrés, yes, doing well, thank you. And how are you? Excellent. Listen, the reason I was calling is that a gringo lawyer is going to show up in your court, probably today, with some local attorney, and he's going to file a motion to be allowed to represent a client here in Villa Rosario. Yes, well, it's a prisoner we have in our jail. We're charging him with murder. Yes, he's a gringo as well. Yes, messy business. I know. Anyway, this gringo lawyer came to my office today. I do not like him. He was very disrespectful to me. I *know*. Well, it's the times we live in. I do not want to see him back in my office. I would consider it a great favor if his motion to practice law was turned down, or at least delayed a few weeks. His name? I have it right here." Don Fernando picked up the business card. "It's Eric Trout, from the law firm of Foucher and Ortega in New York City. Yes, oh well, thank *you*. Yes, of course, I will tell her you said hello. Next Sunday? That would be lovely. Yes. Well, I know you're busy, so I will let you go. Thank you."

Don Fernando hung up the phone and smiled.

"What was that about?" Dan asked.

Andrés Cordela is the judge in Panama City that handles those *pro hac vice* motions that foreign attorneys have to file to practice here in Panama. He's married to my wife's sister. Young Mr. Trout's motion won't get approved."

Dan just laughed. "Is there anyone in law enforcement or the courts that you're not related to?" he asked.

"No, not really," answered don Fernando seriously.

"Okay, shall we go talk to Jacques Foucher now?" Dan said.

Don Fernando nodded and reached for his phone.

CHAPTER TWENTY

Don Fernando had Jacques Foucher brought to the interrogation room. He was seated at a small table with his hands cuffed behind his back. The guard stood a few feet away. Dan thought that Foucher didn't look as cocky as he had two days earlier. He sat slouched in his chair, unshaven and disheveled. Dan and don Fernando took seats facing him on the other side of the table. Jacques raised his head and looked at them without any expression.

"Señor Foucher," don Fernando said, "I am here to inform you that you are being held for investigation of the following crimes: murder in the first degree, burglary in the second degree, and carrying a firearm without a permit. Other charges may be forthcoming. We have informed the US Embassy of these charges."

"I want a lawyer," Jacque Foucher said in a monotone.

"And you shall have one," Dan said. "In due time. But let me explain how the Panamanian judicial system works. Police Chief José Fernando has officially filed what are called 'investigative charges' against you. The law permits him up to a year—a full year—to build his case against you before he has to hand you over to the prosecutor in Panama City. At that point, the prosecutor will file formal charges, and you will be transferred from the jail here over to a jail in Panama City. Then, the actual court proceedings and trial will start in Panama City, and you certainly will have a lawyer for that, one of your own choosing or a public defender. But for the moment, you belong to Police Chief Fernando. There will be a very short hearing here in Villa Rosario, in a few days, to confirm what I'm telling you. There is no right to bail down here, Mr. Foucher. Because of the nature of the charges, the judge will confine you to what is known as 'preventive custody' while the case is being investigated. The court will provide you a public defender for that hearing, but that's the only hearing you'll get here in Villa Rosario. A representative from the Embassy will probably come by to meet with you this week or the next to see if there is anyone in the States they need to notify about your situation."

"I want to call my lawyer in the States," Jacques said, again in a flat tone.

"Sorry, phone calls are not a right down here. As I said, you'll get a public defender in a few days, and you can communicate your wishes to him."

Jacques seemed to slouch further in his chair. "That's not fair," he said softly.

"No, it's not," Dan agreed, "but you chose to come down here to a Central American country *with a gun*, Mr. Foucher. And since you'll hear this at your hearing, I'm not giving away any secrets by telling you that a bullet found in a certain dead body in a local bookstore a few days ago came from your gun. So, while I agree with you that it's not fair that you don't enjoy the same rights here that you might in the States, I would suggest that a certain Romain Martin Groslot wouldn't think it was very fair that he was shot in the back."

"I don't know anything about that," snapped Foucher. "Whatever happened to innocent until proven guilty?"

"That presumption doesn't apply down here, Mr. Foucher. Panamanian law is based on the Napoleonic Code. Once the police file investigative charges against you, you are presumed guilty until you get to trial. None of the legal rights that you would have in the States kick in until you are transferred to Panama City. And as I said, that could be next year. Until that time, you're stuck here with us. I tried to explain your situation to you two days ago, but you didn't listen. But maybe you'll listen to me now."

Jacques Foucher glared at Dan, but Dan could tell he was thinking.

Dan continued. "You're being held on suspicion of murdering Romain Martin Groslot, but as I tried to tell you

Sunday, that is not my concern. You can murder whomever you want as long as they are not friends of mine—"

"I didn't do it!" Jacques interrupted.

"Shut up," Dan said curtly. "I don't care. I only care about one thing, which is why you came to Panama to talk with *me*."

"You can't question me without my lawyer!" Jacques spit out.

Dan sighed audibly, and then spoke very slowly, as if he was talking to a child. "Okay, Mr. Foucher. I'm going to explain this *again*, in very simple terms, so that *even you* can understand this. First, you are not in the United States, so your Miranda rights do not apply here. Second, I am not working for the police. I am not an employee of the police. The only reason I am here in this room with you is because I asked my friend, Police Chief Fernandez, if I could talk with you. So, because I am not an agent of the state, I can ask you any questions I want. But I am not going to ask you anything related to the crimes you are charged with. I only want to know why you came to Panama to see *me*. You don't have to talk to me, it's true. But I will point out that you are stuck in a cell in a small-town jail that is not too comfortable. It doesn't even have a shower, does it? And you are likely to be stuck here for a long time. And I—being a fellow American and, as I say, a friend of the police chief here—am in a position to help you, to at least get you transferred to a cell with a shower, a more comfortable bed, and maybe even better food..."

Dan paused to let his words sink in.

"Police Chief Fernandez is not going to question you. No official here in Villa Rosario is going to question you. That's not how things are done down here. The police here will build their case file without talking to you. The only one who is going to talk with you is me, and the only reason I am talking to you, is because you chose to involve me in whatever you were doing down here! And I want to know why. Why did you come here? Why did you call me? Why did you tell me you were Silas Edwards? That's all I want to know."

Jacque Foucher licked his lips nervously.

"David sent me," he finally said.

"David Ortega?" Dan asked.

"Yeah. David had a deal with Silas, an agreement... but he found out that Silas was going to double-cross him and keep the maps for himself. David knew you were going to send the maps to Silas, so we had to get them first. He told me to pretend I was Silas. I told David it wouldn't work, that you wouldn't believe me, but he said it was our only chance."

"Why did David want the maps?" Dan asked.

But Jacques said, "No! I answered your question. Now answer one of mine. Did you ship the maps to Silas?"

The question surprised Dan. Jacques had just been told he was being charged with murder, yet he was still obsessed with the maps. That made no sense. But Dan decided to take a chance and answer Jacques's question. He shook his head and said, "No. Silas is dead."

Jacques's eyes widened, then he looked away. "Fuck," he said softly.

"He was murdered this weekend, shot in a parking garage," Dan said.

Jacques seemed to sink down in his chair. He just continued to say, "Fuck, fuck, fuck..."

"Now tell me," Dan said, "why did David want these maps?"

Jacques shook his head no. For a second, Dan thought he was going to clam up. But then Jacques sighed and said, "Ricardo Mendes told Silas that he had been working with a man called Matzel Davis. We weren't sure who Matzel Davis really was. But when you told Silas that Ricardo had drawn some maps, you mentioned some of the names on the maps. Silas recognized those names immediately.

"As being in Toledo?" Dan asked.

"Yes. Silas believed Ricardo had somehow cracked the San Servando code."

"And what exactly is that?" Dan asked.

Jacques frowned and then looked up at Dan. "Do you still have the maps?"

Dan hesitated for a split second. He did have the copies he had made of the maps, but his intuition told him to keep that fact to himself.

"No," he said. "While I was meeting with you in front of the Church, someone broke into my apartment and stole them."

Jacques closed his eyes and slumped further in his chair. He looked defeated.

"Fuck," was all he said.

But Dan noticed that Jacques did not seem surprised that his apartment had been burglarized.

"You know who did this," Dan said matter-of-factly.

"Barcus and his crew," Jacques said.

"They work for Ortega?" Dan asked.

Jacques just shook his head no.

"They worked for Silas?" Dan asked.

Jacques shook his head no again. "Silas had double-crossed us... and joined Barcus."

"And this code..." Dan started to say...

But Jacques interrupted him.

"No. No more. I've answered your questions. No more. Now give me a cell with a shower and let me talk with a lawyer."

Dan looked at don Fernando. Don Fernando nodded and said to the guard, "Lleva a este hombre a una celda con ducha y una cama mejor ... y dale un poco mejor de comida."

"Sí, Capitán." And the guard grabbed Jacques's arm and made him stand up.

"They'll take you to a better cell now," Dan said.

"And a lawyer?" Jacques asked.

"The court will appoint one in a few days. I don't have any control over that," Dan said.

The guard took Jacques away.

Dan and don Fernando sat quietly in the room. Finally don Fernando said, "These maps must be very valuable, Dani."

Dan shook his head. "I don't think so, don Fernando. I examined those maps carefully. They were too crudely drawn to show anything. They were just a few lines on notebook paper with a few names. They were like a child's drawing, a doodling."

"And this San Servando code? What is that?"

"I have no idea," Dan said. "There was a weird drawing of a castle tower on Ricardo's maps with the abbreviation *San Serv*, but I don't know if that's connected."

"It sounds like a buried treasure story, Dani."

"Yeah... I think it's more like a wild goose chase, don Fernando. Remember, none of these goons had seen the maps. They were all just speculating what was on them. Jacques said that Silas knew that Ricardo was working with Matzel... but that they *discovered who Matzel really was*. They know something about Matzel that we don't know, because it was the fact that Ricardo was working with Matzel—not the other way around—that made Ricardo's maps valuable..."

Dan sat and thought for a moment, then continued. "In fact, this whole thing started when I mentioned the maps to Silas. He didn't want to let on, but I could tell he was excited. So, yes. You're correct in saying the maps are valuable. But I don't think they're valuable for what they show, because they really don't show anything. So, they must be valuable for what they represent. Whatever Matzel was working on, whatever this San Servando code means, *that* must be something valuable... and all these idiots came down to Panama, because they hoped the maps would lead them to whatever this valuable thing was. They were all speculating. Two people murdered because of this... this speculation. Whoever stole the maps must have been pretty damn disappointed when they finally looked at them."

Dan thought more about what Jacques had said. Then, almost rhetorically, he said aloud, "Silas was going to double-cross David Ortega. Somehow, Ortega finds out. How does he find out? Silas worked for some guy named Barcus. Barcus comes to Panama to get the maps from me. Does Ortega know this too, or does he just guess that is what's happening? Ortega sends Jacques to get the maps first. But now Barcus has the maps. What would Barcus do? He has no reason to stay here anymore. He would go to Spain... Don Fernando, we have to notify the airport to arrest anyone with the name Barcus. Maybe he hasn't left Panama yet."

Don Fernando nodded and said, "Let's go to my office."

Both men stood up and hurried out of the interrogation room.

CHAPTER TWENTY-ONE

Back in don Fernando's office, Dan made more notes on his legal pad while don Fernando made several calls to Immigration at the airport.

Finally, he hung up and said to Dan, "They are going to call me back in a few minutes."

Dan nodded and said, "You know don Fernando, Jacques and his crew arrived here about two and a half weeks before Ricardo came to see me. They couldn't have known anything about the maps then, because I didn't mention them to Silas Edwards until a week after Ricardo left, because I didn't discover them until a week later... I'm trying to figure out the sequence here... All these guys were in Madrid, except for Silas who was back in New York. Jacques said that Silas knew that Ricardo was working with Matzel, so evidently, they all knew something about Matzel that we don't. Something that Matzel had, or something that he knew, was important. David Ortega seems to be in charge of Jacques Foucher and the Frenchman and the Colombian. He sends them from Spain to Panama. Two weeks later, Ricardo comes running to my place, then flies to Spain. I find the maps a week later—no, a week and two days later. I tell Silas. He recognizes the map as being of Toledo. Somehow, Ortega finds out about that, and he also finds out that Silas has asked me to ship the maps to him. And somehow, he also finds out that Silas is going to keep the maps for himself or give them to this guy named Barcus. So, David Ortega tells Jacques to get the maps from me before I can send them to Silas. Since Jacques is already here in Panama, that means that Ortega had to have called or emailed or texted Jacques.... Can you get a warrant to see who Silas talked with on his cellphone? Maybe we can get a cellphone number for David Ortega and use that to track him down. Or maybe there's some texts or emails that will tell us something.

Don Fernando nodded and said, "I can do that. But I don't need a warrant. We have his phone, and I have a new technology forensic expert on my staff now. He can unlock any phone and read all the emails."

"Really?" Dan said. "When did this happen? I thought your budget was really tight."

"Special grant from your government," don Fernando said and smiled. "Another reason I keep on good terms with your FBI."

Just then the phone rang. Don Fernando answered it and jotted down some notes.

After he hung up, he said to Dan, "A man named Dimitrios Barkoxe, spelled B-a-r-k-o-x-e, flew out of Panama City yesterday morning."

"To Madrid?" asked Dan.

Don Fernando nodded yes.

"What's his nationality?"

"He was using a Spanish passport," don Fernando said, "but he listed his nationality on the immigration form as 'Basque.' I understand those Basque people are a very proud people."

"Hmmm, B-a-r-k-o-x-e, huh... That sounds close to Barcus."

"I think this is our man, Dani. He arrived from Madrid last Friday, the day before Matzel's house was broken into."

Dan thought for a minute, then said, "Dimitrios Barkoxe... Can you ask the FBI and Interpol whether they have a file on him? Maybe even send those two fingerprints your men found in Matzel's house? Maybe one of those prints is this Barkoxe fellow."

The phone rang again. Don Fernando answered it, jotted down some more notes, thanked the caller, and hung up.

"That was Immigration again," he said. "Remember you were thinking that a fourth man might have flown into

Panama with Jacques Foucher and the Colombiano and the Frenchman? Immigration keeps a list of the exact order of who is processed through the line at the airport. Jacques Foucher was in line first, followed by the Colombiano Álvaro Renaldo, and then the Frenchman Romain Martin Groslot. Immediately before Jacques Foucher was a family with children, so I think we can rule them out. But, right behind Groslot was a woman named Mariana Ibarra who told Immigration she was traveling alone from Madrid to visit friends. She arrived with an open return ticket to Madrid.

Dan pursed his lips. His experience was that women were rarely involved in organized crimes of violence.

"I don't think she's connected to this case, don Fernando," he said.

"I might agree, Dani, except that she left on the same flight yesterday as Dimitrios Barkoxe, going back to Madrid."

"Really?" said Dan. "Shit, I can't keep track of all these people."

"I will ask Interpol and the FBI about her as well," don Fernando said.

"Please..." Dan shook his head. "I just can't make any sense out of this case, don Fernando." He paused then thought out loud. "If this Mariana woman was traveling *with* Jacques and his crew, and competing *against* Barkoxe to get to the maps first, why did she fly back to Madrid *with* Barkoxe?"

Don Fernando just shrugged. "I don't know Dani, but there's no honor among thieves, you know. Maybe she was with them; maybe she pretending to be with them; or maybe she was just following them; maybe she switched sides."

"Yeah... fuck... I just can't see what connects all these people... There's more to this than just some crappy maps..." Dan shook his head. He hated not understanding things. Finally, he said, "Well, there's not much else I can do here. I guess I'm going to head on back home. Thanks again for lunch."

"My pleasure, Dani. Why don't you come back tomorrow around eleven. We should have some reports from Interpol by then. If something turns up sooner, I'll call you."

"Okay, amigo."

As Dan left the police station, his head was swirling with the names of all the different players in this case: Silas, dead in New York; Álvaro Renaldo and Romain Martin Groslot, both dead here in Villa Rosario, Jacques Foucher, in jail; David Ortega, in Spain, probably in Toledo; Dimitrios Barkoxe and Mariana Ibarra, who both flew to Madrid yesterday; Ricardo and Matzel Davis, who both flew to Madrid in the last two weeks. Maybe the answers lay in Spain. Maybe he would have to go to Spain—and do what? Search for Ricardo and Matzel in either Madrid or, more likely, in Toledo. It would be like looking for a needle in a haystack. Still, it was an idea worth thinking about.

As Dan walked across the Parque Central on his way back to his apartment, he spotted the Todo banners flying on portable flagpoles at one corner of the park. There were five or six electric bikes lined up for rent under the flags. Several locals were standing around looking at the bikes. One of the banners advertised the Todo debit card with the slogan, "Trade Crypto Risk-Free." Ricardo wondered how anyone could trade cryptocurrency risk-free.

He continued walking, thinking about the idea of going to Toledo.

As soon as he got to his apartment, and opened the door, his cellphone in his pocket began to ring. He looked at the caller ID. It was don Fernando.

"Well, that was quick, don Fernando," Dan said.

"Ha, yes, well I wanted you to know what I just found out. This Dimitrios Barkoxe—he was connected with that You-Bank you were telling me about. Interpol says that both Jacque Foucher and Dimitrios Barkoxe were on the Board of Directors of that bank in Belize. They have both men listed as 'under investigation,' but no charges have been filed."

"Wow... wow, okay... do we know what they were under investigation for?"

"No, Dani. All I got was a summary report. But I have sent a request in for a detailed report, along with copies of the fingerprints we found in Matzel Davis's house and your house. We should get something back by tomorrow morning."

"Okay, well, thanks don Fernando. I'll see you tomorrow."

Dan hung up and stepped inside his apartment. So, Jacques and Barkoxe were on the Board of You-Bank together. Was Barkoxe a lawyer too? Did they know each other before You-Bank or did they meet there? Was You-Bank connected to whatever Matzel Davis and Ricardo were working on? It couldn't have been just coincidence that two Board members under investigation for bank fraud turn up in Villa Rosario desperate to get some maps—maps that Ricardo drew while working with a retired Moor who kept file cabinets full of articles on finance... Did Jacques and Barkoxe have a falling out? Maybe he was wrong to assume that they were competing against each other. Jacques had never said that. He had only said that Barkoxe was the one who stole the maps from Dan. Maybe they were all working together... but then, why shoot the Frenchman and the Colombian? And who shot Silas?

Dan looked at his watch. A bit early to drink he thought, but he went and got a beer from the refrigerator. Then he sat down at his desk, turned on his laptop, and opened his beer.

Dan spent the next two hours researching You-Bank and its connection to Todo.

He handwrote several pages of notes. After he had exhausted the internet, reading through all the articles he could find, he typed up his notes on his laptop. Old habits die hard, and Dan's old habit of typing up his research notes was a good one—it helped him organize his thoughts.

He learned that You-Bank was incorporated in Belize eight years ago as a "foreign exchange and processing bank." He knew from his previous research that this meant it wasn't really a bank—it could only issue and process debit cards. The bank listed Todo as its only client for these debit cards, but to Dan it appeared the other way around. Todo wasn't a client of You-Bank. Rather, You-Bank was just the subsidiary of Todo that allowed Todo to market debit cards worldwide. Dan wondered if Jacques and Barkoxe were working at Todo as well.

You-Bank's only role was to host Todo's debit cards. Todo had engineered the debit cards so that they could market them as mini-banks and transfer stations. Clients could deposit money directly on the cards, and You-Bank even paid a small amount of interest if the deposits were large enough. Todo had contracted with Visa to process all the transactions. When someone initiated a transaction, Visa would send the information to Todo, and Todo would complete the transaction, transfer any money, and send the completed information back to Visa and You-Bank. Visa never touched the client's money—they just shunted the transaction information to You-Bank's computer servers. But Visa's logo appeared on the debit card, giving it the aura of legitimacy, and cardholders could use the card everywhere Visa was accepted. The debit cards were set up so that people could easily transfer money to and from any other debit or credit card, allowing people such as web-cam girls to receive payments directly from their customers, or allowing clients to easily transfer money across borders to any bank account or any person who had a Todo debit card. The debit cards automatically converted currencies across borders according to the international currency exchange rates. Recipients of transferred funds could go to their local ATMs and withdraw money in their local currency. The cards even converted money into bitcoin or any crypto-currency and acted as a crypto-wallet.

It was unclear to Dan where the clients' money was actually stored. The computer servers that managed all the financial transaction were in Belize and were owned by You-Bank, but You-Bank was only a "processing bank." They weren't allowed to actually take deposits. Dan could only assume that Todo must control all those funds, but he had no idea where the funds were.

Todo's original debit cards issued through You-Bank had been hugely popular. Millions of people used them. One report estimated that the annual total card usage exceeded seven trillion dollars.

But then, almost five years ago, You-Bank suddenly collapsed. All the debit card holders who thought they were depositing their money in a FDIC-insured US bank discovered that their savings were uninsured... and gone. All the clients who thought that Visa would help them gain access to their frozen accounts learned that Visa had nothing to do with their debit cards. The FBI investigated; the IRS investigated; the World Bank investigated; Interpol investigated; but no one was ever charged.

The reason the investigation produced no indictments was that there was no paper trail for investigators to follow. You-Bank's servers were in Belize, and when the bank shut down, the servers simply deleted everyone's account. Years of financial records simply evaporated from the ethernet in one day. No hard drives, no back-up copies, no duplicates were ever found. Electronic bank statements and emails all mysteriously disappeared from customers' phones as well. Investigators knew there had been a fraud, but they had absolutely no proof that the bank had even existed.

There had been warning signs, of course. The money that Todo was transferring passed through many legitimate banks, and those banks were required to file a SAR form—a suspicious activity report—to the Financial Crimes Enforcement Network, known as FinCEN, of the US Treasury. In the first year of You Bank's existence, the Bank of New York Mellon filed a half-dozen SARs stating they had confirmed that most of You-Bank's transfers were payments to online casinos, pornography websites, and anonymous accounts in off-shore banks. Bank of America soon followed, and filed SARs stating that You-Bank did not know the true identity of many of its customers, a violation of the "know your customer" rule that banks are required to follow. CitiBank filed a SAR stating that their internal investigation showed that a large number of recipients of You-Bank's transfers were escort services. Deutsche

Bank filed a SAR stating that they could not determine the commercial purpose of over $23 million of You-Bank's transfers.

These types of SARs would have triggered investigations into any US-based bank, but You-Bank, being based in Belize, remained just outside the Treasury's jurisdiction. Technically speaking, it did not even meet the Treasury's definition of a bank. In the Treasury's view, it was only a "foreign exchange," not a bank, and this fact stymied many of the early investigations.

By the time the pressure mounted to the point where the Treasury was going to have to do something, You-Bank simply collapsed and evaporated, like a thief closing his tent and disappearing in the night. Todo scrambled to preserve its public image and core business, and quickly announced partnerships with new "banks" in Ireland and Croatia, but similar to You-Bank, these new banks were merely processing centers for Todo's debit card. Customers who could prove that their lost deposits on the debit cards were from legitimate sources had their accounts reopened in these new banks and did receive credit for their lost funds—after a few months delay—in the new banks. But customers who could not prove that their funds were from legitimate sources, i.e. customers who would not be able to sue Todo because that would expose their criminal activities, never got their money bank. Escort services, pornography websites, drug delivery services on the dark web, and people laundering money were simply stiffed and had no avenue to complain.

The big unanswered question, of course, was where all those millions of dollars ended up. Without a paper trail, the government of Belize and the US Treasury could not trace the money; and without complaining victims there was little incentive to do so. Interpol seemed to be the only agency that was keeping up an active investigation.

Dan leaned back in his chair and reviewed his typed notes. He would share this tomorrow with don Fernando. But still, he wondered, how did all of this relate to Matzel and Ricardo?

CHAPTER TWENTY-TWO

Dan's telephone rang early the next morning.

"Ah, Dani. I hope I didn't wake you," don Fernando said.

"No, I'm up, don Fernando. I'm just working on my first cup of coffee."

"Good, good. You should come by my office. That new technology forensic expert we hired is a magician. He was able to open up Jacques Foucher's phone. We have all the text messages between him and that David Ortega fellow. They paint quite an interesting story."

"Really? That's great! I'll be there in twenty minutes. I just gotta shower and get dressed."

"I'll be here," don Fernando said.

*   *   *

Twenty minutes later, Dan was sitting in don Fernando's office, poring over a multi-page printout of text exchanges.

"These are texts from WhatsApp, don Fernando. I thought WhatsApp was encrypted!" Dan exclaimed.

"Ah Dani, our expert was trained by the FBI. He can open anything. He called the FBI and within five minutes, he found out that the cell number that Foucher was texting to was an international cell number owned by David Ortega. This printout you are holding is just the texts between those two phones. He's working on the other people Foucher texted."

Dan was reading as fast as he could, turning the pages, and speaking out loud.

"Look at this, don Fernando. Here's a text from Foucher to Ortega, saying they've located Ricardo and have been watching him all week. Damn... Here, he's complaining about the Panamanian heat... Okay, here Foucher says he's seen Ricardo going to visit someone named Nassim." Dan looked at don Fernando and asked, "Who's Nassim?"

Don Fernando just shook his head. Dan went back to reading the texts out loud.

"Okay, okay, here Foucher is telling Ortega that Ricardo has disappeared, and Ortega says *quote* I wonder if Nassim told him anything about the coins *unquote*... I wonder if he's talking about the coins in Matzel Davis's store... Oh fuck! Here's David Ortega talking about tapping Silas Edwards' phone... Double fuck! He fucking *listened to me* telling Silas about the maps! Jesus!... So *that's* how he knew!... Okay, here Foucher is upset and telling Ortega that he thought he saw Barcus following Nassim... and then Ortega replies and tells Foucher they can't wait any longer, to go ahead and *quote* break into the bookstore and look for the coins *unquote*... Shit! Here Foucher is telling him that they were *quote* interrupted *unquote* and that Renaldo and Groslot are dead... Here Foucher is arguing with Ortega and telling him that him that impersonating Silas won't work... but Ortega tells him to do it anyway... and that's the last text... Oh my God, don Fernando. This is amazing."

Don Fernando leaned back in his desk chair and beamed. "I thought you'd be pleased," he said. "This Jacques Foucher, like most criminals, is an idiot. He has basically given us a confession."

"Well, he didn't actually admit he killed the Frenchman," Dan replied.

"A minor detail. With these transcripts and the ballistic report, in our court system, he is—how do you gringos say?—he is burnt toast."

Dan nodded, then asked, "Do you think we should talk to him again?"

"Let's wait until tomorrow, Dani. He's got his detention hearing today. I think that after he goes through that, he will be more willing to talk with us. The judge is going to let me detain him here for up to a year while I complete my investigation."

"Wow," Dan said softly.

"And by tomorrow," don Fernando continued, "my forensic expert may have pried more information out of Foucher's phone."

"Okay, that sounds good, don Fernando, Dan said. "I haven't eaten breakfast yet, so I'm going to go get some food. I'll drop back in tomorrow morning."

*   *   *

Dan left don Fernando's office in search of food. He knew there were some fondas on the other side of the Parque Central that served breakfast. As he cut through the park, he saw the Todo display again. There was a big white tent over the bikes and a banner advertising the Todo debit card. He saw the same young fellow that he had talked to last Friday standing by the bikes. Dan remembered that his name was Mark. Mark obviously recognized him too, as he waved at Dan and gestured for him to come over to the bikes. Dan walked over.

"Hello, Dan," Mark said. "Did you come back to get one of our Todo debit cards?"

Dan was impressed that the fellow remembered his name. That's the sign of a good salesman, Dan thought.

"I'm still mulling it over," Dan replied.

"Well, we got a new promotion going this week, Dan," Mark said. "If you open up a Todo debit card this week, we will give you $100 worth of TodoCoin."

Dan looked at Mark. "What's TodoCoin?" he asked.

"It's our proprietary crypto token," Mark said. "It's better than a stable coin, because it's pegged to the value of bitcoin. If bitcoin goes up in value, you make instant money, passive income, no effort required. And you can use our TodoCoin anywhere bitcoin is accepted. And, best yet, for every one thousand dollars of TodoCoin you buy, we will give you another one hundred dollars' worth of TodoCoin. That's like ten percent instant interest on your investment."

153

Dan nodded his head. "That is a sweet deal," he said. "But let me ask you this: if your TodoCoin works just the same as bitcoin, and is worth exactly the same as bitcoin, why wouldn't I just use bitcoin?"

"I'm glad you asked that question, Dan," Mark said. "And the answer is because TodoCoin is better than bitcoin. It's better because it's safer; and it's safer because it's in a bank. All your TodoCoins are stored at the Todo Bank, not just floating out somewhere on the internet like bitcoin. Your TodoCoins are totally protected and guaranteed by the Todo Bank."

"But your TodoCoin is still a digital asset?" Dan asked.

"Yes, it is."

"So, what do you mean that it's *stored* in a bank?" Dan asked.

"I'm glad you asked that, Dan. The Todo Bank is a true blockchain bank. We keep all the records of all our investors secured locked in our blockchain at the Todo Bank."

Dan's internal bullshit detection meter was vibrating strongly, but he kept up with his questions. "And where is the Todo Bank located?" he asked.

"We have branches all over the world, including in Panama City. In fact, we are currently in negotiations with the government of Panama to have the TodoCoin become one of the official currencies of Panama," Mark said.

"Really?"

"Yup," Mark said proudly. "Within a few months, you'll be able to use Panamanian balboas, US dollars, and TodoCoins interchangeably in Panama."

"Well, that's amazing," Dan said.

"It is," said Mark. "Opening an account with Todo Bank is as simple as downloading our app. There are no fees to open an account, and the app places a digital wallet right on your phone, so you start trading TodoCoins and other crypto-currencies right away."

"But, in order to trade crypto-currencies, I have to buy them first, right?" Dan asked.

"Of course," Mark said. "Our Todo app links automatically to the other financial apps in your phone, like your credit cards, PayPal, Google Pay, Venmo, Zelle, Apple Pay, etc., and you can use any of them to buy TodoCoin. Just takes one swipe of a finger and you can be trading TodoCoin."

"But I can use the card like a regular debit card, I mean, to pay in dollars?" Dan asked.

"Of course," Mark said. "You can choose to keep your deposits in the Todo Bank, in US dollars, or TodoCoins, or even convert them to any currency worldwide. We have lots of customers here in Panama who keep their deposits in Euros in Todo Bank, because they travel to Europe so frequently."

"Interesting," Dan said, trying to wrap his head around all this information.

"We have a WiFi hotspot right here," Mark said, pointing to a table and chairs set up under the tent next to the electric bicycles. We can hop on the internet and get you a Todo account in thirty seconds."

"Hmm... let me think about it some more," Dan said. "I still have to read that brochure you gave me last week. But thank you for answering my questions. This has been most informative."

With that, Dan walked away from the Todo display and toward the food stalls on the other side of the park. The more he learned about Todo, the more he thought the entire business sounded like a scam.

CHAPTER TWENTY-THREE

The next day, Dan was back in don Fernando's office.

"We're making progress, Dani," don Fernando was saying. "We have much to talk about."

"I'm all ears, amigo."

"We sent the fingerprints that we found on that notebook on your desk to Interpol and the FBI," don Fernando said, "and they made a match. Guess who they matched it to."

"Dimitrios Barkoxe?" Dan asked.

"Correct! So, we can now place him at the site of two burglaries: your apartment and Matzel Davis's house. I told Interpol that I would ask the prosecutor in Panama City to issue a warrant for him. Interpol said that they could not issue an international red notice for him unless we could connect him to the murders. I told them that we are working on that, but that at this time, he was just a person of interest in those murders."

"Okay," said Dan. "Do we know anything more about this guy?"

"Not really," said don Fernando. "As I mentioned yesterday, he was on the board of directors of that You-Bank, along with Jacques Foucher. Both of them are persons of interest in the failure of that bank, but they've been persons of interest for the last five years and no charges have ever been filed, so I don't think that's going anywhere. The FBI doesn't have anything more on Barkoxe, but Interpol said he was a person of interest in an investigation about ten years ago for counterfeit lottery tickets in Spain. But that investigation also didn't go anywhere. He is a Spanish citizen, but it is unclear where he was born or where he lives. That's all I could find on him."

"Okay," said Dan.

"Next, my forensic expert was able to pry more information out of Foucher's cell phone. Its GPS function places him at Matzel Davis's bookstore last Saturday night. The time matches the death of the Frenchman."

"Another evidentiary nail in his coffin," Dan said.

"The GPS also shows that he went back-and-forth from his hotel in Panama City to Villa Rosario every single day since he arrived in Panama."

"An active fellow," said Dan.

"There is also a crypto wallet in his cellphone, inside a Todo Application. Señor Foucher is quite a wealthy man. He has moved over a million dollars worth of cryptocurrency in the past month."

"Really?" said Dan. "A million dollars? What kind of movements?"

"My forensic expert said that someone was transferring TodoCoins into his wallet, and he was exchanging them for dollars and transferring those dollars to someone else using the Todo App. We don't know yet who the money went to."

"Did he withdraw any of that money for his own use?" Dan asked.

"Not that we can tell."

"Interesting. So, he was just washing the money and passing it on?" Dan said.

"Looks like it," don Fernando agreed. "We also found some texts he made to a cellphone with a Madrid area code. We don't know who this person is, but we know it's not Ortega. These were very cryptic texts. I don't understand them. Here's a printout."

Don Fernando handed Dan a single page. Dan read it and shrugged. "These don't make much sense to me either," he said. Then he read out loud: "Tao is killing us... We need to depeg Ching and short bitcoin... and then this other person responds with *quote* Tao just moved 8m to stub account *unquote* and then Foucher texts that someone named Rostow is going to unwind dogecoin... hmm, and here's one that's weird. It's got a lot of exclamation points. It says *quote* Just saw Rostow's report, three exclamation points. Expecting run in three quarters. Keep stacking *unquote* followed by five more exclamation points."

"Gringo gibberish," don Fernando commented. "These were not even sentences."

"No, they're not," replied Dan. "But they all relate to finance. Tao could be a person or a cryptocurrency. Ching is probably some type of crypto-coin. Dogecoin is definitely a cryptocurrency. The phrase 'keep stacking' is interesting. That's what gold collectors—people who buy gold bullion—say to each other. It means to keep stacking gold."

Don Fernando nodded and said, "We're working on trying to find out who this other person is that Foucher was texting to."

"Okay," said Dan.

"Also," don Fernando said with a smile, "remember that laptop we found in Foucher's hotel room? Well, my little forensic expert made a copy of the hard drive, and he was finally able to decrypt it and see all of Foucher's emails."

"Really?" Dan asked. "Um... don't you need a warrant to do that?"

"Technically, no," answered don Fernando. "Under Panamanian law, with a murder case, my investigative powers are pretty broad. Besides, if it turns out I need a warrant, remember that Judge Andrés Cordela is married to my wife's sister."

"Oh yeah, that's right," said Dan.

"Anyway, we're still poring through his emails, but so far, we haven't found much tied to this case. It seems he preferred to communicate by text on his cellphone. But we did find an email to David Ortega."

"Oh?" said Dan.

And here's the best part: my forensic expert was able to follow that email to David Ortega's IP address... and then my little wizard was able to hack into señor Ortega's computer."

"What? Are you serious?" exclaimed Dan.

Don Fernando nodded and smiled broadly. "It was amazing, Dani. I watched this guy do it. It took him five minutes and we were inside Ortega's computer, reading his emails, copying his files..."

"Wait a minute, don Fernando, that's way outside the scope of this murder investigation," Dan exclaimed. "That *can't* be legal."

"True," said don Fernando. "But where would I get a warrant to do such a thing? To open up a computer in Spain from Panama? Who would have jurisdiction to issue such a warrant? The Hague? You know what I learned from the FBI? It's better to ask for forgiveness, than to ask for permission." Don Fernando laughed.

Dan shook his head. "That just doesn't feel right, don Fernando," Dan said, but then he shrugged and asked, "but... what did you find?"

"Well, he's in Toledo, Spain. That was easy to figure out. Most of his files are heavily encrypted, but we're working on them. Like señor Foucher, he is moving millions of dollars in cryptocurrency around the world, transferring from wallet to wallet, and then moving the coins into these cryptocurrency tumblers that obliterate the source..."

"So, he's laundering money, too?" Dan said.

"It certainly looks that way, Dani. He emails daily with a guy named Stan Rostow, no doubt the same Rostow in Foucher's texts. This Rostow fellow is some financial guru; he has a big presence on social media where he pushes people to buy TodoCoin, but privately, he's telling Ortega to dump TodoCoin and buy gold."

"Jeez, these crypto guys are crazy," said Dan.

"Maybe, Dani. But here's a word of caution: we found a file of electronic receipts on Ortega's computer. This guy is also heavily into guns. We found receipts for at least sixteen assault rifles and handguns."

"Figures," Dan said.

"Anyway, that's all we know so far about Ortega. In other news, we finally found a neighbor to Matzel's house who was willing to talk with us. He said he saw five men leave Matzel's house last Saturday night. He said that at the time he didn't think much about it. He didn't see them arrive, and he didn't know how long they were there; he just saw them leave as a group sometime around eleven p.m."

"Five men?" exclaimed Dan and leaned back in his chair. "Wow, that's a big group for a burglary... do you have any idea who they are?"

"No, the neighbor said he didn't recognize them. I asked Immigration to cross-reference anyone who arrived in Panama the same day as Barkoxe with the names of anyone who left Panama on the same airplane as Barkoxe and that Mariana Ibarra. I'm waiting on Immigration to get back to me."

"Oh yeah... Mariana Ibarra," Dan said. "I'd forgotten about her. Any info on who she is?"

"Not a clue," don Fernando said. "Interpol has no information on her. I also talked with that precinct police chief in New York. They have no leads in the murder of that Silas fellow. He says it was a professional hit."

"Hmm," said Dan.

"On a positive note," don Fernando said, "Señor Foucher had his little detention hearing yesterday. We had a translator there for him, and the judge read the charges to him. You should have seen his face when the translator told him that the judge remanded him to our custody for a year while we investigated the case."

"I bet," Dan said. "Did he get a public defender?"

"Yes, but the lawyer they appointed for him doesn't speak English, so he wasn't much use. The judge told him they would try and get an English-speaking public defender appointed for him at the next review hearing."

"When's the next hearing?" Dan asked.

"In about two months. No, señor Foucher was looking very frustrated by the end of the hearing."

"Maybe the reality of his situation is beginning to sink in," Dan said. "Do you think we ought to have a little *come-to-Jesus* chat with him today?"

Don Fernando nodded. "Why not?"

A few minutes later, a weary-looking Jacques Foucher was seated hunched over in the interrogation room with his hands cuffed behind his back. Dan and don Fernando walked in and sat in the two chairs facing the prisoner.

"Mr. Foucher," Dan began, "I hope by now you have a better understanding of your situation, and a better understanding of how slow the Panamanian justice system works."

Jacques Foucher looked up at Dan. The angry visage of a few days ago was gone.

Dan continued: "As I said the other day, I am not going to ask you any questions about the crime you are accused of committing. My only interest in talking to you is to understand why you chose to involve me and my friend Ricardo Mendes in your stupid endeavors. So let me ask you: Why were you following Ricardo?"

Foucher sighed, but then said, "We were hoping he would lead us to Nassim."

"Who is Nassim?"

"Nassim Kahil," said Foucher. "He's David's ex-partner."

"Ex-partner in what?" Dan asked.

"In Todo. They both used to work for Todo."

"The finance company?" Dan asked.

Foucher nodded his head yes.

"Okay, so you were following Ricardo, and then David Ortega tapped Silas's phone and found out Ricardo had drawn these maps, and that I had them." Dan said.

Foucher looked a little surprised, but nodded his head yes and said, "By then, Ricardo had disappeared. David told us to break into the bookstore."

"I don't understand," Dan said. Why break into the bookstore if you knew I had the maps?"

Foucher sat quietly for a moment and then just shook his head. He looked like he was about to cry. For a moment, Dan wondered if interrogating Foucher was going to be a waste of time.

But then Foucher blurted out, "I told David it was a stupid idea to break into the bookstore. We just went over there Friday night to check the place out, but when we got there, the front door was open... so we went in..."

Foucher started to cry. "It was a trap. I didn't mean to shoot Romain! He was my friend. Nassim was waiting for us. He shot Álvaro. I pulled my gun and aimed at Nassim, but Romain got in the way! You have to believe me—it was an accident."

Dan was stunned by this admission. He glanced quickly at don Fernando, and then looked Foucher in the eyes, and said quietly, "Listen Jacques, I'm sorry, but I'm not here to talk about the shooting. You will eventually get a lawyer, and you can explain all of this to your lawyer, but not to me. Just tell me why you went to the bookstore if you knew I had the maps?"

Foucher wiped his nose on his shoulder. "The maps were secondary. They were useless without the coins. I kept telling David that..." His voice drifted off.

"What... what coins?" Dan asked.

Foucher just shook his head, and said, "No! If I tell you, they'll kill me. The same way they killed Silas..."

"No one can get to you in here," Dan said.

Foucher just shook his head. "Nassim saw me in the bookstore. He knows who I am. They can find me."

"And who is this Nassim?" Dan asked.

"He owns the bookstore."

"How is he related to Matzel Davis?" Dan asked.

"Nassim Kahil is Matzel Davis's real name," said Foucher.

Dan looked over at don Fernando. Don Fernando just shrugged.

"Okay," said Dan slowly. "Then what about Dimitrios Barkoxe? We know he broke into my apartment and Matzel Davis's house. We have a warrant out for him."

"You'll never find him... He's... wait..." Foucher looked up at Dan with a sudden panic in his eyes. "What house did he break into?" he asked.

"Matzel Davis's house," said Dan, "north of town, in Santa Rita, in the Ribera neighborhood."

Foucher looked like someone punched him in the gut. He inhaled, squeezed his eyes tight, and then asked, "Was this a white stucco house with a big blue door, down the street from the Santa Rita church?"

Dan looked at don Fernando, who nodded yes.

"Yes," said Dan.

Foucher sunk lower in his chair. "That's Nassim Kahil's house," he said. "Was it ransacked?"

"It was completely torn apart," Dan replied.

"Then he's got the coins... he's got the coins *and* the map. Fuck."

Foucher sunk down in the chair, and muttered again, "He's got the coins and the map. That's it, then. I'm a dead man."

"What's so special about these coins?" Dan asked, but Foucher just shook his head no.

The memory of the Ricardo's maps flashed across Dan's mind. "Okay, okay," he said, "tell me about Barkoxe. We know he flew back to Spain. Has he gone to Toledo?"

Foucher's face looked like he was miles away, but he nodded a barely perceptible yes.

"Is he going to meet up with David Ortega?" Dan asked.

Foucher shook his head. "No," he said, "he's going to kill David."

"I thought all of you were together," Dan said. "You were on the board of directors at You-Bank with Barkoxe," Dan said.

Foucher shrugged. "That was a long time ago," he said, "before I met David. Barkoxe hates David. And now... he doesn't need him anymore... so he'll kill David."

Foucher looked up at Dan and said, "He'll kill you, too. He'll kill your friend Ricardo; he'll kill anyone who gets in his way." Foucher looked down, then said softly, "I should have never gone back to Todo. I should have never got involved with David. This mess is all his doing."

"Why is everyone so interested in Toledo?" Dan asked.

Foucher shook his head no. "No more," he said firmly. "No more."

"Okay," Dan said. For a moment, Dan felt sorry for Foucher. "Is there anything I can get you?" he asked.

Foucher sighed. "A lawyer who speaks English."

Dan looked at don Fernando. Don Fernando nodded yes.

After the guard took Foucher back to his cell, Dan and don Fernando just sat in the interrogation room, each of them wrapped in their own thoughts.

Finally, Dan asked, "Do you know anyone named Nassim Kahil?"

Don Fernando shook his head no.

"Did Matzel have a roommate at his house, or a partner in the bookstore?"

"No, Dani," said don Fernando. "I think this Nassim Kahil *is* Matzel Davis, just like señor Foucher said. Panama has a long history of extranjeros coming here and changing their names. Panama is a place to start over."

Dan nodded his head. "I'm more worried than ever about Ricardo, don Fernando. I think he's gone to Toledo. I think that's where Matzel—or Nassim—told him to go when they met that night at the gas station in El Espino. I think Matzel told to go there and that he would meet him there. I think Matzel and Ricardo are there together right now. I think that's where David Ortega is, and I think that's where Dimitrios Barkoxe is. They're all in Toledo... and Barkoxe has the maps."

"Well, sí, Barkoxe has the maps, but you have a copy," don Fernando said.

"True, but they make no sense to me. Somehow, these maps must mean something to these guys... What a clusterfuck, don Fernando. None of this makes sense. And what coins was Foucher talking about? Matzel—or whatever his name is—had coins at his store, but Foucher and his goons didn't touch any of them... Matzel must have had other coins at his house, coins that were more valuable than the ones in his store... but the ones in his store weren't cheap, and yet Foucher left them alone... But if the coins were at Matzel's house, why is everyone going to Toledo?"

Don Fernando just shrugged, and said, "I don't know, Dani."

"Well, what *do* we know so far?" Dan asked rhetorically. "Foucher and Barkoxe worked together at You-Bank which was controlled by Todo. That bank failed five years ago. Foucher then meets David Ortega, but Barkoxe hates Ortega, so Foucher and Barkoxe are no longer friends... If Matzel is Nassim, then that means that Matzel used to be partners with Ortega. But Ortega sends Foucher here to steal from Matzel. Then Matzel shoots the Colombiano, and Foucher tries to shoot Matzel but hits the French guy instead. Now Foucher is afraid that Barkoxe and/or Matzel will kill *him*... Jesus, it's like a soap opera! These guys keep switching allegiances."

"And don't forget Mariana Ibarra," don Fernando said. "She arrived with Foucher but left with Barkoxe."

"Oh, yeah," said Dan. "I should have asked Foucher about her... You know, don Fernando, the only commonality here is that they all seem to be connected with Todo. But still, I can't figure out what's going on."

"You know, Dani," don Fernando said, "I said this before, and you scoffed, but sometimes the simplest answer is true. You've got a map and a bunch of criminals desperate to find some coins. It sure sounds like a treasure hunt to me."

"Maybe, don Fernando... maybe."

CHAPTER TWENTY-FOUR

The next morning, Dan decided to do more research on Todo. Everyone involved—evidently, even Matzel—was either working for, or had worked for Todo at some point in the past. There *had* to be some connection between Todo, the company, and whatever was so valuable to have triggered the burglary of Matzel's home and store, and the death of two people. Dan had originally thought it had something to do with Ricardo's maps, but now, he wasn't so sure. Foucher had said that the maps were secondary to some type of coin... he had said that the maps were useless without the coins... and then, when Dan had told Foucher that Barkoxe had ransacked Matzel's house, Foucher almost collapsed in his chair. Dan tried to remember Foucher's exact words: "Now he's got the coins *and* the maps." Somehow the two were important together.

Dan opened his laptop and started searching for articles that contained both the words "Todo" and "coin." There was the usual slew of sponsored articles from self-proclaimed influencers praising the value of the TodoCoin. Dan skipped over those. But the first non-sponsored article that popped up was one that had been published a week earlier entitled "Todo to Introduce Gold-backed Digital Currency." He clicked on that link. The first thing he noticed was that the article was written by Stan Rostow. Now, Dan was interested. The article was short, and Dan read it carefully.

Todo had announced that next year it planned to release a gold-backed digital currency called the Oro Coin. This coin was going to be pegged to the TodoCoin, and in fact, could only be purchased with TodoCoins. However, once purchased, Todo claimed the Oro Coins could be redeemed for gold. Todo claimed to have entered into an agreement with the government of Zimbabwe to adopt the Oro Coin next year as an official currency and to back it with its gold reserves.

This seemed like some sort of science fiction, Dan thought. But there were links in the article to other articles, and Dan followed each of those.

Evidently, it was true. Back in 2009, due to overwhelming inflation, Zimbabwe had abandoned the Zimbabwe currency and adopted the US dollar. This helped stabilize the country's economy but hurt Zimbabwe's relations with Russia and China. In 2019, Zimbabwe went back to using the Zimbabwe dollar. Almost immediately, the inflation cycle started again. Zimbabwe then passed a law requiring all companies mining or refining gold to pay royalties to the government in gold. Although Zimbabwe is a poor and a historically corrupt country, it is rich in gold. With this new royalty law, Zimbabwe began stockpiling gold in its National Reserve Bank, looking for a way to once again control inflation without having to be again dependent on the US dollar. Todo came along at the right moment, and offered to create and implement a brand-new currency called the Oro Coin, if Zimbabwe would back the Oro Coin with gold.

Dan learned that as soon as Todo had made this announcement, the price of the TodoCoin had skyrocketed. Speculators from around the world wanted to own TodoCoins so that they could redeem them for Oro Coins next year. The price of TodoCoin overtook Ethereum and Tether, to become second only to Bitcoin.

As Dan read more, he began to admire Todo's tactics. With one announcement—without actually doing anything, without taking *any* risks—Todo had managed to almost triple the value of its TodoCoins in one week. It seemed like the perfect pump-and-dump scheme to Dan. Todo could pump the price of its TodoCoin for a whole year, claiming that the following year, customers could use their TodoCoins to buy Oro Coins in the hopes of being able to redeem those

Oro Coins for gold. What a great scheme, Dan thought. It was the perfect pitch that combined gold fever with crypto fever. So many things could go wrong in a year, Dan thought. Zimbabwe could back out of the deal, or force people to travel to Zimbabwe to redeem their coins. Anything could happen! As long as Todo cashed out it's TodoCoins before the scheme collapsed, Todo would be filthy rich, without any liability.

But still, Dan thought, how did this connect to the burglary in Matzel's house? Todo was selling *digital* coins; coins whose only existence was a string of numbers on a blockchain. Was Foucher referring to real coins, or to digital coins when he said that Barkoxe got the coins from Matzel's house? Maybe Matzel had a computer, or a thumb-drive with a digital wallet on it... maybe that's what everyone was after. But if that was the case, what value were the maps?

Dan was sitting at his desk, pondering these things, when there was a knock at his door. This startled him, as no one ever came to his apartment unannounced. The memory of the burglary and his feeling of being violated was still fresh in his memory. Although his rational mind knew that Barkoxe had flown back to Madrid, that didn't stop his adrenaline from instantly starting to pump. He jumped out of his chair, went to the kitchen, and grabbed a knife from the drawer.

He walked over and peeked through his window blinds. There was a young man standing there, in some kind of uniform.

"Quién es?" asked Dan from inside.

"DHL," came the reply.

Dan placed the knife on the table by the door where he could reach it easily, and opened the door.

"Dan Landes?" the young man asked.

"Sí," Dan said.

The young man held out one of those electronic clipboards with a signature window.

"Firma aquí," the young man said pointing to a small screen at the top of the clipboard.

Dan signed his name as best he could, writing a squiggly line with his finger across the small screen. The young man then handed him a DHL express-mail envelope, nodded his head, turned and left.

Dan looked at the envelope. It was addressed to him, all right. He stepped back inside his apartment, closed the door, and tore the seal on the envelope to open it. Inside was a handwritten note that read:

> *Dan,*
> *I hope you are alright. Things are a little sketchy here. Can you come to Toledo? If so, meet me next Tuesday at 5 p.m. at the Charla Café, on the Paseo de la Rosa.*

It was signed *Ricardo.*

The handwriting looked like Ricardo's, Dan thought. But why would Ricardo go to all the trouble to send him an express international letter, when he could have just texted him or called him?

Dan sat down at his computer and pulled up Google Maps and typed in Paseo de la Rosa in Toledo, Spain. It popped up right away: a short street, on a hill east of Toledo, on the other side of the Tagus River. He didn't have to type in Charla Café—it was right there on the map, at the top of the hill. He also noticed that further down the hill, overlooking the river, was the Castle of San Servando. That's no coincidence, Dan thought. San Servando. That was same name as the code that Foucher had mentioned.

Dan thought about the hassle of dropping everything and just hopping on a plane to Spain. Tuesday—that was just four days away! It's a ten-hour flight to Spain. Plus, he knew he would lose another day to jetlag. He would have to fly out today or tomorrow!

Dan picked up his cellphone. He was going to call Ricardo right now and find out what this was all about. But just as was starting to dial, the question occurred to him again: why would Ricardo go to all the trouble to send him an international letter when he could have just texted him? Then Dan remembered that David Ortega had somehow hacked into Silas's phone system and listened to Dan talking with Silas. Maybe Ortega had done the same to Ricardo's phone... maybe that's why Ricardo reverted to the old-fashioned letter to communicate with Dan—to prevent Ortega from knowing where Ricardo was and what he was up to. Dan wondered if his own phone was tapped. He put his cellphone back down on the desk.

Fifteen minutes later, Dan was in don Fernando's office, showing him Ricardo's letter.

"This is good news, Dani," don Fernando said. "It means that your friend Ricardo is still alive."

"But he sent me a letter, don Fernando."

"Yes, I can see that Dani. And he wants you to visit him. How wonderful!"

"No, what I mean, don Fernando, is that he sent me a letter rather than call me or text me. The only reason he would do that is if he thought his phone—or my phone— was being tapped."

"Ah, yes... I see your point," don Fernando said. "Well, that means that when you get to Spain, you should buy a burner phone, so that you can stay in touch with me."

"What?" asked Dan.

"Yes, I learned all about burner phones in the online FBI course I am taking. In fact, when you get to Spain, would you buy one for me, too? Villa Rosario is too backwards of a town to have burner phones, and I would like to have a burner phone."

Dan just looked at don Fernando, then said, "So you think I should go?"

"Of course, you should go, Dani! Everyone else is already there except you. Matzel Davis, Ricardo, David Ortega, this Barkoxe person. No one is left in Villa Rosario except you and me. No, you should go! How else are we going to get to the bottom of this mystery? I would go with you, but someone has to stay here and maintain law and order."

Dan just nodded his head. "Okay... I'll go," he said. "I'll go home and try and find a cheap ticket for tomorrow."

"Well, Dani," don Fernando said, "why don't you use my computer? If there's a chance that your phone might be tapped, maybe, in the realm of infinite possibilities, your computer might be monitored as well. I was amazed at how fast my little forensic expert was able to tap into David Ortega's computer."

Dan was taken aback by this. He sat and thought about it for a moment, but he had to concede that don Fernando was right. He had been drawn into this whole mess from the beginning. He had better start playing it smart.

"You're right, don Fernando. Let me borrow your computer for a minute," he said, reaching for his wallet and his credit card.

CHAPTER TWENTY-FIVE

The next two days were a fog to Dan. Travel does that. The faster you go, the more the details blur. Dan remembered booking his airplane tickets on Don Fernando's computer; but then, when he woke up in his hotel room in Toledo, Spain, in what seemed like light-years later, his body aching and dull, he could only recall a jumbled mix of images and sensations: the crowded airport; uncomfortable metal chairs in the waiting areas; constant noise; stale air-conditioning; physical pain; trying to sleep on the plane; and how bright and harsh the sun was when the plane landed in Madrid. He had skipped the tourist bus from the airport to the Atocha Train Station and had opted for the faster taxi, only to sit for an hour on the hard wooden bench at the train station waiting for the next train to Toledo. He couldn't remember how he checked into his hotel in Toledo. His only clear memory was crawling, fully clothed, onto the hotel bed and falling instantly to a heavy sleep.

When he awoke, it was afternoon. He felt horrible. He wasn't sure what day it was. Evidently, he had rented an expensive room with a sitting area, a sofa, and a kitchenette, but he was just grateful that there was a coffee maker. While his coffee was brewing, he checked his cell phone and determined that it was Sunday afternoon. His meeting with Ricardo was Tuesday. He moved the window curtain a few inches and looked outside. All he could see was a narrow street and long shadows. This was insane, he thought. Why was he here? He was too old for wild goose chases, too old for overnight airplane travel, too old for everything...

The coffee helped. He showered and dressed and drank a second cup of coffee. He realized he was hungry. He checked his watch again. Almost five p.m. He wanted breakfast. He still needed to unpack his suitcase and arrange his clothes, but first he needed to eat. He gathered his wallet and passport, and then noticed there were two cell phones on the dresser. For a microsecond, his brain did not understand why he was seeing two cell phones, but then he remembered. He had followed don Fernando's advice and bought a cheap cell phone with a SIM card for Spain at the Madrid airport. He put both cell phones in his pocket and then checked himself in the mirror to make sure he appeared normal. Then he stepped out into the hallway, found his way downstairs into a bright modern hotel lobby and asked the receptionist where the nearest restaurant was.

She told him there was a nice outdoor café at the end of the block. He thanked her and stepped out of the hotel's front door into a dark narrow cobblestone street. He could see bright sunlight at the corner where the street seemed to open up to a plaza, but the front of the hotel was completely shaded. Dan realized that the narrowness of the street and the tall buildings on either side meant that the street would be in perpetual shadow except for midday. He wondered again how he had checked into the hotel. He had a vague memory of catching a taxi from the train station, but the street the hotel was on was too narrow for any vehicle. The taxi must have dropped him off at the corner and he must have walked the block to the hotel entrance. He couldn't remember.

Dan walked to the corner. The narrow street did indeed open up to a sunlit plaza, where five other streets joined to make a wide free-for-all of cars, taxis, and pedestrians. Dan noticed that none of the streets were level. They all were at different angles, some going uphill, some going downhill. Even the plaza itself was tilted. It was disconcerting to look at, like being a bit seasick.

The outdoor café was on his right. He found a seat under a large umbrella and adjusted his chair as best he could to be level on the cobblestone pavement. A bored-looking waiter brought him a menu without saying a word. Dan quickly asked for a coffee as he took the menu. He felt like he needed to drink a whole pot.

There were no breakfast options on the menu, of course. The waiter came back with his coffee and a basket of bread. Dan ordered salmon and potatoes. The waiter took his order without saying a word.

As Dan chewed on the bread and drank his coffee, he began to feel better. He took out both of his cell phones, looked up don Fernando's number on his old phone, and then typed that number into his new phone, and texted don Fernando that he had arrived safely in Toledo.

More details of why he was here began to come back to him. Maybe the coffee was beginning to work, because for the first time since he had woken up, Dan's brain began to think. Matzel Davis had to be the lynchpin that connected everyone. But it wasn't him they were after, it was his coins. But not just any old coins, because everyone ignored the coins in his store which were worth a lot. No, everyone was after some type of coin that was much more valuable, so valuable that they would kill for it. Matzel clearly was not the man who Dan thought he was. Don Fernando had warned him early on that Matzel had killed three Colombianos years ago who had robbed and murdered one of Matzel favorite clients. And Jacques Foucher claimed that Matzel had shot Alvaro Renaldo. Clearly, Dan had misjudged Matzel. He knew nothing about his past. Maybe his name really was Nassim Kahil, and he had changed his name and fled to Panama with some coins. But Jacques Foucher couldn't be underestimated either. He had broken into Matzel's bookstore armed. He had come armed to his meeting with Dan, pretending to be Silas Edwards. Yet, even he was afraid of Dimitrios Barkoxe, whom he claimed was going to kill David Ortega. And Dimitrios had been brazen enough to break into both Dan's apartment and Matzel's house. No, none of these guys should be underestimated; they were all murderers.

The non-communicative waiter brought Dan's food. And just in time, because Dan was starving. A huge portion of grilled salmon with some boiled potatoes covered the plate. Dan dug into it. The waiter reappeared to bring a glass of water and to refill Dan's coffee.

And somehow, Dan thought as he ate, all of these murders and burglaries had something to do with Todo. He had no proof, but there was the fact that both Foucher and Barkoxe had been on the board of directors of Todo's bank. And Foucher had claimed that Matzel Davis a.k.a Nassim Kahil and David Ortega both had worked for Todo in the past. And then there was the fact that Foucher and his two goons all had Todo credit cards in their wallets. Everybody seemed connected to Todo. It was all circumstantial evidence, but Dan had never believed in coincidence. Everyone had been after Matzel because of his coins, and at the same time Todo was starting to market their new digital TodoCoin. Improbably as it seemed, Dan felt in his bones that these two facts were connected. How Ricardo's maps fit into all this, Dan didn't know. Foucher had said that the maps were useless without Matzel's coins. That statement still nagged at Dan. How were they connected? How could coins and paper maps be connected? It made no sense.

He looked down the street. The sunlight was turning yellow. It would be sunset soon. Tuesday he would find this Charla Café and hopefully find Ricardo. Maybe Ricardo could connect the dots for him. All he could do now was wait.

Dan finished his dinner/breakfast and signaled to the waiter for another cup of coffee. He was starting to feel human again. The waiter brought the pot by, filled up Dan's cup, and slid the check under the napkin holder. Dan wondered if all the waiters in Toledo were as stoic as this guy.

Suddenly, as he took a sip of his coffee, he became aware of someone standing beside his table, close to him, hovering over him, and exactly at the same time that his peripheral vision indicated this looming presence, he smelled perfume. He looked up from his cup, and there was a woman standing there, looking down at him. She was stylishly dressed, in a short skirt and white blouse, with her hair pulled back, a shoulder bag clutched underneath her arm.

"Dan Landes?" she asked.

He nodded slowly.

"May I sit down?"

He nodded again and gestured toward the chair opposite him. He could feel adrenaline throbbing in his brain. He didn't like surprises, even if they were pretty. She sat down, looked at him, and half-smiled.

"I'm afraid you have the advantage of me, Miss..." he said.

"Ibarra, Mariana Ibarra," she replied.

CHAPTER TWENTY-SIX

Well, Dan thought to himself. *This changes everything.* He nodded slowly and turned his head casually to gaze around to see if there were any suspicious-looking characters loitering nearby.

Mariana must have noticed his looking around.

"I came alone," she said.

The fact that she had noticed his glance at the surroundings and had surmised that he was checking to see if she had come with anyone else told Dan to proceed very carefully, to play his cards close to the vest.

"Yes?" he said, and nothing more.

"Mr. Landes," she smiled, "I'm here on business. You must forgive my boldness, but the desk clerk at your hotel told me you might be eating here, so I took the chance of finding you. I work for the Lamanca Recovery Agency."

She reached into her purse and removed a wallet, from which she extracted a business card. She handed the card to Dan. It simply read "Lamanca Recovery Agency" under which was her name and the title of "recovery specialist" followed by an address in Madrid and two phone numbers.

It took Dan a moment to register what a recovery agency was.

"I thought bounty hunting was illegal in Europe," he said.

She shrugged and smiled. "We can't legally arrest anyone, but we can locate them."

She pronounced the word "locate" with a certain coldness.

"I see," Dan said. "And what has this to do with me?"

"We are looking for someone who is known to you, a certain despicable criminal by the name of Nassim Kahil, or as you know him, Matzel Davis. Nassim Kahil is wanted in Greece and Bulgaria for several murders, and in Spain for armed robbery and attempted murder. There is a substantial reward offered for his arrest."

She paused as if she were waiting for Dan to say something. He said nothing.

"There are several governments and many people looking for him," she continued. "We want to be first. We are prepared to offer you one hundred thousand dollars if you find him and turn him over to us... alive, of course."

"That's a lot of money," Dan said.

"We are very intent on finding him, Mr. Landes. He has done a lot of damage, and has always managed to avoid consequences."

"I see," Dan said, and slid her card into his shirt pocket. "Let me ask you this, Miss Ibarra. How did you find me? I mean, how did you find me here in this city? How did you know what hotel I was staying at? And how did you know *I* knew Matzel Davis?"

Mariana Ibarra just shrugged. "We're in the recovery business, Mr. Landes. That's what we do. We locate people. The world is a small place, and everyone is plugged in to the electronic fog that surrounds us. You cannot go anywhere without us knowing."

Dan's eyes narrowed. Was she threatening him or just speaking generally?

"And yet Matzel Davis has eluded you," he said.

"He is very cunning, Mr. Landes. I promise you, he will kill you if he thinks you are in his way, if you stop him from getting what he wants... he will kill you in an instant. You will be much safer if you turn him over to us... not to mention one hundred thousand dollars richer."

She stood up. Evidently, the meeting was over.

"The second number on my card is my personal cell phone," she said. "I have it on me twenty-four seven. If you find him, even if you just see him, call me."

And with that, she turned and walked away.

Dan watched her walk down the street, turn the corner and disappear. *What a cold, calculating woman,* he thought to himself. He reached for his coffee cup, but noticed his hand was shaking. *Cold, calculating, and dangerous,* he thought.

He waved the waiter over and asked for a glass of whisky with ice. The waiter picked up Dan's bill and returned a minute later with the whisky and a new bill.

The obvious question, Dan realized as he sipped his whisky, was how it was so easy for Mariana Ibarra to find him. We're all "plugged into the electric fog that surrounds us," she had said. He began to think back. He had made his plane reservations and the hotel reservations on don Fernando's computer. Of course, he had used his real name and paid for the reservations with his credit card. Had he used his own computer to do anything? He thought hard. No, no, he hadn't. Wait: yes, he had. He had looked up Toledo on Google Maps on his computer in his apartment to find the Charla Café... no, wait... he had only entered Toledo and Paseo de la Rosa as his search terms. He had never typed in "Charla Café." Maybe they didn't know about his upcoming meeting with Ricardo there Tuesday night. And who *were* they, exactly? And how many of them were there? Mariana Ibarra was with Dimitrios Barkoxe, obviously, because they flew out from Villa Rosario together... so that's two people. And Dimitrios Barkoxe's fingerprints were found in Matzel Davis's house; and the neighbors saw five people enter that house... so that's six people... but Mariana Ibarra arrived in Panama with Jacques Foucher, who works for David Ortega. And David Ortega might not know that Mariana was with Barkoxe... Jesus! How many people was he up against?

He glanced around the plaza nervously, looking for anyone who might be following him. There was a middle-aged couple sitting a few tables over on his left, a young woman with a small dog on a leash two tables over on his right. People were walking back and forth across the plaza. Two boys with bicycles were standing and talking on the opposite corner...

He gave his head an involuntary shake, to get these thoughts out of his head. *It's so easy to be paranoid,* he thought, *so easy*. He forced himself to focus. Mariana Ibarra didn't know he was eating at the restaurant. She only knew what hotel he was staying at. She had to go ask at the hotel for him. The hotel clerk had simply told her that he might be eating at this restaurant. She didn't know what he looked like, so she had to approach his table and ask. He was the only tourist-looking male sitting by himself, so her approaching his table and asking was logical. Just because she found him did not mean he was being watched... But still, he would be extra careful. He reached into his pocket and took his old Panamanian cellphone out of his pocket, turned it off, and removed the battery. He would only use the new burner phone from now on.

CHAPTER TWENTY-SEVEN

Dan awoke the next morning feeling less ragged than the previous night. Maybe he was getting over his jetlag. A card in his room stated that the hotel served a simple breakfast in a large room off the lobby. On his way downstairs to that breakfast, he stopped at the front desk and got a map of Toledo.

Over coffee, fruit, and toast, he studied the map. The Castle of San Servando appeared to be walking distance from the hotel. Dan decided to walk there after breakfast. There was really nothing to connect this castle to this whole case except Foucher's cryptic reference to a San Servando code and that sketch of a castle marked "San Serv" in Ricardo's maps, but he had the whole day to himself, so he could afford a little walk.

He thought about Mariana Ibarra and the Lamanca Recovery Agency. He ran through the mental exercise of imagining that she was telling the truth—that Matzel Davis was really an international fugitive murderer on the run and that she was working for a bounty hunter agency trying to track him down. Part of that story fit with what don Fernando had told him about Matzel killing the three Colombians years ago, and it kind of fit with Dan's impression of Matzel as a man who liked to be in charge... but the problem was not with Mariana Ibarra's story; it was with Mariana's associates. She had arrived in Panama with Foucher and his gang of thugs, and she had left with Dimitrios Barkoxe—the same Dimitrios Barkoxe whose fingerprints were found at the burglary of Matzel Davis's house and at the burglary of his apartment. No, Mariana Ibarra was not to be trusted. That didn't mean that her story about Matzel Davis being wanted for murder was false; it just meant that she was not to be trusted any more than he would trust Foucher, Barkoxe, or even Matzel Davis. As far as Dan was concerned, they were all birds of the same feather.

It occurred to him that he could test Mariana Ibarra's story. He took out his burner cell phone and texted don Fernando and asked him to check with Interpol see if there were any warrants out for Nassim Kahil. He realized that it was one a.m. Panama time, but there was nothing he could do about that.

On his way back to his room after breakfast, Dan noticed that the hotel had several computers set up in a room off the lobby for hotel guests to use. He stepped into the room and googled the Castle of San Servando. There were conflicting stories of its origin. One article said that the building was built by the Romans around 200 BC and used as a temple. Another article said it was built by the Moors after they invaded Spain in 711 AD and used as a mosque. Another article said it was built after Toledo was recaptured from the Moors by the Spanish Reconquista in 1085 AD and then given to the Knights of Templar. Evidently, the Knights of Templar occupied it, fortified it, and added castle towers, but it fell into disuse in the mid-1300s. However, in 1874, it was named a national monument by the Spanish government.

Dan's eyes glazed over as he quickly scanned through the articles, that is, until he came across a recent article which said that the castle was currently closed to the public in order to do major internal structural modifications, and that restoration project was being financed and managed by... Todo Financial Services, Ltd.

Dan leaned back in his chair and reread that article. He couldn't believe it. Todo had entered into a contract with the Spanish government whereby Todo had total control over the San Servando Castle, had closed all public access, and was doing some type of major reconstruction inside. This project was expected to take at least another year to complete. Evidently, the Spanish government eagerly agreed to this contract because Todo was providing the financing— arranged, it was claimed, from private sources. Dan thought back to don Fernando's comment about buried treasure. What a perfect cover to dig for buried treasure: to dig under the guise of doing remodeling. But he quickly dismissed this fantasy. Todo had been working on this project since last year. If Todo had determined that there was something of value buried under the Castle of San Servando, why would Foucher, Ortega, Barkoxe, and Ibarra all be so interested in Matzel's and Ricardo's maps? If they already knew there was treasure buried under the castle, no one would need the maps. Dan once again dismissed the "buried treasure" angle. It made no sense, and besides, the maps were too crude, too simple, to lead anyone to buried treasure.

Still, all the more reason to take a walk and scope out this old castle.

*   *   *

The walk from the hotel to the San Servando Castle turned out to be more of a hike. As Dan had noticed at dinner the night before, none of the streets in Toledo were flat; they all were either uphill or downhill. Plus, there were no straight roads. They all curved around the hills in a circular fashion. By the time he got to the road that led up to the castle, he was out of breath and sweating.

He looked up at the castle. It was not that impressive. It was a solid two-story building, very rectangular looking, constructed with large brown stones, and seemed to be built directly into a solid rock hill. The building had many small windows, secured by iron bars. Dan could only see one turret, built into one of the corners of the building. That turret and the usual embrasures at the top of the building were the only architectural features that made it look like a castle. Otherwise, it could have passed as any solid ancient building appropriated by the government for modern use.

After he caught his breath, Dan walked up the hill to the castle, looking for an entrance. As he got closer to the building, he could see that each corner had a small turret, giving it more of a castle look. He had to walk all the way around the top of the hill, to the east side of the building, to

185

finally find the entrance, which consisted of a large iron gate, which was closed and locked. Next to the gate was a nearby official sign, bearing the seal of the government of Spain, saying the historical site was closed for renovation. Todo was not mentioned on the sign.

Dan could hear the sound of machines and construction coming from inside the building. He followed the road around the castle, and at one point, through the bars of the iron fence, he saw a large concrete mixer with a rotating drum being attended to by several workmen. Well, he thought to himself, if someone was digging for treasure, they wouldn't need to be mixing concrete. Maybe they were just restoring the building.

Dan looked around. It was a very scenic site. The castle had a perfect view of the Tagus River. His eyes followed how the road he was standing on continued to switchback up the next hill. He looked up that hill and realized that that was where the Charla Café was. He also realized he was in no shape to do this hike again tomorrow night. He would take a cab to meet Ricardo tomorrow.

CHAPTER TWENTY-EIGHT

Dan awoke early Tuesday morning with a feeling of dread. His meeting with Ricardo was not until five p.m. He had the whole day to kill. Maybe it was the fact that he had to wait all day that made him anxious. But he could not shake that feeling that something bad was going to happen.

He checked his burner phone while still lying in bed. Don Fernando had texted him at some point while he was asleep to say that that Interpol had no record of anyone named Nassim Kahil. No warrants, nothing. That proved that Mariana Ibarra was lying, Dan thought. She had lied straight to his face. Knowing that, however, did nothing to alleviate his anxiety. He hoped he would feel better after breakfast.

His walk downstairs to the breakfast area in the hotel took him past the reception desk. There were free copies of the city's newspaper—*La Tribuna de Toledo*—on the front desk for guests to take and read. He picked one up to read over breakfast and glanced at the headline as he walked into the breakfast room. The headline read, in Spanish: "Man Killed in Drive-by Shooting." Strange, Dan thought, to have a drive-by shooting in such an ancient city. First of all, Toledo was not a car-friendly place. All of the twisting, narrow roads were built before cars were invented. It was impossible to drive fast in Toledo. Secondly, he associated drive-by shootings with gang warfare, or poor cities with drug problems. Toledo was ancient, but it was a prosperous tourist city. He sat down at a table and scanned the first paragraph as the waiter brought him coffee. Evidently, a man was sitting in a car parked near Toledo's Provincial Hospital when a second car pulled up alongside of him and riddled the car with bullets. The second car sped away, and no one got a description or a license plate number. The man in the parked car was hit multiple times and was dead when the police arrived. At least twenty bullet casings were found at the scene.

It wasn't until the third paragraph that the article gave the name of the victim. He was an American tourist... named David Ortega.

Dan's heart leapt to his throat. He reread the article several times. The victim was driving a rental car and had parked by the side of a road that led towards the hospital's parking lot. A bicyclist who had passed the car moments before the shooting noticed that the victim was just sitting alone in the car. The police surmised that he was waiting for someone.

Dan took out his burner phone and looked up the hospital on Google Maps. The hospital was nearby, located just east of the San Servando Castle. The road where the shooting occurred intersected the road surrounding the castle, maybe a block from where Dan had been walking just yesterday, and a mere three blocks from the Charla Café where he had to go tonight. The shooting happened about two hours after he had returned to the hotel from his walk.

Dan's mind was racing. He remembered Jacques Foucher saying that Dimitrios Barkoxe would be coming to Spain to kill David Ortega. Could this really be the same David Ortega? How could he find out? He took his burner phone and typed a text to don Fernando saying a man named David Ortega had been murdered here in Toledo and asking don Fernando to contact the Toledo police and see if they would give him more information. That was the only thing Dan could think to do.

Once again, he was aware of the extreme disadvantage of his position. Here he was: in a foreign land, completely out of his element, completely in the dark, dealing with dangerous people, one of whom—Mariana Ibarra—had already tracked him down. He felt completely vulnerable. Even though he did not like guns, and even though he knew it was illegal for a tourist to possess a gun in Spain, still, he wished he had one on him.

The waiter brought him a plate with toast, a hardboiled egg, and three slices of cheese. Dan wasn't the least bit hungry, but he knew he should eat something. He reached for the knife to butter his toast and noticed it was a small sharp steak knife rather than a regular butter knife. He looked around, and then slid the knife up his sleeve, securing it under his watch band. He was glad he had put on a long-sleeved shirt today. He knew it was silly, but somehow, having that knife made him feel better.

He wondered what he would do with himself until his meeting with Ricardo. He wondered if Ricardo would even show up. And if he did show up, would he be able to explain what the fuck was going on?

CHAPTER TWENTY-NINE

Late that afternoon, Dan stepped out of the front door of the hotel. He was wearing a light jacket to help conceal the small steak knife that was up his sleeve, still secured by his watch strap. He walked up the narrow street to the plaza and hailed a cab to take him to the Charla Café. His body was tense, hyper-alert. As the taxi approached the café, Dan noticed three black sedans parked, one after the other, on the opposite of the street. The windows were tinted so Dan could not see in. If there was anyone watching the café from inside the cars, they weren't being very discrete about it.

Dan paid the taxi driver, stepped out of the car, and looked at the front of the Charla Café. It had a large outdoor seating area with six or seven tables, all of which were empty, giving the impression that the café was closed. But Dan could see lights on inside. He glanced back at the three dark sedans, then stepped up the front steps and went through the front door.

It took his eyes a moment to adjust to the low light. He stood there, blinking, looking around the inside of the café. It was a large space with tables, but it seemed to be almost completely empty. Over in the corner there was one table that held three men, but that was it. No other customers, and Dan didn't see any staff. He wondered if this whole trip was just one wild goose chase. He scanned the entire room. Where was Ricardo? He blinked again and looked over at the table of three men. Two of the men were in dark suits, but wait... He squinted. The person in the middle was Ricardo.

Dan's vision was better now. He could see that Ricardo was looking at him, but not waving, not making any kind of gesture. Dan's instincts told him that this was a trap, but he still started walking towards the table. He could see Ricardo watching him as he walked closer—watching, but not making any facial movements. Dan wondered if he was drugged.

Dan got to the table. To the left of Ricardo sat a thin man with a slight moustache. He was wearing a very expensive suit. His graying hair was slicked back. His skin had a slight olive tone to it. He was smiling slightly, but it was not a warm smile. Dan noticed that his hands stayed underneath the table. The man sitting to Ricardo's right was shorter and heavier, a beefy man with a dull thuggish look on his face. Dan looked at Ricardo. His face was expressionless, listless, and pale.

The thin man with the moustache spoke. "Thank you for joining us, Mr. Landes. Please have a seat."

The man gestured with his head to the empty seat across from him. His hands remained below the table.

"What's in your hands?" Dan asked.

The thin man's eyebrows went up slightly. He seemed annoyed by the question. He raised his right hand slightly to show Dan the top of a small pistol.

"You can put that away," Dan said as he pulled the chair back to sit down. "You hardly need that."

The thin man smiled slightly and said, "I prefer to keep it."

"A man who keeps his options open," Dan said dryly as he sat down. "I respect that." Then he added, "What have you done to Ricardo?"

"Oh," the thin man responded, "I apologize for that. We had to give him a small... *potion*... to induce him to come with us quietly. He'll be fine in a couple of hours."

"And you are?" Dan asked.

"Dimitrios Barkoxe, a su servicio," the thin man replied.

"I figured," Dan said.

Dan glanced at the fat man sitting to Ricardo's right. There was no point in asking his name. He was clearly a subordinate, just there for the muscle.

"And what's the point of all this?" Dan asked.

"It's a long story," Dimitrios said. "But the short version is that we are waiting for your friend."

As Dan pondered that response, there was a crackling of static. Dimitrios lifted his left hand up from under the table. It held some type of small walkie-talkie device. It crackled again and a scratchy voice came out of it. "A taxi drove by but kept on going. There were no passengers in it."

Dimitrios pressed a button on the device and said "Okay."

It dawned on Dan what was going on. He understood now why the three cars were parked so visibly out in the open in front of the café.

"I see," Dan said. "You're waiting for Nassim Kahil... and you're using Ricardo and me as bait."

"Very astute, Mr. Landes."

"And what makes Nassim Kahil so important?" Dan asked.

Dimitrios's eyes narrowed. "He has my coins," he said coldly.

Dan was surprised. Jacques Foucher had said that Barkoxe had ransacked Matzel Davis's house in order to steal the coins. Foucher had asserted that Barkoxe had found the coins hidden in the house. Dan realized that he had always assumed Foucher was correct."

"I thought *you* took the coins from Matzel's... or rather, Nassim Kahil's house in Villa Rosario," Dan said.

Dimitrios slowly shook his head no. "Nassim got there before we did. He took the coins—*my* coins—and fled."

Dan pondered this. Foucher had said that the maps were useless without the coins. No wonder everyone wanted Matzel Davis so bad. Had Matzel been one step ahead of everyone the whole time? Did he leave the front door of his shop open to lure Foucher and his gang to come inside? Once they were inside, did Matzel shoot the Colombian as Foucher had claimed? Then what? Foucher escaped and Matzel ran back to his house to retrieve the coins and then went straight to the airport before Barkoxe and his gang arrived? Dan ran the timeline in his head. It didn't make any sense. The coroner said the Colombian and the Frenchman were killed around ten p.m. Matzel's neighbor said he saw five men leave Matzel's house around eleven p.m. The amount of damage to Matzel's house meant that Barkoxe would have been there at least an hour. There wouldn't have been enough time for Matzel to get to his house before Barkoxe showed up.

"Okay," Dan said slowly. He decided to take a stab in the dark. "And so... why did you shoot David Ortega?" he asked.

"I didn't," Dimitrios said and smiled. "I merely sent him to deliver a message to Nassim—a message that conveyed that I wanted to meet, to combine forces. Ortega was an idiot. He believed me when I told him I wanted the three of us to get back together, like the old days. I told him to tell Nassim that as a gesture of my good faith, I would deliver his two friends from Villa Rosario to him. Of course, I knew Nassim would kill Ortega. But that is just as well. He saved me the trouble of doing it."

"What makes these coins so important?" Dan asked. "What makes them worth killing three people?"

"Three people?" Dimitrios said with a sneer. "Hundreds have died for these coins, Mr. Landes. And, if all goes well, thousands more will die."

Barkoxe's words sent a chill down Dan's back.

The walkie-talkie crackled again. "Still nothing, bossman."

"What do you mean, 'thousands more will die'?" Dan asked.

Dimitrios looked at Dan. There was an icy coldness in his eyes, as if he was taking stock of an insect he was about to step on.

"Do you know what Todo is, Mr. Landes?"

"My understanding is that it's a money-transfer business and bitcoin platform that wants to be a bank," Dan said.

"Ha," Dimitrios snorted in disdain. Then he asked, "And do you know what the Gran Ventura is?"

Dan shook his head no. He had never heard that term before.

"Yes, your friend told us that you didn't know anything," Dimitrios said, then asked, "Did Nassim ever show you the coins?"

Again, Dan shook his head no.

"Yet, you had the maps. Those maps could have only been drawn by using my coins," Dimitrios said and raised his eyebrows in a questioning manner.

"The only reason I had those maps was because Silas Edwards asked me to mail him Ricardo's notebooks." Dan said.

"Ah yes, Silas Edwards, what a bitte," Dimitrios sneered, using the French slang word for dick. "He wasn't a Todo. He knew nothing of our history, our destiny. He was a greedy American bitte who thought he could steal our gold. David Ortega played him like a violin. What a fool. He got exactly what he deserved."

Dimitrios looked at his watch. He paused for a moment, then said, "I will tell you this much, Mr. Landes: I can trace my family's history back over seven hundred years. Those coins were *my* family's coins. We minted them! It was our project! It was our idea! Fate *wrenched* them from our control, but twenty-two generations of my family have worked and slaved and schemed for seven centuries to reclaim what God originally gave us! Coin by coin, we clawed them back. And those coins were passed down in my family to me. *To me*, Mr. Landes! Ten years ago, Nassim Kahil stole them from me. Now he will be forced to give them back!"

"Dude, I don't know anything about all that," Dan said. All I know is that you broke into my apartment."

Dimitrios just shrugged and looked at his watch. Then he picked up the walkie-talkie, put it to his mouth and said, "Okay, it's time to move."

He slid the walkie-talkie into the side pocket of his suit jacket, then said to Dan, "Let's go. We need to take a little walk."

Dimitrios stood up and made a small gesture with the hand that held the pistol. Dan stood up. The fat man took Ricardo's arm and picked him up like he was picking up a tissue. Ricardo was completely compliant.

"May I ask where we are going?" Dan asked.

"We're just going to walk down to the castle and wait for Nassim," Dimitrios said.

And so, they did. The castle was about three blocks below the Charla Café, down a steep road. It made for a strange parade, the four men walking down the road, followed by the three dark sedans. The fat man and Ricardo led the way, the fat man still guiding the zombified Ricardo by the arm. Dan followed them, with Dimitrios slightly behind him, his right hand with the gun in his suit jacket side pocket.

"This is quite a spectacle," Dan said to Dimitrios.

"I want to be sure he sees us," was Dimitrios's only response.

They approached the large iron gate that Dan had seen the day before. Dimitrios pulled out a key, unlocked it, and swung it wide open. The four men stepped inside, followed by the three sedans. Dan could see seven workers dressed in dirt-smeared overalls over by the cement mixer, adding sand and water to the mixer, completely unconcerned by the men and the three cars that had just entered their domain. After the cars were parked inside, Dimitrios swung the gate halfway shut, but did not close it. The doors of the three sedans opened and nine men climbed out. These were big men, hired guns, thugs, enforcer-types. Dimitrios pointed to a large wooden door on the side of the castle. The fat man guided Ricardo through it. Dan followed with Dimitrios's gun at his back, and then the nine men from the cars followed behind them in single file. They walked through a large open room, then down a massive hallway to an even larger room. The floor in the center of this room had been torn up, and a large pit had been dug in the center measuring at least twenty feet in diameter and almost ten feet deep, circled by a walkway. The bottom of the pit was covered with about a foot of water. Shovels, picks, and several wheelbarrows were stacked on the walkway on the other side of the pit.

The fat man guided Ricardo over to the corner by an open door and leaned him against the wall. Ricardo looked like he was about to fall asleep. The fat man held him up with one arm. Dimitrios stood on the walkway with Dan, facing the huge pit. The nine thugs stood on the walkway behind Dimitrios.

A small smile crossed Dimitrios's lips. "Do you like our work?" he asked Dan.

"What is it?" Dan asked.

"It's going to be our latest vault. We're going to have to knock a wall out to get it into this room, but after we build the concrete foundation, we will lower the vault into the pit."

"Okay..." Dan said slowly, "I'll bite. What's the vault for?"

Dimitrios laughed. The reflection from the water in the pit seemed to give his eyes an eerie yellow gleam. "Todo built this castle, Mr. Landes, more than nine hundred years ago. It belonged to us, and we are taking it back. It will be the crown jewel of the Todo banking system, and our first deposit will be the treasure of the Gran Ventura."

Just then, the seven workers who had been mixing cement outside shuffled into the room. Dimitrios frowned. He looked at his watch and then yelled out to them, "It's quitting time! Go home. There's no overtime!"

"We just need to get our tools," one man yelled back, and pointed to the stack of shovels and picks by the wheelbarrows.

"Okay, but hurry up," Dimitrios yelled back.

The men walked over to the pile of tools and started moving the wheelbarrows into position as if to load the tools. Dan noticed that each wheelbarrow had a small tarp over its contents. Dimitrios turned to Dan and gave him a little push, indicating he should walk over to the corner where the fat man was holding Ricardo up. Dan was still watching the workmen in his peripheral vision. Suddenly, he saw them, as if on cue, all moving in unison, pull the tarps off the wheelbarrows and pick up some type of machinegun-like weapons from the wheelbarrows. They all picked up these weapons and started firing simultaneously, aiming across the pit at the nine men who were walking behind Dimitrios.

Nobody understands how the brain works when disaster strikes, but people all over the world report the same phenomenon. In a microsecond, the brain is flooded with chemicals with only one purpose: survival. Time stops, or slows down to a crawl. Sound disappears or becomes distorted. Vision narrows and becomes super-acute.

At the exact moment that Dan saw the men across the pit start to pull their triggers, he felt himself leave his body. He was outside of his body watching the events unfold before him in slow motion. He could tell there was a thunderous noise coming from across the pit, a noise that echoed off the stone walls of the room and grew louder and louder, but none of the sound seemed to reach his ears. He felt he was floating in total silence. He saw white fire coming from the gun barrels across the pit. He smelled burning sulfur that burned his eyes. He tried to move, but the air around him felt thick, as if he was stuck in molasses. He saw some of the nine men tried to reach inside their jackets or toward their waists for their guns, but they had no time. The machine gun fire hit them where they stood, knocking them backwards, flying against the wall, blood gushing from their torsos, backs, arms, and heads. They seemed to crumple to the ground in a grotesque dance of flailing arms and legs.

Dan turned his head towards Ricardo. The fat man had let go of him and pulled a gun from a shoulder holster. Without the fat man to hold him up, Ricardo slid down the wall to a sitting position to the floor. The fat man aimed his pistol at the workmen across the pit, but before he could fire a single shot, a stream of bullets blew the top of his head off. Blood shot upward. He hit the wall behind him, then fell forward into the pit.

Dan felt an arm reach around his neck and jerk him backwards. Dimitrios had grabbed him from behind and was trying to get behind him and use him as a shield. In that moment, something popped inside Dan's head and the world seemed to snap back into place. Dimitrios was shooting at the workmen across the pit; they had stopped firing and were now ducking for cover. Dan could move in real time now. He reached over to his left forearm and grabbed the steak knife from under his watch band. He held it like an ice pick and swung it downward as fast and hard as he could into Dimitrios's thigh and then yanked it upward cutting a deep gash into Dimitrios's leg. The knife's handle broke off in Dan's hand. Dimitrios screamed and let go of Dan's neck. Dan pulled away and threw himself to the ground. In that instant, one of the workers across the pit aimed his machine gun. There was a rapid burst-fire, and a line of black holes stitched across Dimitrios's chest. His mouth flew opened and he fell backwards and collapsed on the floor.

Dan looked up from the dirt walkway where he lay. No one on Dan's side of the room was left standing. The workers across the pit were running out of the room. Dan looked over at Ricardo. He was just sitting there on the floor leaning against the corner, looking dazed. Dan picked himself up and scrambled over to him. Dan realized he was still gripping the broken handle of the steak knife tightly in his hand. He stuck in in his jacket pocket and then patted Ricardo's chest. No bullet wounds. There, by Ricardo's feet, was a small 9mm pistol that the fat man had dropped when the workmen blew off the top of his head. Dan quickly picked it up and shoved it into his jacket pocket. Then he grabbed Ricardo's arm, hoisted him up, and began to drag him out of the room through the large wooden door that lead outside.

When he got outside, the workers were nowhere to be seen. Instead, just outside the gate, there was a large green car waiting, with both passenger doors open. A man was standing outside of the car waving frantically to Dan to come to the car.

"C'mon! C'mon! Hurry!" the man was yelling.

Dan dragged Ricardo, half falling, to the car.

"Get in the front!" the man yelled as he grabbed Ricardo out of Dan's hands and pushed Ricardo into the back seat of the car, shutting the door after him. Dan dove into the front seat. The man slammed the front passenger door shut, and the car took off, leaving the man standing there in front of the castle.

Dan was sprawled out in the front seat. The car was speeding down the road. He untwisted himself and sat up in the seat and looked at the driver. It was Matzel Davis, driving the car like a maniac.

Matzel glanced at Dan and said, "Carlos will handle the police when they arrive. I don't know what drugs they gave Ricardo, so we need to take him to a hospital. The Provincial Hospital is going to be swarming with police because it's the closest to the castle, so I'll take you to the Quirósalud Hospital. Now listen carefully. Do not tell the hospital you were anywhere near the castle. Your story is you were at a bar downtown, and your friend took some drugs, but you don't know what kind. Do not mention anything else, you understand?"

Dan nodded his head.

Matzel continued: "You're just two American tourists who were out drinking and partying, got it? Ricardo won't remember a thing about this evening, so he can't say anything. Hopefully, they'll just keep him for a couple of hours and then release him, but I'm afraid you'll have to stay there with him until he comes out of it so you can reassure him when he wakes up, and also keep him from saying anything stupid. Once they release him, take him back to your hotel and let him sleep it off. I'll come by tomorrow evening around six p.m. and see how's he's doing.

Dan nodded his head again. He became aware he was breathing heavily, that his head was throbbing, and his ears were ringing. He realized he was coming out of shock. What had just happened? Matzel took the bridge over the Tagus River and then sped onto the freeway that wrapped around the ancient city. Dan had so many questions, but right now he just focused on getting his breathing under control. He had to make himself presentable to the hospital staff.

CHAPTER THIRTY

The hospital kept Ricardo overnight. Dan found it impossible to sleep sitting in the waiting room. The florescent lights were too bright; the plastic chairs too hard; and the adrenaline in his system was still pumping. He couldn't stop his hands from shaking. Plus, he was paranoid that someone might somehow discover the pistol that was in his jacket pocket. He tried to position the gun so that it didn't make a bulge. In doing so, he discovered the broken knife handle he had placed in the same pocket. He had totally forgotten about that. He discretely deposited the knife handle in a nearby trash bin. He picked a chair in the corner, away from other people, and tried to make himself as comfortable and as inconspicuous as possible.

As the hours went by, his cop brain slowly took over, and he began to reorganize all his previous assumptions about this case. There might not be a warrant out for Matzel under the name of Nassim Kahil, but clearly Mariana Ibarra was not wrong about him being a murderer. He had just massacred eleven people inside the Castle of San Servando. It's true that Dimitrios had kidnapped Ricardo and Dan and was using them as bait; and equally true that Dimitrios would have murdered Matzel in order to get those coins—those damn coins!—but in Dan's view, both Matzel and Dimitrios were cut from the same cloth. It was the classic criminal scenario: Ortega, Barkoxe, and Matzel had all been partners at one point, but had had a falling out. Dan had seen it a million times back when he was a detective in the States, but never with this kind of body count.

First, the two bodies in Matzel's shop; then Silas in New York; then Ortega in a drive-by; then Barkoxe and his gang of thugs; Dan wondered how many more murders had happened that he didn't even know about. Dimitrios had said that hundreds had died for those coins.

Still, Dan was in the dark as to why. Dimitrios had said that his family had minted those coins hundreds of years ago, but that they were somehow taken from them. Was this a blood feud, that went back centuries? But, a feud between who? What made these coins so valuable? And what was that Gran Ventura that Dimitrios had asked him about?

From the beginning, Dan had felt confused and out of the loop. That pissed him off. Ricardo hadn't clued him in that night when he showed up at his apartment; Silas had lied to him; Matzel had toyed with him in his shop; Dimitrios didn't tell him anything. Even Foucher knew way more than he had let on. Dan hated not knowing. He was fed up with being used as a patsy. He decided to get to the bottom of this, even if he had to drag the truth out of Matzel the next time they met.

*   *   *

The next morning, at dawn, the hospital released Ricardo to Dan's care. Ricardo was still woozy, but he at least recognized Dan, and was glad to see him. In the taxi ride back to Dan's hotel, Ricardo told Dan that all he wanted to do was sleep. As Matzel had predicted, Ricardo remembered nothing about the night before. The only thing he remembered was being grabbed outside of his hotel and being forced into a car.

As Matzel had instructed him to do, Dan took Ricardo back to Dan's hotel. He had Ricardo lie down on the sofa and covered him with a blanket. Ricardo fell asleep immediately. Dan then climbed into his own bed.

*   *   *

Dan awoke at about four in the afternoon. Ricardo was still asleep. Dan took a shower and then ordered several sandwiches from room service. While he waited for room service, he made a pot of coffee. He figured Ricardo would be just as hungry as he was.

The smell of the brewing coffee seemed to awake Ricardo. He opened his eyes, looked around, sat up on the sofa, and said to Dan, "Where am I?"

Dan explained that he had brought him to the hotel that morning. Ricardo had no memory of the hospital or coming to Dan's hotel. Dan suggested he take a hot shower, that food would be delivered soon, and that he might remember more after he ate something. He handed Ricardo a clean towel and pointed to the bathroom. Ricardo nodded and got up.

While Ricardo was in the shower, Dan turned on the TV. The story of what was being called the San Servando Massacre dominated the news. But every channel carried the same explanation: that this was a revenge killing between two rival drug gangs. There were no actual witnesses to the shooting, but there were interviews with workers at the castle who all spun the same story: that they had seen drug dealing in the neighborhood, and had heard threats. There were promises to beef up security, and calls for an investigation.

Dan turned the TV off when Ricardo got out of the shower. The food arrived shortly after that. Dan was right: Ricardo was starved. He tore into the sandwiches. Between bites, he peppered Dan with questions.

"So, you're saying that it was Dimitrios Barkoxe who kidnapped and drugged me?" he asked Dan.

"Yup. Did you know Dimitrios? Had you ever met him before?" Dan asked.

"No," Ricardo replied between bites. "Matzel had told me about him, but I had never met him."

"What did Matzel tell you about him?" Dan asked.

"That he's a purebred Todo; that he could trace his family lineage in Todo back more than seven hundred years."

Dan frowned. He did not understand Ricardo's answer. "Um... exactly *how old* is Todo?" Dan asked.

Ricardo took another bite. "Todo, the organization? Oh, it's old. It's been around more than three thousand years, I guess. So, what happened to Dimitrios? How did I get away from him?

Dan still didn't understand Ricardo's answer. How could Todo be three thousand years old? But he responded, "Dimitrios is dead."

"Dead? How?"

"Matzel's men shot him."

"What? Fuck, was I there?"

"You sure were," Dan answered, and proceeded to explain to Ricardo exactly what had happened the night before. Ricardo stopped eating and just listened to Dan with his mouth open.

"You're shitting me," Ricardo said when Dan finished.

"No, buddy, that's exactly what happened."

Ricardo shook his head. "All because of some stupid coins."

"Yes," said Dan. "And I would very much appreciate it if you could tell me about these coins, and about why everyone is so willing to risk their lives for them. I'm sick of being in the dark."

Ricardo finished the last bite of his sandwich, took a swig of coffee and said, "I can try. It's kind of complicated. Matzel can explain it better than I can, but I'll give it a shot... I guess for me, it started fifty years ago. As you know, I was living in Madrid after I got out of college. Madrid was much different back then. Franco had just died, and things were very chaotic. Of course, I was much younger and wilder. But anyway, back then, I used to buy old Spanish coins from street vendors or coin shops. I collected them. It was a hobby of mine, a diversion. They were cheap, and I thought they made good souvenirs. I used to have a nice collection. But over the years, I sold most of them, except for three coins that were my favorite. I kept those three coins, I guess, for sentimental reasons. Anyway, about a year ago, I decided to sell them. I just didn't need them anymore. I guess I was trying to simplify my life. I didn't know what they were worth, but I had heard that Matzel Davis was an expert in old coins. I didn't know him well at the time, but I took the coins over to his shop to ask for an appraisal."

Ricardo paused to take another sip of coffee. He was about to speak again, when there was a soft knock on the door. It made Dan jump. He looked at his watch. Six o'clock. It must be Matzel, he thought.

Dan stood up and went over to the chair by the desk where he had hung his jacket that morning. The fat man's gun was still in the pocket of the jacket. Dan slipped the jacket on and walked over to the door. He looked through the peephole—it was Matzel. Dan opened the door and Matzel stepped inside.

CHAPTER THIRTY-ONE

Matzel nodded at Dan but went right over to Ricardo, sat down on the sofa next to him, and put his hand on his shoulder.

"How are you feeling my friend?" he asked Ricardo.

"Alright, I guess," said Ricardo. "Dan was filling me in on what happened. I guess yesterday was pretty wild."

Matzel nodded.

"So Barkoxe is out of the picture?" Ricardo asked.

"Finally," said Matzel, "and Ortega too."

Ricardo looked amazed. "Ortega's dead?"

Matzel nodded. "He had an unfortunate accident."

"I think his unfortunate accident was knowing you," Dan blurted out. Dan then looked at Ricardo and said, "Ortega was sitting in his car when *someone*," and Dan looked over at Matzel, "drove up and fired about twenty bullets into him."

Matzel smiled, shrugged his shoulders and said, "Very unfortunate."

"Wow," Ricardo said, but then looked at Matzel and asked, "then we're free to proceed?"

Matzel nodded. "I think so, my friend. Do you feel up to traveling?"

"I think I can handle it," Ricardo said.

Matzel stood up. "Then let's go. We have work to do."

"Whoa, whoa, not so fast," Dan said forcefully. He felt his anger welling up. He wasn't going to be ignored or jerked around again. He pulled out the gun from his jacket pocket and pointed at Matzel.

"Sit back down," he said slowly.

Matzel shrugged and sat back down. He sat there, saying nothing, but with a slightly amused expression on his face.

"No one is leaving until someone clues me in as to what is happening!" Dan said. "I want to know who these people were, what the fuck is going on, what these coins are all about, and why these coins and the damn maps are so important... I want to know the whole fucking story!"

Dan was almost shouting now.

Matzel made an acquiescing gesture and opened his hands. "Of course, Mr. Landes, of course. You are owed an explanation. We have treated you rather poorly. But it is a long story, Mr. Landes, a very long story."

"I've got nothing but time, buddy," Dan said, and waved the gun at Matzel. "And I'm sick and tired of being kept in the dark. I want to know *everything*, from the beginning!"

Matzel laughed. "From the beginning, eh?" he said. "Well sir, as a historian, I can appreciate that. In fact, there is no way to understand the importance of these coins without going all the way back to the very beginning. Okay, well then, since you insist, I will tell you everything, from the beginning."

Matzel glanced at Ricardo, and Ricardo nodded, as if to say, "Go ahead."

And so, Matzel began: "What I am about to tell you, Mr. Landes, may seem fantastic, unbelievable, even insane, but I assure you, it is all absolutely true and historically accurate. To explain it in full requires a bit of a history, thirty-eight centuries to be precise, but if you will bear with me, I think you will find it very enlightening, and it will answer all of your questions. You've heard of the Knights of Templar, I presume?"

Dan nodded. "I've heard of them. Part of the Crusades, right?"

"Yes," said Matzel, "that's the part everyone knows. But the story starts earlier, much earlier, almost two millenniums before the birth of Christ, around 1800 BC, when the city of Jerusalem first became fortified. Of course, Jerusalem had existed as a settlement for two thousand years before that, but by 1800 BC, the city had become rich, very rich indeed. It was rich enough that the city needed walls built around it, to keep out invaders, and to protect its richest and most important building, the Temple of Moriah. The Temple of Moriah was built in the center of Jerusalem, high on a hill. The ruins of that temple still exist, Mr. Landes, in the same location. It is known today as the Temple Mount, and it is the holiest site in Jerusalem. But in 1800 BC, it was known as the Temple of Moriah. And back then, the Temple of Moriah was more than just a place of worship; it was also the center of all of Jerusalem's commerce and business. And that Temple made Jerusalem rich. How? Through trade. By sheer luck of location, Jerusalem existed at the crossroads of two major trade routes: the Silk Road to Afghanistan and Asia, and the sea routes to Cyprus and the Iberian Peninsula, or as we now call most of it, Spain. And what made these trade routes so important? Bronze, Mr. Landes, bronze. This was the Bronze Age, and bronze, as you may or may not know, is made from ninety percent copper and ten percent tin. Copper was plentiful. There were huge copper mines on the island of Cyprus, and the businessmen of Jerusalem controlled all the contracts for the copper that came out of those mines. Not that they were great sailors, no, far from it, but they were brilliant negotiators. They didn't know how to build ships or how to sail, but they knew how to negotiate contracts with the coastal people who had those skills. And so, contract by contract, the businessmen of Jerusalem bought and controlled all the copper mines on Cyprus.

"But tin was a harder commodity to find. The only substantial supply came from Afghanistan in the east, or from the mines in the central part of Spain, and Jerusalem wanted to control those routes as well. But they had competition for tin. The Hittites to the north also had trade routes to Afghanistan, and the Philistines from Crete had shorter sailing distances to Spain.

"But Jerusalem found a way to eliminate competition from the Hittites and the Philistines. Egypt was expanding into what they called their New Kingdom, and by 1500 BC, the city of Jerusalem had been surrounded and absorbed by Egypt. But Jerusalem wasn't conquered by Egypt—no, no. The city of Jerusalem negotiated a peace treaty whereby they retained a certain independence and retained the right to engage in trade. Businessmen never care who's in power, Mr. Landes, as long as they can continue making money. By this time, Egypt controlled the entire eastern Mediterranean coast, all the way north to what is now Turkey and all the way west along the African coast to what is now Tunisia. Egypt's New Kingdom was vast! To get to the Mediterranean Sea, all of Mesopotamia, Assyria, and Arabia had to pass through Egyptian land, and pay monetary tributes and taxes. Thus, the Egyptians needed copper and tin more than anyone. Why? To make bronze armor and weapons, because they had the biggest army and the most territory to protect, so they needed the most bronze. And the Egyptian overlords recognized that it was easier to let Jerusalem continue running their trade routes in exchange for a guaranteed supply of copper and tin. Egypt blocked the Hittites and the Philistines from trading in tin, giving Jerusalem a monopoly in the tin trade. It was a good arrangement. The Jerusalem traders were free to travel east to Afghanistan or sail west to Spain, and in return, Egypt got copper and tin to make bronze. Both sides flourished.

"So, by 1400 BC, Jerusalem controlled the tin routes to Afghanistan and Spain and the copper mines in Cyprus, which meant that Jerusalem controlled the production of bronze for the Bronze Age. This monopoly brought vast wealth for the businessmen and upper class of Jerusalem. But this monopoly did not come about just because they had the protection of Egypt. No, Mr. Landes, Jerusalem's monopoly came from a brand new and more far-reaching development: the invention of credit, or to be more precise, letters of credit.

"Ah, you look surprised, Mr. Landes. Let me explain. I mentioned that the Temple of Moriah was more than just a religious site—it was center of Jerusalem's trade business. You see, back then, temples were not simply churches. Temples were the center of every city. They were the marketplaces where people bought groceries; they were where people gathered to hear the news of the day; they were where all the major businesses were located; they were cultural centers with art galleries and libraries. The Temple of Moriah was the biggest temple ever built. It was the business, cultural, and economic center of Jerusalem. And economic centers need banks, so the Temple of Moriah became the banking center of the Holy Land. You'd go to the temple to pray, and afterwards, you could pay your mortgage. It was one economic monolith. And I don't mean there were banks *inside* the Temple of Moriah, Mr. Landes. I mean that the temple itself was *the central bank* of the Mediterranean! They built and controlled all the currency exchanges in all the countries surrounding the Mediterranean; they set the rate of exchange for the different currencies; and they controlled the flow of gold and silver between countries. These bankers were the shrewdest minds of their day. And they weren't all Jews. There were Greeks, Turks, Arabs....This was a thousand years before the birth of Mohammad and Christ. The urge to make money brought people together. If you were a lawyer or a young man with financial smarts back then, your religion didn't matter—you worked as a banker or trader in the Temple of Moriah. Almost all the inventions we have now regarding money, came from that temple. They invented interest, compound interest, mortgages, and, most importantly, lines of credit. The whole invention of lines of credit came from the money lenders at the Temple of Moriah. If the money lenders thought you were credit-worthy, they would give you a letter of credit, written in cuneiform with a reed stylus on a clay tablet, and you could carry that clay tablet to foreign lands to do business..."

Matzel paused. He looked at Dan and furrowed his brow, as if he was gathering his thoughts.

"You have to understand two things, Mr. Landes: Number one, how revolutionary these clay letters of credit were, and how they completely transformed trade. And number two, how there is a direct connection, down through the centuries, from those clay tablets to Todo, to You-Bank, to the bitcoins of today.

"Let me explain how these letters of credit worked. You see, in order to do trade, you have to have contracts. For example, a tin mine promised to provide a certain amount of tin, and someone else promised to pay a certain amount of gold for the tin upon delivery. So, you had to have some kind of written contract to memorialize these promises, and all these contracts had to travel to foreign lands. The traders from the Temple of Moriah had to travel thousands of miles from Jerusalem to Spain or Afghanistan to make these trades. And those trade routes were constantly raided by thieves and bandits. The traders could not risk traveling with money. If they carried gold or silver to conduct trade, they would be slaughtered. So, they carried these clay tablets that served as letters of credit. These tablets were not just the promise of money—no-no-no. They were brilliant. They were personalized to the bearer. They were letters of introduction. They would identify and describe the particular trader who was carrying them. Only that person could use them to trade for a contract for goods. If a bandit robbed a trader of a clay tablet, it would be worthless to the bandit. He couldn't exchange it for anything. Only the person identified and described in the tablet could negotiate the tablet for goods. The tablet contained a promise to deliver a certain amount of gold when the trade was completed. However, what made the clay tablet valuable was that it contained a coded message at the bottom. Think of it as the first two-factor authentication system. Here's how it worked: A trader would travel, say, to Afghanistan, to negotiate the purchase of a certain amount of tin. He would carry a clay tablet identifying him and his mission. The tablet would contain a code at the bottom indicating what symbols would appear on a second clay tablet should the contract be successfully completed. A deal would be struck with a businessman in Afghanistan, who would arrange for the delivery of said tin to Jerusalem. When the tin was delivered, the delivery man, or more accurately, delivery caravan, would receive a second clay tablet indicating that the tin was satisfactorily delivered. This second clay tablet contained various symbols. The delivery man would go back to Afghanistan and give this second clay tablet to the

Afghani businessman. Remember I said that the Temple of Moriah controlled all the currency exchanges in the Middle East? Think of those currency exchanges as the Temple's regional banks. The Afghani businessman could take the two clay tablets to the local currency exchange and show the two tablets side by side, one tablet being the contract for the purchase of tin, and the other showing the successful delivery of tin, and if the second tablet contained the symbols that the code on the first tablet predicted, then the currency exchange would give the Afghani businessman the agreed-upon amount of gold in exchange for the two clay tablets. Understanding the code at the bottom of the clay tablets was a closely-guarded secret, and only the top man at the currency exchange was trained in the code by the Temple of Moriah. The code was impossible to decipher because it changed with the date. Each clay tablet was dated, and that date determined how you would read the code. It was a very good system and allowed commerce to flourish for centuries. But... all good things must come to an end. And just after 1200 BC, the entire Bronze Age civilization collapsed and all the civilizations around the Mediterranean fell into a dark age that lasted almost three hundred years."

"I've heard about this," Dan said. "Something about the Sea People."

"Ah, yes," Matzel laughed, "the so-called Sea People. That is the common explanation for the collapse of the Bronze Age: Sea People invaders. The Sea People were real, alright, but they were not the cause of the collapse of the greatest civilization that Europe and the Middle East had ever known—no, not at all. They were not the *cause*; they were the *effect*. The collapse of the Bronze Age created millions of refugees, and like a tsunami, they flooded every Mediterranean country. It was the biggest migration of people that the world had ever seen. They overran and completely destroyed the cities of Greece, Turkey, Canaan, Babylon, Cyprus and Assyria. The Egyptians called these refugees the Sea People, because they traveled to Egypt by boat, but in fact, most of them traveled overland, from the East and North. They were refugees, Mr. Landes, refugees with nothing to lose. It wasn't that they were well-armed. They weren't, but there were so many of them. Millions and millions of refugees. They weren't an army of warriors; they were an army of migrants. They were migrating, looking for food and shelter. And what created these millions of refugees? The *collapse of credit*, Mr. Landes, the complete and utter collapse of credit in all the civilizations that surrounded the Mediterranean."

"Well," Dan said, "I appreciate the history lesson, but how does any of this connect to Todo, to Barkoxe, or to these coins?"

"Bear with me, Mr. Landes," responded Matzel, "I told you that this was a long story, but it will all make sense. Recall that I mentioned that the traders in the Temple of Moriah were not all Jews. Anyone could come and do business there. After all, if the Temple of Moriah was making trades all along every trade route, it stands to reason that ambitious businessmen from the other end of the trade routes would want to come to Jerusalem to get a piece of the action. Everyone always wants a piece of the action, Mr. Landes! And the Temple did not discriminate against anyone. All were welcome to come and set up shop. But unfortunately, one of the groups that came to Jerusalem in about 1250 BC were the Ancient Celts from the islands that now form the United Kingdom. It is my belief that they traveled to Jerusalem originally from Cornwall, because there were tin mines in Cornwall, and there are clay tablets that still exist that reference trade between the Temple of Moriah and these mines in Cornwall. But they could have come from anywhere in the British Isles. Back then, the Ancient Celts controlled almost all of the British Isles. And the ruling class of the Celts—who we now call the Druids—were very advanced, very interested in power, very practiced in the art of religion as a way to organize the masses. After all, they built Stone Hedge. They were the priests and judges of their day. They were engineers, mathematicians, and astronomers, but most damaging to the Temple of Moriah, the Ancient Celts were code breakers.

"You see, back in 1250 BC, the British Isles were a wild and ragged place. Rebellions and local wars were common. So, to maintain their control over the people, the Ancient Celts had learned to use magic and superstition and even human sacrifice to keep the people in fear of them. The Ancient Celts were extremely disciplined and ruled their world by fear. They created a system of spies throughout the British Isles to keep them appraised of anyone fomenting rebellion. If they suspected someone of being a dissident, the Druid priest would cast a spell against that person, then they would have their spies secretly poison that person to make the spell appear to come true. In order to communicate with their spies, the Druid priests developed a whole system of codes. Over time, these codes became a complete language, only known to the Druid priests. So, when the Ancient Celts came to Jerusalem to trade, they immediately understood that the symbols at the bottom of the clay tablets of the Temple of Moriah were a type of code. It took them decades to decipher the clay tablets, but eventually... they broke the code."

Matzel paused and pursed his lips. "The Ancient Celts envied the fantastic wealth of the Temple of Moriah. They wanted that wealth for themselves, but rather than earn it by engaging in trade, they decided to steal it. They broke the code of the Temple of Moriah and began to counterfeit these clay tablets, these contracts for the delivery of copper and tin. They would send their spies and accomplices throughout the Middle East with these counterfeit clay tablets, and these spies would go to the currency exchanges and exchange the clay tablets for gold. These clay tablets were perfect counterfeits. The currency exchanges couldn't tell the difference, and neither could the accountants back at the Temple of Moriah.

"So, the Celtic traders in Jerusalem were slowly becoming rich by passing off these counterfeit clay tablets at the currency exchanges all along the trade routes. But they were greedy. They weren't satisfied with merely being rich. They wanted to have fabulous wealth, so they began to speculate with these counterfeit tablets. They created the first Futures Market, Mr. Landes. They would claim that there were trade deals pending in Spain or Afghanistan, and that they represented the foreign businessmen who needed the money quickly. The Celtic traders would then sell clay tablets called Ikons—from the Greek word *eikón*— that represented a future trade. An investor could buy an Ikon tablet at a discounted price, wait a few months, and then go back to the Celtic traders and trade the Ikon for two clay tablets that represented the completed trade. The investor could then redeem the two clay tablets at a currency exchange for full value. For example, the Celtic traders would tell a potential investor that they knew of a trade for tin that was worth four hundred grams of gold. The Celts always claimed the deal was in a far-away place like Afghanistan, and that it would take three months for the tin to be delivered, and they would always claim that the foreign businessman couldn't wait for the full payment for the tin and would accept a discounted payment. The Celts would show the investor an Ikon that described the deal. If the investor bought that story, the Celts would sell him the Ikon for three hundred grams of gold. The Ikon couldn't be redeemed until the supposed tin was delivered—that gave the Celts time to counterfeit the clay tablets that represented the fictitious trade. The investor would hold onto the Ikon for three months and then redeem the Ikon for the two clay tablets. He could then take the two clay tablets to a currency exchange and redeem them for four hundred grams of gold, and thus realize a profit of one hundred grams of gold from his initial investment. But if the investor didn't want to wait the three months, he could sell the Ikon to another investor for, say, three hundred and twenty-five grams of gold, and thus make an immediate profit of twenty-five grams of gold. And that's what most of the investors did. They would buy an Ikon from the Celtic traders and turn around and sell that Ikon to other investors. Well, the market for Ikons exploded. Everyone wanted to buy them and flip them for a profit. People were mortgaging their homes to get cash to buy Ikons. The Celtic traders could barely keep up with the demand. They were making more and more Ikons and, of course, more and more counterfeit clay tablets to support those Ikons. They were able to keep this ruse up for about fifteen years, during which time, in today's terms, the Celtic traders became multi-millionaires.

"But sometime after 1200 BC, it all came crashing down. The central bankers at the Temple realized that their currency exchanges were redeeming an ever-increasing number of contracts, but that the supply of copper and tin was flat. It made no sense. There were just too many contracts that had to be paid, and the Temple was running out of money, and they didn't know why. No one ever figured out that the Temple of Moriah had been flooded with worthless counterfeit clay tablets. The Celtic traders, however, realized that the jig was up, and they took their vast reserves of gold and went into hiding. Eventually, the Temple started to default on the contracts it had to pay. Investors suddenly lost confidence in the Temple and in the entire banking system. The Ikons became worthless. The word spread like wildfire, and there was a run on the bank like the world had never seen. But the damage was irreversible, and the Temple went bankrupt. Understand, the Temple of Moriah was *the central bank* of the entire Bronze Age civilization—it had created the entire economy of the Middle East—and when it failed, the fabric of society began to unravel. Without trade, there is no civilization! There was no liquidity left in the money system: no money to lend, no credit for new businesses, no money to pay employees, no money to pay mortgages or buy food. This affected every single country of the Mediterranean world. Everyone went bankrupt. Middle-class people were suddenly homeless, destitute, and angry... very, very angry. The world's biggest refugee population was created within a matter of months. It didn't matter who you were or what class of society you occupied— you were now broke and homeless, and this indescribable mass of people went on a rampage. It was a riot that lasted more than two years. They began to migrate, and as they traveled, they destroyed everything in their path: buildings, cities, temples... Even the Temple of Moriah was destroyed. They weren't Sea People; they were bankrupt people. And the Bronze Age didn't just collapse—it was ransacked and burned to the ground. From the Hittite cities to the north, all the way south through Assyria and Babylon, all the way east to Jerusalem and Canaan, everything was destroyed. But, by the time this army of refugees reached Egypt, they were beginning to run out of steam, and the Egyptians were finally able to defeat them. Egypt managed to survive, barely, but the rest of the Bronze Age civilization was completely destroyed. All because of the Celtic traders. The Celtic traders had essentially skimmed all of the gold out of civilization.

"Fast forward a hundred and sixty years or so, and King David of the Jews comes to power, and restores Jerusalem. Forty years later, King David's son, Solomon, becomes king and rebuilds the Temple of Moriah, only now he modestly calls it the Temple of Solomon. He wanted to make the temple an economic powerhouse again. He created new money regulations. Credit and letters of credit are restored, but strictly controlled. And guess who reappears? The Celtic traders, only now they are the chief money lenders, because they were the only ones who held onto their gold through the collapse of the Bronze Age, so they are the only ones who had money to lend. They were so important to King Solomon's plan to jumpstart the economy, that he makes the Celtic traders the protectors of the Temple of Solomon. They were known as the Knights of the Temple, a title that later evolved to Knights of Templar.

"So... just like the Italian mafia who came to your country, Mr. Landes, the Ancient Celts managed, over a period of two hundred years, to transform themselves from unscrupulous conmen to the most respected businessmen of their day. They no longer needed to counterfeit clay tablets at the Temple of Solomon, because now they were in charge of all the money-lending at the temple. They made their money off the high interest rates they charged. They walked around with their heads held high. You know that old joke about the golden rule, Mr. Landes? He who has the gold makes the rules... Well, the Celts were the wealth class of ancient Jerusalem, and no one could touch them. And they continued that way for the next six centuries. They survived every invasion of Jerusalem: the Greeks, the Romans... Remember the story about Jesus throwing the money lenders out of the temple? That was the Celts he was berating. He threw them out of the temple alright, but they returned to their money-lending stalls the very next day, and it was business as usual. Not even Jesus could stop them. They *owned* Jerusalem.

"But you know the problem with having too much gold, Mr. Landes? If you have too much money, you have nowhere to put it. The Celts had nowhere to invest their gold reserves because they *were* the bank. There were no bigger banks where they could deposit or invest their wealth. So, they bought up as much land as they could, and built secret vaults underneath their houses to store their gold. They built currency exchanges in Spain and stored some of their gold there. All the while they were building up their reputation as the pious Knights of Templar, they were shipping tons of gold back to the British Isles to fund wars and expansions of Celtic territory into Germany. But they still had more money than they knew what to do with.

"But the party ended in 614 AD when, in a sudden and violent attack, the Persians captured Jerusalem. The businessmen of Jerusalem thought they could negotiate with these Muslims the same way they had negotiated with every previous invasion, but they were wrong. These Muslim warriors had no use for the Celts and their pseudo-religious Knights of Templar act. In fact, the Persians hated the Celts more than they hated the Jews. The siege of Jerusalem lasted three weeks, and the Persians killed over 60,000 inhabitants. The Celts had to flee Jerusalem with what gold they could carry with them. And they couldn't return because the Muslims maintained control over Jerusalem for the next four hundred and eighty-five years."

Matzel gave a little laugh. "As you might imagine, that pissed the Celts off to no end, because they had to leave behind these huge reserves of gold buried in secret vaults under their houses in Jerusalem. They tried negotiating with the Persians but to no avail. The Celts were forbidden to re-enter the city. And, to add insult to injury, in 711 AD, the Muslim Moors from Northern Africa conquered Spain, and took control of the Celtic currency exchanges, so the

Celts lost the gold they had stored there too. Yes, the Celts were very pissed. Of course, they were no longer purebred Celts by then—that bloodline had been mixed with so many other groups. They were simply known as the Knights of Templar now, but they still had their skills at organizing, at finance, and for using religion to achieve their ends. They used the gold they had carried out of Jerusalem to finance the Reconquista to take back Spain. They paid the Spanish King Alfonso VI to attack the city of Toledo, which the Moors had turned into their capitol of Spain. In 1085 AD, after a long siege, King Alfonso captured Toledo and drove the Muslims out. Recapturing Toledo gave the Knights of Templar hope that they could recapture Jerusalem. They also regained control over their banks in Toledo and the gold inside those banks. The Knights of Templar moved their headquarters to Toledo and began pressuring the Pope to declare war on Jerusalem. It was the Knights of Templar, Mr. Landes, who organized and financed the Crusades to take back Jerusalem. The Crusades had nothing to do with religion—religion was just a front that the Knights of Templar used to convince the Pope to declare the First Crusade... and all the Crusades that followed... just so the Templars could re-enter Jerusalem to get their gold. The love of money, as Paul the Apostle once wrote, is the root of all evil."

Matzel paused and shook his head. "Well, you must forgive me, Mr. Landes. History has always held such a fascination for me, and I can talk for hours, but let me get to the point. The Knights of Templar wanted to return to Jerusalem because that's where their gold was buried. But as the Crusades wore on, the Templars had to raise more and more money to continue funding them. So, what did they do? They reverted to their old trick of selling futures. They raised money by selling the promise of paying back investors with gold—gold that was buried in Jerusalem. And they funded the entire Crusades this way—in the same way that they raised money centuries earlier in Jerusalem: by selling Ikons that promised a gold return. Only this time, they didn't make these Ikons out of clay tablets. They used a much smaller and easier-to-carry Ikon—silver coins. By this time, the Knights of Templar had built the Castle of San Servando and were using it as a bank and a mint. They had huge presses there where they manufactured these tokens out of silver with a code indicating the amount of gold each Ikon could be redeemed for once the Crusaders liberated Jerusalem. The code represented a promise to pay twenty times the value of the coin once Jerusalem was liberated. The Knights of Templar called these Ikons 'San Servando Righteous Investments,' which in Spanish is *San Servando Inversiones Justas*, and so these Ikons became known simply as Justas coins. And this wasn't a cult secret—this was an open market sale. The people of the day knew what was going on. They knew the Knights of Templar had gold in Jerusalem. They knew what the code represented. And, like all speculators, they bought these Justas coins hoping to make a quick profit because they expected the Crusaders to win a quick and easy victory. Plus, of course, they were doing this for the glory of God and the Pope and all that bullshit, but it was still greed that made the people buy those Ikons.

"But... as you know... the Crusades dragged on for two centuries. Eventually, the Knights of Templar *were* able to re-enter Jerusalem, dig up most of their gold, and were rich again. But then, they made a fateful decision. They decided not to repay their investors. All of the young men who had bought Justas coins as an investment had long since died. And as for those people who had inherited Justas coins from their fathers, well, the Knights of Templar simply claimed that the Justas coins had not been an investment, but a donation to the Crusades and to the glory of God. That was a lie, of course. The Knights of Templar had clearly sold the Justas coins as an investment, and now they were simply refusing to pay. In their defense, the Templars had no choice, because they had sold more Justas coins than all the gold they had buried in Jerusalem. The Justas coin business had been so profitable to the Knights of Templar that they had oversold them. Greed, Mr. Landes, always goes hand in hand with fraud."

Matzel paused and looked at Dan.

"Are you seeing a pattern here, Mr. Landes? Perhaps you are wondering if the modern-day Todo organization that you know—this confederacy of thieves that David Ortega and Dimitrios Barkoxe chose to die for—has any connection to the Knights of Templar; whether Todo might, in some fantastic way, have some connection with the original Celts that caused the collapse of the Bronze Age; whether the Todo debit card is in any way similar to the Celtic counterfeit letters of credit; whether the digital TodoCoin might be similar to the worthless Justas coins that the Knights of Templar sold with such religious zeal to fund the Crusades just so they could return to Jerusalem and dig up their gold. Well, the answer is yes! The fact is... the Knights of Templar never went away. Their descendants, trained in the same deceits, walk among us today. Of course, they don't call themselves the Knights of Templar anymore. They call themselves the board of directors of the Todo Bank, but they are, in fact, members of a secret society still engaged in fraud and deceit. That's the thing about wealth and power, Mr. Landes: once you have it, you never want to let it go. And organizations behave just like individuals. They repeat what has worked for them before. The business you know today as Todo is, in fact, run by the descendants of the Knights of Templar. Their reach is worldwide, but their base of operations is right here in Toledo. And this Todo debit card that they constantly promote is just a dressed-up version of the clay tablet Ikons that they were hawking three thousand years ago. And this so-called crypto-currency that they are selling—this TodoCoin—is just a digital version of the silver Justas coins they sold in Spain to finance the Crusades. They are running the same frauds that has worked for them for centuries. The Todo debit card is a counterfeit letter of credit, and the TodoCoin is a complete and utter fraud, Mr. Landes. And Todo is just as dangerous to our civilization as their ancestors were to the Temple of Moriah. They are skimming all the money off their debit cards and off their TodoCoins. People think they are depositing their dollars into the Todo Bank when they open up an account and get a Todo debit card. They think they are depositing their dollars in some safe and secure crypto-wallet when they buy TodoCoins, but it's all illusion. The Todo Bank and the Todo crypto-wallets are just metaphors, Mr. Landes, just smoke and mirrors. There is no actual bank or wallet. All those deposits are converted to gold the instant Todo gets their hands on them. And all that gold is hidden in secret vaults all over Europe. And why? Why this desperate push to open Todo bank accounts and sell TodoCoins? Why this massive hoarding of gold?"

Matzel stared at Dan in a way that gave Dan a shiver.

"Because the Todos are recreating the collapse of credit that they engineered in 1177 AD," Matzel explained. "Say what you want about end times, Mr. Landes, but the fact is, the Ancient Celts did very, very well in 1177 AD when the Bronze Age collapsed. Some people, and some organizations, want chaos, because they are at their best in chaotic times. When the Bronze Age collapsed in 1177 AD, the Celts were the only ones with gold, the *only ones!* They hunkered down until the dust settled and then emerged as the Knights of Templar. They were only ones who could restart the world economy at the Temple of Solomon, the only ones with gold, the only ones with liquidity. They became the ruling class, the rich elite. And the modern-day Todo organization wants that again. They want the world's economy to collapse, so that they can emerge on top after the dust has settled."

Matzel was quiet for a moment. Dan thought about what Matzel had said. Was there any truth to this, he wondered, or was he simply dealing with a paranoid conspiracy-theorist madman? Then he asked Matzel, "So how does all this connect to Ricardo's maps and these coins of yours that everyone seems to want?"

Matzel smiled. "Ah yes, the maps and the coins. That all relates to the Gran Ventura, and in order to explain that, I have to tell you a bit more about the Knights of Templar. Where was I? Oh yes... so, by 1300 AD, the Crusades were over, and the Knights of Templar were sitting pretty. They had recouped their gold from Jerusalem; they had annulled the debt that the Justas coins represented; and they now owned almost all of the currency exchanges in Spain and France. They were richer than ever. But they were no longer admired. In fact, they were roundly hated for refusing to redeem those Justas coins. People thought that it was not very Christian of the Templars to renege on a religious debt. Some governments thought this as well. France, in particular, did not approve, because the government of France had been foolish enough to invest in those Justas coins. And so, in 1307, King Philip IV of France declared that the Knights of Templar were blasphemers, seized all their currency exchanges in France, and burned many of their leaders at the stake. The remaining Templars fled to Spain. There, they found protection under King Alfonso IV. In Spain, the Templars weren't quite so hated because they had helped the ancestral King Alfonso recapture Toledo, but also because the Spanish government had never invested in any Justas coins. Nonetheless, the Knights of Templar decided it would be best to change their name. After all, there were no more temples for them to protect. They needed a new identity. Since they were still in the money changing and loan business, they formed a corporation in Spain called the Table of All Exchanges, or in Spanish, La Tabla de Todos los Intercambios, which over time, simply became known as Los Todos, and business went on as usual. Are you seeing the connection now, Mr. Landes?

"The Los Todos organization was organized similar to your US Mafia, in that there were different families that controlled different enterprises. Some ran legitimate banks; some ran loansharking services; some ran churches; each family had their specialty. One of the Todo families, the Barkoxe family, ran the various gambling rackets: lotteries, betting, casinos, and the like. Yes, indeed, Mr. Landes, the Barkoxe family—the forefathers of our late friend Dimitrios Barkoxe. They had escaped France and resettled here in Toledo. King Philip IV of France had seized much of the Barkoxe family's gold back in France, and the Barkoxes were looking to rebuild their wealth in Spain. They hadn't forgotten the old Knights of Templar methods of raising money using Ikons, and so, in 1320, with the blessings of the rest of the Todo organization, the Barkoxe family invented a new type of Ikon. Do you know what that was? It was a treasure hunt game, Mr. Landes—a simple, stupid, idiotic treasure hunt game. It started off small. The Barkoxe Todos would hide a small amount of gold in a treasure chest somewhere in Spain; then they would mint these silver tokens called venturas, and they minted them in the same Castle of San Servando that their ancestors used to mint the Justas coins of the Crusades. But these venturas were different. The Barkoxes didn't mint them out of pure silver. They used a copper and silver mixture called billon that looked like silver but was ninety percent copper. They had no value by themselves; their only value was in the game. Each ventura had a different design and a different shape. If someone managed to collect all the different venturas and arrange them on a table in the right order, like a jigsaw puzzle, they would see that the different designs on the venturas formed a map on one side and had clues on the other side. And if they figured out the clues and followed the map, they might find the treasure. But the operative word here is 'might,' as the map was both complicated and purposefully vague. There were only one hundred different ventura coins to each map, but the Barkoxe Todos minted thousands of copies of these Ikons, and sold them for the modern equivalent of ten dollars each, so it was a very profitable business. The whole Todo organization got behind this project. But of course, the game was rigged. There were key pieces that you needed to solve the map. Those key venturas had the most important clues, and each map had four or five of these key pieces. And the Todos only minted one of each of these key pieces, in order to make the game more difficult, and to make the game last longer, so they could sell more venturas.

"Well, these ventura games turned out to be wildly popular. Because the venturas were minted in the Castle of San Servando, these treasure games became known as the San Servando games, and the clues on the backside of the coins were called the San Servando code. Everyone wanted to solve the San Servando code. People all over Spain were buying and trading these Ikons, trying to accumulate enough clues to solve the puzzle. Every time someone would figure out one of the maps and dig up one of the treasures, the demand for more games soared. And with each new game, the Todos would increase the amount of treasure they hid and raise the price of each ventura coin they sold, until 1346, when they held their biggest contest ever—which they called the Gran Ventura. They hid one hundred and twenty bars of gold. Do you know how much gold that is, Mr. Landes? One hundred and twenty bars of gold weighs about two tons. But because gold is so heavy, two tons takes up less than four cubic feet. Very easy to hide. But, in today's market, that amount of gold is worth over one hundred and thirty million dollars."

Matzel's eyes seemed to glisten. He paused and looked at Dan. "And did anyone ever dig up the treasure of the Gran Ventura? No, Mr. Landes, because one year later, in 1347, the game was abruptly halted. In fact, everything in Europe came to a grinding halt. That year, Mr. Landes, 1347, was the year that the Black Death came to Europe, the most devastating plague the world had ever seen. Over twenty-five million people died. Bodies littered the streets. Europe lost sixty percent of its population.

"Spain was hit fast and hard, and the overcrowded cities were hit the hardest. The wealthy fled to isolated villas in the mountains, hoping to escape the horror of the plague. And those fleeing included the remaining Todos and their families. Some of their diaries survived all of these centuries, and in those diaries, the Todos bemoan the fact that they had to leave the buried treasure of the Gran Ventura behind. Because the biggest irony of all, Mr. Landes, was that the secret of the Gran Ventura, the location of the treasure, had only been known to the top two leaders of the Todos, and the Black Death had killed both of them. So the location of the Gran Ventura treasure was completely lost to the remaining Todos who survived the Black Death. That plague lasted four years and decimated everything, including the Todo organization, and afterwards, the remaining Todos had to scramble like everyone else to find venturas, in an effort to try and accumulate a complete set of one hundred tokens to have the map and all the clues so they could find the very treasure that their own organization had buried. For almost seven hundred years, the descendants of the Todos have been trying to regroup and solve the mystery of the location of the Gran Ventura treasure, but they never had all the clues, because they never could accumulate all one hundred venturas. That is... until now. And that brings us to our mutual friend, Ricardo."

Matzel turned and gestured to Ricardo that it was his turn to speak.

"Well, as I started to tell you, Dan, I had these three old Spanish coins from my days in Madrid, and last year I took them to Matzel to get them appraised. I didn't know it at the time, but one of those three coins wasn't a coin—it was one of the ventura Ikons made by the Todos. I knew it was unusual—it had an odd shape—but I just thought was just an old weird Spanish coin. I had no idea what it really was. But when I showed it to Matzel, well, he got so excited. He offered me five thousand dollars for it. Back then, of course, I had no idea that he had been working on the riddle of the Gran Ventura for five decades."

"I couldn't believe it when he walked into my shop," Matzel said. "He walked in holding one of the rarest venturas. I had been searching the entire world for it, and it was right in Villa Rosario the whole time."

Matzel began to laugh. "Life is ironic, don't you agree, Mr. Landes? Always trying to trip us up. The rarest ventura had been under my nose all this time."

"So... you have all one hundred Ikons?" Dan asked.

Matzel's smile lighted up his face. He nodded his head, and said, "Thanks to Ricardo... I do."

Ricardo continued, "There's a little bit more to it. You see, Dan, fifteen years ago, back in Europe, David Ortega and Matzel used to be partners. As a young man, Matzel had inherited eleven venturas from his father, who was a coin dealer in Berlin. His father had opened a chain of coin shops in Europe after World War II. Lots of families were pawning old coins back then, simply to raise money to buy food, so his father had access to a constant supply of old coins to examine. Matzel's father had learned about the treasure of the Gran Ventura from *his* father, who had been a coin dealer in Morocco. Call it a family obsession. Anyway, Matzel had inherited eleven venturas from his father. And, early in his career, he managed to find five more. So, he had a total of sixteen venturas. Then he met David Ortega in Amsterdam. Ortega was in Amsterdam attending coin shows, also looking for venturas...”

“He was a filthy mongrel Todo,” Matzel interrupted.

Ricardo sighed. “The Todos tried to keep their bloodlines very pure—they thought they were royalty, God's chosen people. Ortega wasn't descended from the original Todos. But his family had worked with the Todos as lawyers for generations, so Ortega was trusted by the pure-bred Todos, which turned out to be a mistake. They made him an advisor, a consigliere, to Todo's board of directors, where he began to embezzle money from them undetected. Eventually, they put him on the board of You-Bank where he continued his embezzlement activities until You-Bank collapsed.

“He was extremely greedy,” Matzel interrupted.

“Anyway, Ortega had managed to accumulate twenty-four venturas,” Ricardo continued. “So Matzel and Ortega put their venturas together for a total of forty pieces, enough to make a good portion of the map, almost half, but it still wasn't enough to make any sense out of the clues. But Ortega had money, and he offered to fund a joint venture to travel Europe together searching every trade show and every coin shop, searching for more venturas.”

“The problem with the venturas is not in finding them,” Matzel said. “The Todos minted thousands of them. You can find them if you look hard enough. The problem is finding the right ones. The most important pieces are very rare.”

“Anyway,” Ricardo said, “David Ortega and Matzel scoured Europe for almost five years, and they managed to collect six more venturas which meant that together they possessed forty-six of these Ikons. Then they met Dimitrios Barkoxe in Barcelona.”

"Another filthy Todo, but a purebred one," exclaimed Matzel.

"Matzel is right about that," Ricardo said. "Dimitrios could trace his family tree back almost eight hundred years. He was definitely a Todo. And his ancestors had gathered and passed down the line a huge number of venturas. When Ortega and Matzel met him, Dimitrios had thirty venturas... actually, Dimitrios had more, but some were duplicates of ones that Ortega and Matzel already had. But Dimitrios had thirty venturas that Ortega and Matzel didn't have."

"I never trusted him," Matzel said, "because he never trusted us. He always acted like we were going to steal his venturas. He only showed them to us once, when he was fully armed, and even then, only for a few minutes."

"But he finally did show his venturas to Ortega and Matzel," Ricardo said. "He had to. None of them alone had enough of the tokens to form the map. So, the three of them agreed to collaborate. And so, one night in Barcelona, they sat down, all of them armed, and put all their venturas together."

"Together, we had seventy-six venturas, three-fourths of the map," Matzel explained. "We put all of the pieces together, and all three of us just stared at the map in awe."

"As the three men studied the map, some of the clues started to make sense," Ricardo said.

"Yes, it almost came together," Matzel said, "We could tell that the treasure of the Gran Ventura had to have been hidden in Toledo—we didn't know where exactly, but we could tell it was near the Castle of San Servando. We agreed to meet again the next night, to look at the map again, and to make plans to go to Toledo and scout the area out. But then, the next night, we had a... a small disagreement."

"They had a major fight," Dan corrected Matzel. "Ortega pulled his gun and tried to steal all the venturas from both of them."

Matzel made a gesture with his hands and said, "And I was forced to go into hiding."

"Why?" Dan asked.

"Because Matzel shot Ortega," said Ricardo.

"It was self-defense," Matzel protested. "Unfortunately, he didn't die."

"Wait! What happened?" asked Dan.

"After Dimitrios showed up for the meeting, Ortega pulled his gun, trying to rob both of them," Ricardo explained, "but Matzel knocked over a lamp, and then shot Ortega," Ricardo said. "Dimitrios tried to pull his gun, but Matzel was already aiming right at him. Matzel grabbed all three satchels of venturas and ran out of the building.

"Wait! Matzel stole all the coins?!" Dan asked.

"I only did what they were trying to do to me," Matzel exclaimed. "I thought Ortega was dead, and the dead have no use for money. As for Barkoxe, I should have shot him, too. It has been my life's biggest regret."

"Anyway, Matzel left Barcelona," Ricardo explained, "eventually found his way to Panama, changed his name to Matzel Davis, opened a book and coin shop, and tried to live under the radar.

"And his original name was... Nassim Kahil?" Dan asked.

"At your service," Matzel said and gave a little bow.

"Jesus fuck," Dan said and shook his head

Ricardo continued, "By this time, the internet had grown so much that Matzel found he could search for coins online. The internet was a tremendous advantage and allowed him to remain anonymous. Over the next nine years, he managed to locate and buy twenty-three more venturas, giving him ninety-nine pieces to the map."

Matzel smiled broadly. "And then, the Magnificent One smiled on me and sent me Ricardo with the last of the rarest venturas."

"On this map, there are four rare pieces, and each one shows key information, without which, the map is incomplete—useless," said Ricardo. "Matzel had three of these key pieces. Evidently, I had the fourth, and last, rarest Ikon. With the venturas he had accumulated... well, *stolen*, from David Otega and Dimitrios, Matzel almost had the complete map, but he needed my ventura to make it complete. When I first showed it to him, he almost shit his pants.”

“It was so beautiful,” Matzel said.

“He immediately offered me five thousand dollars for it. I was suspicious, because I didn’t know him well at the time. I thought if it was worth that much to him, it must be worth much more in the open market.”

Matzel shook his head. “I was so excited,” he said, “that I let my greed get the upper hand. I had to have that coin.”

“But eventually, as I got to know him,” Ricardo continued, “I began to trust him. He didn’t tell me the whole story of the Gran Ventura at first. He only told me that there was an ancient treasure map made out of old coins. I thought it had something to do with pirates or something... anyway eventually I agreed to share my ventura with him. I remember the day he took me into a back room of his bookstore. He had all of his coins fitted together on a table, like a jigsaw puzzle, and we placed my coin into the one open space, to form the complete map.”

“So beautiful,” Matzel said.

“But we still had to make sense out of it,” Ricardo said. “Even with all the pieces, the map was still a riddle. Some of the venturas were worn down, the clues were mysterious, and the map was crudely drawn. We had to figure out the clues, unravel the puzzle. That took us months. I began to draw different maps in my notebook depending on how we were interpreting the clues. And as we worked on the puzzle, he began to tell me more and more of the history of the Todos and the Gran Ventura, always telling me just enough to get me to help him.” Ricardo glanced sideways at Matzel. “I didn’t find out all the details until recently.”

“You were on a need-to-know basis,” Matzel said sheepishly.

“Perhaps,” Ricardo said sarcastically, “if he had shared the whole story with me from the beginning, I wouldn’t have mentioned to Silas Edwards that I had was working on an old treasure story that had to do with the Knights of Templar. Unbeknownst to any of us, Silas knew David

Ortega, and Silas must have mentioned it to him. Silas began prying me for information. One day, Silas stupidly asked me if I knew of anyone named Nassim Kahil. I lied and said I did not. But that's when I figured out that Silas had been lying to me all along. I knew that Matzel real name was Nassim Kahil, but I had never mentioned that to Silas, so there's no way he could have known that name. Of course, Ortega had been searching for Matzel for over ten years. So sent Jacques Foucher and his crew to Panama to see if Matzel was, in fact, Nassim Kahil."

"That Foucher fuck was another filthy mongrel Todo," spat out Matzel. "I spotted him right away. I saw he was following Ricardo. I told Ricardo to go ahead to Toledo and that I would take care of this punk. I set a trap for him, but things did not go as planned. I did not realize Foucher had brought others with him."

"And that trap was leaving your store unlocked so he would walk in?" Dan asked.

"Exactly," Matzel said. "I knew Foucher was following me, so I made a very obvious exit out of my house that Friday night after I met you, and drove to my shop, so Foucher could see me. Then I left the front door open and turned off the alarm system and waited for him to enter. I didn't know about Foucher's companions. My plan was to shoot Foucher and claim it was a burglary, but he brought those two other men. I let them ransack one room and then I popped up and shot them, but... Foucher got away."

"*You* shot both men?" Dan asked.

"No, I shot the big man first, but Foucher shot the other one," Matzel laughed, "shot him in the back."

"Why did Foucher shoot him?" Dan asked.

"Because he's stupid," Matzel said. "Foucher was aiming at me but hit his own man instead. Ha. Todos are so stupid. Anyway, I was just about to call the police, to report a burglary, when I got an alert on my cell phone that my house was being burglarized. My home security camera system, you see, is tied into my phone. I looked at my phone and saw Dimitrios in my house. Imagine my surprise—Dimitrios in *my* house! He was tearing the place apart, looking for my venturas. He thought I had hidden the coins in my house, but of course, I had them safely hidden in my office. But this changed everything. I had to grab my venturas and run. I drove straight to the airport and flew here to join my new partner: Ricardo."

Matzel beamed at Ricardo and patted him on the shoulder.

Dan sat there nodding his head, trying to digest all that he had been told. "So... this treasure, this Gran Ventura, is buried in the Castle of San Servando?" he asked

"Oh, no," Matzel laughed. "Definitely not. I mean, Barkoxe might have hoped it was. He might have hoped he would stumble across it while he was digging, but it's not there."

"So why were they digging up the floor of the castle?"

"Ha! They want to turn the castle back into a bank," Matzel explained. "As I said, back in the early 1300s, the San Servando Castle was their main bank and mint in Toledo, and they are living out some mad fantasy that they can return to those days. But the main reason that they are digging up the floor to install a huge underground vault where they can store their gold. But this vault is not for the gold they are currently skimming off TodoCoin and the Todo debit cards. No, Todo already has plenty of hidden vaults all over Europe that they are using for that gold. No, the vault that they are building under the San Servando Castle is a special vault. It will be used just to store the gold that they plan to steal from Zimbabwe."

"Zimbabwe?" said Dan. "Oh yeah, I read about this—the Oro coin."

"Exactly," Matzel said. "Zimbabwe desperately wants to adopt the Oro Coin as a way to control their inflation. Their own currency is virtually worthless. The World Bank won't loan them any more money. They owe so much money to China and Russia that if their economy goes bankrupt, China and Russia will own all their land—and there's more gold in the hills of Zimbabwe than any other country in the world, almost thirteen million tons underground. But they can't get to it. They don't have the capital to open up new mining operations. They're totally fucked. But Todo has promised to solve all their economic problems by replacing their currency with the digital Zimbabwe Oro Coin and administering their economy for them. In return, Todo gets to create the world's first crypto-currency backed by gold. Todo is going to finance their gold mines. And the only catch is that Zimbabwe has to agree to store their gold with Todo. And where will all that gold be stored? In Toledo, Mr. Landes, in the vault underneath the Castle of San Servando."

"And how much gold are we talking about here?" Dan asked.

"The current contract between Todo and Zimbabwe is for five hundred and eighty tons of gold to be placed under Todo's control," Matzel said.

Dan gave a low whistle.

"That's almost forty billion dollars' worth of gold," Matzel said. "Ironic, isn't it, Mr. Landes, that Dimitrios would risk his life for the treasure of the Gran Ventura, a mere one hundred and thirty million dollars worth of gold, when he was about to inherit forty billion dollars' worth of gold from Todo's scam of Zimbabwe."

Dan nodded and said, "So what happens now?"

"Now?" Matzel said. "Well, we go dig up the treasure of the Gran Ventura and disappear into the night like the thieves that we are, but we will be rich thieves, Mr. Landes. One hundred and thirty million dollars of gold will buy a lifetime of sweet anonymity."

"So, you've solved this... this map, this treasure map?" Dan asked.

Matzel and Ricardo looked at each other and then both nodded together. "We think so, Mr. Landes," Matzel said. "In fact, we are headed there tonight. Would you be interested in joining us?"

Dan stared off into space. His head was spinning, but he considered Matzel's offer. He didn't want to say yes. He didn't want anything more to do with Matzel, but he had come so far he had to know how this was going to end. He sighed, slid the gun into jacket pocket and said, "Sure, why not?"

"Excellent, Mr. Landes, excellent. We can use the extra muscle. I have rented a heavy-duty cargo van. It's parked down the street. It's got a good payload, but we may need to make several trips. Well, gentlemen, there is no time like the present," Matzel said and stood up. "Let's go."

CHAPTER THIRTY-TWO

Matzel drove the large cargo van, with Dan and Ricardo sitting on the bench seat beside him. Dan sat in the middle, scrunched between the two. The suspension in the van was stiff, and the ride was loud and bumpy.

"Where are we going? Dan shouted at Matzel.

"To an old, abandoned Templar House," Matzel explained. "During the Crusades, the Templars built a number of cheap hotels and boarding houses—more like barracks, really—where they would house soldiers on their way to fight for Jerusalem. Back in those days, these hostels were called Templar Houses, and they were all clustered around churches. This one is near the old Iglesia de San Miguel el Alto. That church was abandoned in the 1800s, and this particular Templar House is barely standing."

The van hit a bump that lifted everyone on the front bench seat. Dan almost hit his head on the roof.

"Is it far?" he shouted at Matzel.

"No, maybe five minutes away, on the southeastern part of the central district."

"I have a bunch of questions," Dan shouted. "If Barkoxe had the maps, how come *he* didn't go to this Templar House?"

"What maps?" Matzel asked.

"Ricardo's maps. I found them in Ricardo's apartment, and Silas asked me to send them to him. That's how this whole thing started. But Barkoxe broke into my apartment and stole them."

"The maps in Ricardo's notebooks? Those drawings?" Matzel asked.

"Yes."

Matzel started laughing hysterically. "Oh, that's funny! Those maps are useless!" he said between laughs. They were just crude sketches that Ricardo and I made when we were trying to figure out the coins. We didn't even divine the true directions on the coins until recently. Oh, that's funny. That just goes to show how stupid Todos are."

The van hit another bump.

"Alright," Dan said, "let me ask you another question. Barkoxe said that the gold from the Gran Ventura was going to be the first deposit in his new vault inside the Castle of San Servando. If Todo is getting five hundred and eighty tons of gold from Zimbabwe, why do they need the two tons of gold from the Gran Ventura?"

"Todo wants that gold to jumpstart the Oro Coin," Matzel replied. "With every Ponzi scheme you have to have some capital to pay back the very first investors. Remember, you have to own TodoCoins in order to buy the Zimbabwe Oro Coins. Some investors stocked up on TodoCoins while they were cheap. As soon as the Oro Coins become available, those investors are going to buy Oro Coins and trade them in immediately to get gold to make a quick profit. Zimbabwe won't ship any gold to Toledo until they are sure that adopting the Oro Coin as their currency will save their economy, so Todo needs gold to pay those initial investors until Zimbabwe starts shipping gold. But, as soon as investors are convinced they can get gold easily, greed will take over, and everyone will keep investing and reinvesting in TodoCoin. Nobody will want to cash out because the value of the TodoCoin will keep rising, and nobody ever wants to cash out too early. Todo will use that success to convince more and more countries to adopt TodoCoin as a valid currency. Eventually, when Todo has bled as much gold out of Zimbabwe as they can, something will happen to cause the Oro Coin to drop. Then, Todo will come up with some excuse de-peg TodoCoin from Oro Coin so they don't have to pay anyone in gold. Remember, Todo's only goal is to accumulate gold. As soon as someone invests in TodoCoin, Todo skims that investment and buys gold, leaving the buyer with just a digital receipt. If TodoCoin becomes accepted worldwide—a true universal cryptocurrency—then, when it finally collapses—which it will, eventually—then the entire world economy will collapse. And Todo will be the only organization with a stockpile of gold, with no debts or obligations. It'll be like the collapse of the Bronze Age all over again. Millions will be starving and homeless. Entire countries will become migrating armies. Wars will break out everywhere. Everything we know today will be destroyed. And when the dust settles, Todo will emerge, not as the Knights of Templar, but as the Knights of the New World Order."

Dan thought about this for a moment, then asked, "Do you think Todo will convince the world to adopt the TodoCoin?"

"They're well on their way," Matzel replied. "It's available worldwide; an estimated five hundred million people already use it; investors have poured almost ten billion dollars into it; it's been adopted as an official alternative currency in four countries, including Panama; seven other countries are considering legalizing it... Even China, which has banned bitcoin, has said that it might allow TodoCoin if Todo is successful with this Oro Coin project. Todo has convinced the world that a digital currency is somehow real if its value is backed by gold. It sounds good, but it's a fraud. It's the same fraud that Todo has run over and over, for three thousand years. People just never learn, Mr. Landes; they never learn."

Matzel turned down a deserted street, parked and turned the engine off. The silence startled Dan.

"So... so, how do we stop Todo?" Dan asked.

Matzel turned and looked at Dan with a puzzled expression. "Stop Todo? You can't. Todo is huge; it's worldwide. It's too big to stop. Whatever is going to happen is going to happen. The best we can do is to stockpile as much gold as we can so that *we* are protected when the collapse comes!"

Matzel opened his car door and stepped down onto the pavement.

"Come on," he said.

CHAPTER THIRTY-THREE

Matzel had been right about this old Templar House. It was barely standing. The entire neighborhood looked completely abandoned, but this building looked the worse. Dan wondered if it had been through an earthquake, maybe several earthquakes.

Matzel grabbed a flashlight and a large crowbar from behind the driver's seat and led the way to the back side of the house, with Ricardo and Dan following. In the back of the house, hidden by overgrown shrubs, was a stairwell of three steps that led down to a basement entrance. The door to the basement was partially off its hinges. Matzel pushed it aside, and the three men entered.

Dan whispered to Ricardo, "Have you been here before?"

"Not inside," Ricardo said. "Matzel and I drove by a few days ago to scope it out, then we had to go back and study the coins to be sure this was the place."

Matzel switched on the flashlight and handed the crowbar to Ricardo. Matzel and Ricardo walked down a short hallway, with Dan following. The hallway opened up into a large room. Matzel shined the flashlight around the room. Several internal walls had collapsed. Parts of the roof were missing. The floor was littered with pieces of broken tile and stone.

"Over there," Ricardo said, pointing to a corridor that led off this large room. Matzel nodded and headed down the corridor. Ricardo and Dan followed, picking their way through the rubble. Then they came to a T-intersection of two hallways.

Matzel looked at Ricardo and asked, "Left, then right?"

"Correct," Ricardo said, and the three men started down the left hallway. The hallway came to another T-intersection. Matzel took the right passage.

They walked about thirty feet. Then the passage came a massive solid door.

"This must be it," Matzel said, shining his flashlight and examining the door. There was nothing to grab onto to open it, no handle or lock or even a keyhole. It was made from old wooden beams, held tight together by iron plates. Matzel tried pressing against it, but the door was clearly locked or bolted from the other side. Matzel slowly shined his flashlight all around the edges of the door. Dan could see that time and moisture from standing for centuries in the damp dark hallway had taken its toll. Black mold had eaten away at the wood, and had even invaded the mortar that held the stones of the wall to the doorframe. There was a time, Dan thought, that this door would have been impenetrable But not now. Too much time had passed.

Matzel handed his flashlight to Ricardo and took the crowbar. He tapped on the black mortar around one of the stones of the wall next to the doorframe. The mortar crumbled. Matzel worked at it for a few more minutes, knocking out pieces of mortar until he had enough space to wedge the straight claw end of the crowbar between the stone and the door frame. He pressed his weight against it. The door frame splintered. He turned the crowbar the other way around and applied all his weight against the stone. It began to move.

Matzel stopped, handed the crowbar to Ricardo and said, "That's how we'll do it. We need to bust pieces of the wall out and pry the door out from the frame. But I'm too old for this. You two will have to take turns on it."

Ricardo nodded and handed the flashlight to Matzel and took the crowbar.

Ricardo and Dan took turns chiseling away at the stones around the door frame and the frame itself. After about thirty minutes they had knocked out several stones from the wall and splintered the doorframe into several sections. After an hour, they busted a small hole through the wall, about chest high, next to the doorframe. Matzel took the flashlight and shined the light into the chamber behind the door.

Suddenly Matzel got excited. "I see what's holding the door," he said. "It's this wooden bar across the back of the door. It probably fits into two metal brackets bolted into the wall. We might be able to lift it up."

Matzel moved so that Dan and Ricardo could see where he was shining the flashlight. Then he handed the light to Ricardo and inserted the end of the crowbar into the small hole and levered against the wooden bar. The hole was small and he didn't have much room to move the crowbar, but he felt the wooden bar move just a little.

"We need to knock this stone and this stone out," he said, handing the crowbar back to Ricardo.

After another hour, Dan and Ricardo had knocked the two stones out. The hole was big enough so that Matzel could stick his whole hand through the wall.

"Here, give me the crowbar," he said. He levered the crowbar against the wooden bar and pressed his whole weight down on it. The wooden bar lifted an inch.

"Reach in and try to hold the bar up while I reposition the crowbar," Matzel grunted.

Ricardo reached through the hole and tried to hold the wooden beam up with the palm of his hand.

"Hurry," Ricardo said. "It's heavy and I can't hold it."

Matzel repositioned the crowbar and pressed his weight down on it again. The wooden bar went up another inch. Ricardo pushed his hand upward to hold it in position and grimaced. Matzel moved the crowbar back one more time and pressed downward. There was a sudden release to the crowbar, as Matzel fell to the ground, and a huge bang on the other side of the wall as the beam hit the floor.

"We did it!" Matzel exclaimed as he picked himself up and rubbed his wrist. Then Matzel looked at the door for a moment. He had an odd look on his face, almost a look of reverence, Dan thought.

Then Matzel gave the door a push. Nothing happened. Matzel pushed again, using both his hands and all his weight. Dan and Ricardo added their weight. The door began to move. But it didn't open on hinges. It just fell straight over with a thunderous crash. Dan realized that the door was never meant to open like a regular door. It was probably never meant to be open at all. The wall had been built around the door to hold it in place.

Matzel, Ricardo, and Dan stepped into the room, standing on the door they had just knocked over. Matzel shined his flashlight around the room through the thick dust that the falling door had kicked up. The room was empty, just four walls. Dan had expected something different.

But Matzel and Ricardo did not seem deterred. They seemed focused on the floor. Matzel was moving the flashlight beam back and forth across the floor in a grid pattern. Both men's heads followed the beam.

"There it is," Ricardo shouted, pointing at the edge of the circle of light. Both men stepped quick over to a stop in the middle of the room and just stared down. Ricardo squatted down and brushed the dust away from one of the floor tiles with his hand. Dan stepped over and looked to see what it was. It was a white and red tile, situated in the midst of a floor of brown tiles.

"This doesn't make sense," Matzel said. "The tile should be bigger, much bigger."

He shined the flashlight around the room. As far as Dan could see, all the tiles were the same size, about sixteen-by-sixteen inches, and this tile was the only tile that wasn't brown.

"This has to be it," Ricardo said. "Let's dig it out and see."

Matzel held the flashlight while Ricardo took the crowbar and, lifting his arms above his head, slamming the straight claw end into the grout around the white and red tile. Each bang of the crowbar echoed around the tiny room. The grout splintered and flew in all directions. Slowly, Ricardo was able to carve a trench around the tile. Finally, after about twenty minutes of hammering, he placed the bent claw end of the crowbar under the edge of the tile and began to pry it up. He repositioned the crowbar several times, and on the third try, the tile popped up and fell to the side with a loud clang.

Underneath the tile was a shallow hole. Matzel shined the flashlight down into it. Dan could see there was something shiny in the hole. Matzel handed the flashlight to Ricardo and then reached in and lifted the object out of the hole. It looked to Dan like a thin picture frame, but it was obviously heavy as Matzel was struggling to lift it. Dan strained his neck to see what it was. Matzel stood up, wiped the dust off the object, and said, "It's gold, but..."

"It's inscribed!" Ricardo exclaimed.

Matzel turned the object over in his hands. Dan could see that one side was smooth, but the other side seemed to have an inscription carved into it.

Matzel held the object to his face, took a deep breath, and blew hard against the inscribed side. Dust flew everywhere. He took out a small pocketknife and dug dirt out of the crevices of the carved words. Matzel blew several more times, looked at the object, and then set it down on the floor. All three men squatted down to look at it.

Dan had a better view now. He could see that this object was a gold tablet, approximately six by eight inches and maybe half an inch thick. It had words cut into one side.

"Hold the light at an angle," Matzel said to Ricardo, "so that the words make shadows."

When Ricardo held the flashlight at an angle, the shadows of the engraved letters made the words legible. Dan looked at the inscription. *Macte. Gran Venturam solvisti. Hanc tabulam redime pro praemio tuo apud Castrum Sancti Servandi.*

"It's Latin," Matzel said. "Hold on... here, move the light back and forth."

Dan could see that Matzel was slowly translating the words to himself, his lips moving silently.

Silence hung in the air as Dan and Ricardo waited for Matzel to read the inscription. Suddenly, Matzel fell back in a sitting position, holding his knees and just rocked back and forth. His mouth was open and his eyes seemed glazed over. Dan wondered if he was having a stroke.

"Fuck me, fuck me," Matzel said over and over as he rocked back and forth. "Fuck me."

He shook his head left and right, but then he began to laugh. Dan and Ricardo looked at each other.

"What does it say?" Ricardo asked Matzel

Matzel didn't answer. He just continued laughing.

"Matzel?" Ricardo asked.

"It's a coupon!" Matzel shouted. "A fucking coupon! You have to take this gold tablet to the Castle of San Servando to redeem the treasure! I can't believe I didn't foresee this! Of course the bloody Knights of Templar would hold onto their gold! Of course, they would use a coupon! Of course, it would be a tablet! I'm such an idiot! Oh my God!"

Matzel was laughing hysterically now. He rolled over on his side, still holding his knees, laughing, almost crying.

Dan and Ricardo just looked at him, not knowing what to do. Matzel was gasping for air now, between laughs. After a few minutes, he seemed to compose himself and catch his breath. He sat back up on the floor and said to Dan and Ricardo, "The inscription basically reads, 'Congratulations. You have solved the Gran Ventura. Please redeem this tablet for your prize at the Castle of San Servando.' That's all it says. Back in 1346, the castle of San Servando was Todo's main bank in Toledo. It was their mint, their lottery headquarters, their stronghold, their center of operations. The amount of gold in the Gran Ventura was too much to risk burying outside of their bank, so they simply buried this...this, this golden coupon... I just never saw this coming."

"Is the gold still there, at the castle?" Ricardo asked.

"No, no," Matzel said. "There's been so many renovations and restorations of that castle over the centuries, someone would have found it. No, when the Black Plague hit, the Todos took all their gold out of the bank and hightailed it to the mountains. No, my friends, I'm afraid the treasure of the Gran Ventura is gone."

Matzel picked up the gold tablet and stood up. He turned the tablet over in his hands and started to laugh again. Ricardo shined the flashlight on the tablet and all three men stood there looking at it, with Matzel laughing.

They were so intent on examining the gold tablet that they didn't notice a figure standing in the doorway of the chamber.

"Enjoying yourself, gentlemen?" came a female voice.

All three men turned and starred in the direction of the voice. There, standing in the doorway, holding a pistol in one hand and a small flashlight in the other, was Mariana Ibarra.

CHAPTER THIRTY-FOUR

"Mariana!" Matzel explained. "How good to see you. I see you you've arrived just in time, after all the hard work has been done, as usual."

"Don't be a smart-ass, you old fool," Mariana. "This time, *I've* got the gun."

"Yes, I see that," said Matzel, "but I was being sincere. You have arrived just in time. We were just about to carry the treasure of the Gran Ventura out of here." Matzel gave a little laugh.

Mariana took two steps, moving the flashlight back and forth on the three men, tilting it downward to the hole in the floor, and then to the tablet in Matzel's hand.

"Have you found it?" she asked with a certain tone of incredulity in her voice.

"Oh, yes," Matzel said, and laughed again. I have it all right here." He lifted the tablet up about an inch.

"What do you mean?" Mariana asked.

"Come over here and take a peek," Matzel said. "Your Latin was always good. You'll get quite a kick out of this."

Mariana didn't move. "What do you mean?" she asked again.

Ricardo spoke up. "We followed the map on the venturas and dug where it said. We found this gold tablet with an inscription."

"Come over here and take a look," Matzel said again.

"Just read it to me, Nassim," Mariana commanded.

"Of course, my dear," Matzel said. He lifted the tablet and read the inscription in Latin out loud.

Mariana was silent for what seemed like an eternity. The three men just stood there.

Finally, she said, "If you're shitting me, Nassim, I will put a bullet through your head."

"Come over here and read it for yourself," Matzel replied.

"Put it on the ground, and all three of you step back."

Matzel did as he was told, then all three men stepped backed up ten feet to the wall. Mariana stepped forward, keeping her gun and the flashlight on the men. When she got to the tablet, she moved it with her foot so that the inscription faced her. Then she hunched down, still keeping her flashlight, her eyes, and the gun on the men.

She moved the flashlight up and down from the men to the tablet and back to the men. But finally, she focused the flashlight on the tablet.

"Fuck," she said softly, and lowered her gun. She reached down and rubbed the tablet with the hand that held the flashlight. Finally, she stood up.

"I don't believe it," she said.

"Come back to my hotel, my dear," Matzel said. "I will give you all the venturas, and you can see for yourself. The coins are worthless to me now. You can have them. This is the exact spot that the coins show, and that gold tablet is the only treasure that is here."

"I still don't believe it," she said. "Twenty years..."

"Pfft," said Matzel. "Twenty years for you, but a whole lifetime for me... and for my father, and my father's father! All for naught!"

Mariana raised her gun again and pointed it at Matzel. "You know, Nassim, there are still people who would pay me a good sum to turn you over to them."

"True, my dear, but then, you'd have to kill these two innocent ones." Matzel gestured at Ricardo and Dan. "And that's not your style. But I tell you what I'll do, mi amor: I will let you take the tablet. It's about four kilograms of pure gold, probably worth a quarter of a million dollars. Not a lot, but more than you would get for me. Take it and go."

Mariana shined her flashlight on the tablet, then in the hole in the ground, then back to the men, then on the tablet again.

"Deal," she finally said, and then she bent down and, still holding the flashlight and the gun, managed to lift the tablet with both hands, and stood up.

"About those coins..." she said.

"I'm staying at the Alfonso Hotel. Come by later and you can have them," Matzel said.

Mariana nodded, then without another word, turned and left the room quickly.

Dan blew out a breath of air. "Whew, I was worried there," he said.

"You and me both," said Matzel. "Let's give her a minute to get out of the building, and then we can leave."

Ricardo picked up the crowbar and stuck it several times into the dirt in the hole. There was only dirt.

"What a waste," Ricardo said under his breath.

"But let's look at the bright side," Matzel responded. "We are alive, and Barkoxe and Ortega are dead, so all in all, it's been a good week."

"Are you absolutely sure that this is all there is?" Dan asked.

Matzel nodded. "Ricardo and I studied those coins carefully. There is no mistake. This is the place. That tablet was gold. That inscription was real. And that would be the exact trickster style of those Todos..."

Matzel looked around the room. "We can go now. I'll drop you both off at your respective hotels. I'm sure Mariana will be waiting at my hotel to collect the coins. She will want to see for herself... By the way, I would recommend that we all return to Panama as soon as possible. We could all fly out together. No point in hanging around. Yesterday's little incident at the castle will make Toledo a bit hot for a while."

The three men walked out of the room.

CHAPTER THIRTY-FIVE

The next afternoon, Matzel, Dan, and Ricardo were sitting in the waiting area of the Barajas Airport in Madrid. They had taken the train from Toledo that morning, and were now at the gate, waiting for their flight to Panama.

The three men sat away from the other passengers so they could talk freely.

"I have so many questions, Matzel," Dan said.

"Go ahead. We have time."

"You said that the Barkoxe family was *just one* family group in Todo," Dan said.

Matzel nodded yes.

"How big is the Barkoxe family, and how many families are in Todo?"

Matzel rubbed his chin. "I would say there are about two hundred purebred Barkoxes, and probably another three hundred employees and hangers-on. But they're a small family. The core of Todo is made up of fifteen purebred families, some of whom can trace their lineage all the way back to Jerusalem. The top two families go back even further, to the original British Isles. The heads of the fifteen families control Todo. In fact, the Italian mafia modeled their organization after the Todo family."

"Wow," said Dan. "And how big is Todo?"

"It's impossible to say," Matzel replied. "They are worldwide. They have so many subsidiaries, and own hundreds of companies in many countries, all under different names. They probably have over a million employees and subcontractors, but that's just a guess."

"Aren't you afraid of revenge?" Dan asked. "I mean, if Todo finds out that you were...um... *involved* with the incident at the castle, won't they come after you?'

Matzel shook his head no. "Revenge is not part of the Todo philosophy. They are only interested in wealth, nothing more. If they have to kill someone to get money, that's one thing. But a revenge killing... no, they won't do it. Besides, Dimitrios Barkoxe was kind of a renegade in the Barkoxe family, not particularly well liked. I'm not the only one who won't miss him. No, no, I'm more worried about Mariana Ibarra. She might be capable of revenge."

Dan frowned and looked at Matzel. "Why would she be out for revenge? You gave her a quarter of a million dollars."

"Maybe," Matzel said. "Maybe. I told her that tablet was pure gold, and it may be, but it might also be billon, that mixture of gold and copper, in which case it wouldn't be worth much at all. If it's gold, and she's happy, then I'm happy. But I don't want to stick around if it's not gold. The only reason I'm going back to Villa Rosario is to collect certain, um... investments that I have there, but I'll be moving on. The world is a big place, and it's important to reinvent yourself from time to time."

Dan thought about something Matzel had said the other night in the van, about the only defense against Todo was to stock up as much gold as possible. "You've got gold in Villa Rosario," Dan blurted out. "You've been stockpiling gold for ten years."

Matzel just smiled, then said, "Longer than that, my friend."

Dan thought about that for a moment, then asked. "What about the Oro Coin? How will Todo prime the pump on that project without the gold from the Gran Ventura?"

"Oh, Todo has plenty of other gold they can use. They were just looking for a windfall. No, the Oro Coin project will go on as scheduled. The end of the world will go on as scheduled. That's the one thing you can count on with history, my friend, it always repeats itself."

Ricardo spoke up. "But Zimbabwe is just one small country, and the Oro Coin might fail before it gets off the ground. I mean, there's been plenty of crypto-currency frauds that have collapsed without taking down the world's economy."

"True," Matzel said, "but Todo will try again, again, and again until they get it right. As long as there are people with money to lose, Todo will keep reinventing the Justas coin, or the ventura coin, or the TodoCoin or the Oro coin... People love lotteries; people love get-rich-quick schemes; people just love to gamble; it's in their blood. They love the thrill of anticipation; they love the fantasy of how they will spend their millions once the Knights of Templar conquer Jerusalem and liberate their gold; they love the idea of a treasure hunt, and the idea of finding free money; they love to dream of being singled out by God as the big winner... we just can't help it. Yes, the Oro Coin might be a flop. But if it is, I guarantee you Todo will just start another gold-backed digital currency. It's too good of a racket to give up."

"I don't know," Ricardo said. "The world's economy is pretty big. It might be too big to fail."

"Ha," laughed Matzel. "That's what they probably said about the Bronze Age civilization—too big to fail. The biggest civilization the world has ever known, and it only took three months to kick it back to the dark ages once credit collapsed. What makes any economy too big to fail—quote unquote—is its interdependence. That's what makes it big, and that's what makes it vulnerable. If central banks ever get behind a digital currency, and that digital currency gets adopted by even just a handful of countries... well, fuck... just watch out. It's going to fail. I mean, think about it! All you need is for electricity or the internet to go out, and all digital currency disappears. One massive solar flare and pfffft—there goes your bitcoin, your crypto-wallet, your digital bank... all gone."

Dan and Ricardo were silent.

Finally Ricardo asked, "What about what happened at the castle? Will there will be any repercussions from that?"

Matzel shook his head no. "No," he said. "Carlos and his men have the police convinced that it was a squabble between two drug gangs. Besides, both Todo and the Spanish government have an interest in downplaying that whole incident. They can't let anything interfere with their plans to have Todo buy that property from the Spanish government."

"Is that what is going to happen?" asked Ricardo.

"Yes, the deal is in the works. The castle was a financial burden to the government. Todo will take it off their hands and turn it into a bank. Everyone wins."

"And who exactly is Carlos?" asked Dan.

"Carlos is from one of the more—how shall I describe them?—one of the more *progressive* families in Todo. Like all families, Todo has its black sheep. He's still part of the organization, but he does a little *reconnaissance* work for me from time to time."

Dan nodded. "You were part of Todo?"

Matzel nodded. "I was."

"What happened?"

Matzel got a faraway look in his eyes. "Oh... time... external circumstances... and... personal ambition."

"Is your name really Nassim Kahil?"

Matzel slowly shook his head no. "I've had so many names..." he said, and his voice trailed off.

"And what are you going to do now?" Dan asked.

Matzel shrugged. "I'll go somewhere new, hunker down, wait for the inevitable collapse. Ha, maybe I'll bury my gold. Ha, yes. Bury my gold and leave clues. That would make for an interesting treasure for someone to dig up in a thousand years."

Just then the woman at the gate made an announcement to line up to board the airplane.

"Well, gentlemen," Matzel said standing up, "let's go home."

-FIN-

ABOUT THE AUTHOR

Robert Rahula was born in Spain to an American father and Spanish mother but grew up in Virginia on the farm of his paternal grandparents. He returned to Menorca, Spain in the 1960s to pursue his writing career. Over the past thirty years, Robert has published dozens of books of prose and poetry in Spain and in the United States. Readings of his poems appear on his YouTube channel, his Facebook page, and his website robertrahula.com. He travels Europe and Central and South America for several months a year, giving readings and lectures, and spends the rest of his time writing.